Permed
To
Death

Permed
To
Death

NANCY J. COHEN

KENSINGTON BOOKS
KENSINGTON PUBLISHING CORP.

http://www.kensingtonbooks.com

DEDICATION

This book is dedicated to the members of my critique group: Cynthia Thomason, Charlene Newberg, Lisa Manuel, Ann Reynold, and Marilyn Jordan. Thank you, my talented fellow writers, for your suggestions, support, and encouragement. Not to mention the appetizing snacks! Our bimonthly meetings are the highlight of my week.

ACKNOWLEDGMENTS

I'd like to express my thanks to:

Sharon Kozyra from Blondinas Hair Salon, for being so gracious in answering my many questions about her roles as salon owner and hairstylist.

Judy Carter and Janice Sklar, for their creative input as stylists.

Lieutenant Jeff Riffle, Plantation Police Department, for his review of police procedure.

"Marla, if the coffee is ready, I'll have a cup while my perm processes," Mrs. Kravitz said, squinting as Marla squeezed the pungent solution onto her scalp. "Be careful! I feel it dripping down my neck."

"I'll be done in a minute." Marla gritted her teeth as she bumped her hip against the shampoo sink. Already this promised to be an aggravating day. She'd had to come in early to accommodate Mrs. Kravitz, and the rest of her morning was fully booked. Not that Bertha Kravitz cared; she never considered anyone's needs except her own.

With an efficiency born of years of practice, she wrapped Mrs. Kravitz's rods in a plastic cap, then set the timer for twenty minutes. After washing her hands, she poured her client a cup of coffee and added a package of sugar.

"Don't forget my powdered creamer!" Mrs. Kravitz called.

"I've got it." Marla mixed in two spoonfuls from a

reserved jar, frowning when her spoon scraped bottom. Damn, she hadn't realized the supply had dwindled so low! Sparing a moment to rinse the container at a sink, she tossed it into the trash while making a mental note to buy more later.

"Here you go," she said, handing Mrs. Kravitz the steaming mug.

"Marla, was that my jar you just discarded? I hope you have another one in stock because I'll want more coffee." Taking a sip, the woman grimaced. "Ugh, this tastes like medicine! How long has it been standing?"

"I just brewed a fresh pot before you came."

"Give me another package of sugar." While Marla complied, Mrs. Kravitz scanned the room like a vulture searching for prey. "Where's the bagels? I could use something to eat."

"I haven't had a chance to get them yet. Why don't you try to relax? You have less than fifteen minutes left on your timer. I'm going into the storeroom for some clean towels."

Scowling, Mrs. Kravitz took another sip of coffee.

Hoping to escape before the woman issued a new command, Marla rushed into the storage area. Her gaze scanned the shelves of chemicals, alighting on the neutralizer solution she'd selected earlier. She plucked it off its perch and was reaching for a pile of towels when a strangled sound struck her ears. A loud crash followed, like glass shattering.

Sprinting into the salon, Marla stared at Mrs. Kravitz, who slumped in the shampoo chair. Her bagged head lolled against the sink. The plastic cap wrapped around her rods had become dislodged, partially shading her face. Marla's gaze dropped to the floor where broken shards of the ceramic mug lay scattered amid a trail of dark liquid.

"Mrs. Kravitz?" she rasped, her heart thumping.

When there was no response, Marla stepped closer. She stared in disbelief as she got a better view.

Mrs. Kravitz's face was distorted into an ugly grimace. Wide-set eyes, pupils dilated, stared blankly at the ceiling. She didn't appear to be breathing, unless her respirations were too shallow to notice.

"Mrs. Kravitz?" Marla repeated, her voice hoarse. Maybe the old woman had fainted or been overwhelmed by fumes from the perm solution. Or she'd fallen asleep. But then her chest would be moving, wouldn't it? And her eyes wouldn't be wide-open like a—

Oh God.

Bile rising in her throat, she prodded the woman's arm, then jumped back when Mrs. Kravitz's hand flopped over the side of the chair, dangling like a cold, dead fish. A surge of nausea seized her as images from the past clouded her mind. *You can't freeze up now, girl. Call for help.*

Rushing to the phone, she dialed 911.

"Police, fire, or medical?" replied the operator.

"Medical. I'm Marla Shore at the *Cut 'N Dye* Beauty Salon. One of my clients has stopped breathing. I think she's dead!" Her voice cracking, she gave her address.

"I'm notifying the rescue unit. They'll be there soon."

Marla replaced the receiver in its cradle, her hand trembling as a sense of *déjà vu* washed over her. Stiff with fear, she stood immobilized as memories from another time, another place haunted her thoughts. A child's limp form, cradled in her arms. Her screams, echoing through a summer afternoon. Accusations, harsh and unforgiving.

She hadn't known what to do then. Maybe she could make a difference now.

She dashed over to check the body for a pulse, forcing herself to feel the clammy wrist. She felt nothing. A faint odor, vaguely familiar, assailed her nostrils. Briefly, she wondered about performing CPR, but logic told her it was too late. Sirens sounded outside, accompanied by the noise of screeching brakes. Any decision became unnecessary as a team of paramedics thundered in the front door. She stood aside while they performed their assessment.

A police officer arrived on the scene. After conferring with the medics, he asked Marla some preliminary questions. Numb with shock, she leaned against a counter while he notified his sergeant by cellular phone. She heard him mention something about a crime unit, so when several techs and a detective walked in, she wasn't surprised. Still, she wondered why they'd been called. Surely Mrs. Kravitz had a heart attack or a stroke.

Ignoring the technicians who scoured the salon, she focused on the steely-eyed detective approaching her. She could tell he was used to being in command just from the set of his wide shoulders, his determined stride, and the hawklike expression on his sharply angular face. Bushy eyebrows rose above a nose that might have been rearranged in his youth, indicating he wasn't averse to physical action when required. Faced with such a formidable symbol of authority, she quaked when he stopped in front of her.

Nervous, she began babbling. "I didn't realize she was ill. If I'd have known, I would have called for help sooner. It wasn't my fault."

He held up a hand. "I'm Detective Vail. Please tell me

what happened from the start, Miss Shore." When she'd finished, he studied his notes. "Let's see if I've got this straight. You wrapped her hair, gave her a cup of coffee, then went into the back room. Hearing a noise, you returned to find the deceased slumped in her chair."

Marla nodded. "That's right." Her knees weakening, she sank onto a seat at the closest hair station. A quick glance in the mirror shocked her. Her short, glossy brown hair curled inward at chin length, wispy bangs feathering a forehead creased with worry lines. A stranger's fearful eyes, dark as toffee, stared back at her. Surely, that ghastly complexion couldn't be hers. She looked ill, which was certainly how she felt, but this wasn't as horrible as that day when—

"You made a fresh pot of coffee just before Mrs. Kravitz came in?" Detective Vail asked, ripping her away from painful memories.

She nodded, glad for the distraction. "I poured some coffee into her mug, then added a package of sugar and two spoonfuls of powdered creamer. My other customers prefer Half & Half, but Bertha insisted on using the dry variety. I kept a jar just for her."

A gleam entered his gray eyes. "Where is it?"

"I'm afraid I threw it out. I'd used up the last spoonfuls. She said the coffee tasted bitter," Marla recalled. "I didn't think much of it because she complained about everything."

"Did you notice the color of the creamer?"

"Not really."

"Any unusual odors?"

"No . . . yes. I did smell something after Mrs. Kravitz . . . when I went to feel her pulse. It reminded me of"—she wrinkled her nose—"marzipan. Yes, that's it."

His eyes narrowed. "You mean almonds?"

"I believe so."

He scanned the tabletop holding the coffeemaker and related supplies. "Where do you normally keep the foodstuffs?"

"In a rear storeroom."

"Who's allowed back there?"

"Everyone. Even our clients go into the storeroom sometimes. Our regulars are pretty familiar with the place."

"You said the creamer jar was nearly empty. Did you recall using most of it the last time the deceased was here?"

"Not really." An idea dawned on her. "Surely you don't think it was something in her drink?" she said, horrified.

"We're just collecting evidence, ma'am. The medical examiner will determine cause of death. Is there anything else you can think of that might be relevant?"

She frowned. "The back door was open when I arrived this morning. I meant to speak to the cleaning crew about it later."

"I see. Please excuse me." He held a hushed conference with two techs, one of whom veered off to examine the trash and another who headed for the rear entrance. They'd already scooped up the dribbled remains of coffee on the floor, collected pieces of the broken mug, and dusted everything for fingerprints. The medical examiner had taken charge of the corpse. Finished with his initial assessment, he'd called the body-removal service.

Please get here soon, Marla thought, looking everywhere but at the dead woman. To distract herself, she calculated the cost of a new shampoo chair.

Vail returned to resume his interview. "Tell me, how would you describe your relationship with Bertha Kravitz?"

She compressed her lips. "She was a regular client."

"When did she start coming here to get her hair done?"

"Ever since I opened the shop, eight years ago."

"Did you know her before that time?"

Marla hesitated a fraction too long. "Sure," she said, careful to keep her tone casual. "I'd met her at local charity events."

"Excuse me," said a young officer, approaching them. "There's a couple of women up front who say they're stylists."

Getting Vail's nod of approval, Marla slipped off her chair and hurried to the door. Her face lit up when she spied two familiar faces among the crowd gathering outside. "Lucille! Thank God you're here. And Nicole, I'm so glad to see you! Officer, please let them in," she begged the burly policeman standing guard.

"I'm sorry, miss, no one is allowed inside."

"That's okay, Officer," called Detective Vail. "You can let them inside but keep them near the door."

Marla hugged Nicole when the slim dark-skinned woman entered. Nicole had always been her staunch supporter, and she needed her strength now. She wasn't disappointed. Nicole embraced her, as though sensing her need for comfort.

"What's going on?" Lucille snapped. For a woman in her fifties, she presented herself in an attractive manner. Her light application of makeup was just the right tint to complement her colored reddish gold hair.

Quickly, Marla filled her colleagues in on what had

happened. Her voice shook with emotion, and Nicole laid a comforting hand on her arm. The tall woman looked sleek and elegant in an ivory pantsuit, her thick raven hair tied in a low ponytail.

"Are you okay?" Nicole asked, her initial shocked expression changing to concern.

Marla drew in a shaky breath. "I've been better."

"This wasn't your fault. You couldn't have known the old lady would become ill."

"I should have been more attentive." Her voice faded, and she remembered that other time a life had depended upon her. She'd failed miserably then and hadn't improved this time.

"Marla." Nicole's sharp tone brought her back to the present. "Don't think about what happened before. That's irrelevant to this situation."

No, it isn't, Marla agonized. Both times, she'd been in a caretaker role and someone had died as a result. Her mother said things happened in threes. Was she doomed to repeat her mistake for a third round? *Get a grip. You've already wallowed in enough sorrow. No more!*

She managed a weak smile. "I called our customers to notify them we'll be closed for a few days. I said we had an emergency but didn't go into details."

"What about Miloki and the other staff members?"

"I got hold of nearly everyone. You two had already left for work."

"Good thinking, honey," Lucille cut in, her pale blue eyes approving. "Sounds like you have things well under control."

"Ms. Shore."

Dear Lord, it's that detective again. She summoned her

strength to face him as he bore down on her. "Yes?" His probing gaze made her feel like a criminal.

"I don't understand why you and Ms. Kravitz were here at eight this morning. Didn't you say your salon normally opens at ten?"

His jaw moved, and she wondered if he were chewing on a piece of gum. Unable to meet his eyes, she glanced at his charcoal suit. "Mrs. Kravitz needed a Thursday appointment, but I didn't have any openings today. Usually, I book two hours for a perm so I had her come in at eight. I can be flexible for my regular customers."

"Couldn't she make an appointment for another day?"

"She was scheduled to be a guest speaker at the library luncheon this afternoon. She wanted to get her hair done early."

"Did anyone among your staff dislike the deceased?"

Her gaze flew to his face, and she inhaled a sharp gust of air. Could he possibly—?

"Detective Vail!" called one of the technicians, saving her from having to answer.

"I'll be right there," he replied. "We'll talk more later," he promised Marla in a deceptively congenial tone. His slate gray eyes met hers, his look of cool assessment seeming to suck the guilt from her soul. She swallowed apprehensively, wondering how much he already knew about her, and how much he'd find out.

"When do you think we'll be allowed to reopen?" she asked, concerned about the customers scheduled for that weekend. She hoped they wouldn't lose too many days. The drop in income would be devastating, not to mention how annoyed her clientele would be to have their appointments canceled.

"I'll let you know," Vail said, stuffing his notebook

into a pocket. "We should be able to complete our work here over the weekend." He paused, frowning thought-fully. "I'll need a list of your staff members: names, addresses, phone numbers. Oh, and your appointment calendar." His sharp gaze pinned Nicole and Lucille. "Don't go away. I'll have some questions for you in just a few minutes."

His words caused a ripple of shock to tear through her. Questions about what? Didn't he believe her story?

Shaken, she turned to Nicole. "I'm sorry you got involved," she said, feeling bad that her friends were drawn into the quagmire.

"It's okay," Nicole reassured her, patting her shoulder. "You look awfully pale, Marla. Maybe you should go home."

"Detective Vail hasn't said I can leave yet. Besides, I won't let you face him alone."

Lucille grinned. "Don't get so worked up over this, honey. Think of the good side: the bad publicity might be a godsend. Once the commotion dies—forgive the pun!—people will swarm here to satisfy their curiosity."

"That's just great." She knew her friends were trying to help, but anxiety addled her mind. "Carolyn Sutton will take advantage of the situation. She wants our lease, which is due for renewal next month. From what I hear, she's already been soliciting the landlord, and this inci-dent could turn him against us. He'll boot us out and give the place to Carolyn."

"Nonsense!" Nicole scoffed. "You've fought her off before. You can do it again."

"I hope so."

Vail returned to interview Lucille and Nicole and to collect the list of staff members that Marla had printed from the computer. "You need to come down to the station to make your formal statements," he said. "I'll drive you in my car."

Outside, the warm, humid Florida air blasted her lungs. She followed Vail to an unmarked sedan and got in when he wordlessly held the door open. Mindless of the air-cooled interior, she huddled in the backseat with her companions. At least the last time she hadn't needed to go to police headquarters. She'd been a hysterical nineteen-year-old, and the cops had interviewed her in the home where the accident happened. They were sympathetic, not accusatory. She was the one who'd blamed herself for the tragedy. And later, the child's parents . . .

"You'll be all right," Nicole said, grasping her hand.

Tears squeezed from Marla's eyes. How could she bear to go through another inquiry?

Somehow she survived giving her taped statement at the police station and answering more questions in detail. Thankfully, her involvement in that other incident wasn't mentioned. It was bad enough that she remembered.

Relieved when the ordeal was over, she sagged against the cushion in Vail's car as he drove them back to the salon.

"I'll be in touch," he promised as he dropped them off. His face was impassive so she couldn't read his expression, but his eyes spoke volumes. They never once left her face when he spoke, as though he knew she had a secret to hide.

"Arnie must be wondering what's going on," Nicole said, when they were standing in the parking lot.

Marla glanced at the deli located two stores down the shopping strip from her salon. She didn't want to go home yet. Too many blank walls to face. Too many memories. "I'll talk to him."

"Tell him not to worry, everything will be fine. You, too, honey. Call us later," Lucille urged, waving goodbye.

Exhausted, she nodded, waiting until the two women left. After reassuring herself the salon was properly locked up, she strode to the eatery. The tantalizing aroma of freshly baked bagels wafted into her nostrils as she entered.

"Hi, Arnie," she greeted the dark-haired man behind the cash register. He flashed her a disarming grin. His teeth gleamed white beneath a droopy mustache, dimples creasing his cheeks. She glanced at his trim figure encased in a T-shirt and jeans and quickly looked away.

"What's wrong?" he asked, sobering. "You didn't come in to get your usual order of bagels this morning, and then I saw police cars outside."

She took a deep tremulous breath. "Mrs. Kravitz is dead."

"What? The old lady?" She'd told him about her demanding customer before. "How is that possible?" Delegating his post to an employee, he gestured to her. "Come on, sit down. You look like you're about to keel over."

Taking her elbow, he led her to a vacant table. "Two coffees, Ruth," he called to a passing waitress.

Sniffing the aroma of garlic and hot brewed coffee, Marla became aware of an empty gnawing in her stomach, but her appetite had long since departed. Wiping sweaty hands on her belted tan jumpsuit, she related her story.

"Did she have any medical problems that you knew about?" Arnie probed.

"No, and I've seen her every eight weeks for a trim. Her hair was so resistant that she needed a perm often, too. No matter what I did, she'd *kvetch* about it, but I don't recall her ever saying a word about having a medical condition."

Arnie nodded sympathetically. "I know what you mean about her being a whiner. She came in here for breakfast and was a lousy tipper."

"Tell me about it."

Arnie stroked his mustache. "So the detective thinks it might have been something in her coffee that killed her?"

Marla shuddered. "I hope not, since I served her the drink myself. Vail seemed to find it significant that I smelled almonds near the body."

Arnie leaned forward. "Cyanide."

"Huh?"

"Didn't you ever watch old spy movies? When caught, the guy would take a cyanide pill. He'd be dead in minutes, and his breath smelled like bitter almonds."

"I don't believe it." Although that might explain why the presenting officer had called in the crime unit.

"Whoa, if this is for real, who'd want Bertha Kravitz out of the way enough to do her in?"

Marla snorted. "Who wouldn't?" Refusing to face the horrifying possibilities, she sought another explanation. "Perhaps this isn't about her at all. Maybe someone wants me out of the picture." She twisted her fingers together under the table. "Carolyn Sutton has been itching to discredit me so she can take over my lease. Her shop is going downhill. Maybe she planned to make a customer of mine sick so people would be afraid to come to the salon."

"Mrs. Kravitz isn't sick. She's dead." Arnie's dark eyes regarded her with concern. "You're going out on a limb with that one. I hope you didn't mention Carolyn's name to the cops."

"Of course not. You think I'm *meshuga?*" The waitress brought their coffee and Marla fell silent, staring at her cup. It would be awful if she'd given Bertha a beverage containing a lethal substance. Then there was the matter of who'd tampered with the coffee supplies. Someone must have added poison with deliberate intent to harm. But who?

Wait for the medical examiner's report, she chided herself. Bertha could still have had a sudden stroke.

Grimacing, she looked at Arnie. "Sorry, coffee doesn't appeal to me right now. Got any hot chocolate?" Her throat was parched, and she craved a drink.

The waitress changed her beverage, and she sipped the hot cocoa, seeking solace in its sweetness.

"If this does turn out to be something sinister, I hope you'll let the cops handle it," Arnie warned her.

"What do you mean?"

"Sticking your nose into a murder investigation could be dangerous. You're not responsible for what happened, Marla."

"Yes, I am. My customer's well-being is my responsibility. But this could mean nothing," she retorted. "Mrs. Kravitz probably had an attack of some kind."

"I hope you're right. Look, if you need anything, don't hesitate to call me."

Touched by his concern, she sipped her drink to hide her swell of emotion. "Thanks for the offer, but it's bad enough that my staff is involved."

"Say, I've got tickets for the Florida Philharmonic this

Saturday," Arnie said in an obvious attempt to cheer her. "Want to keep me company?"

"Tally and I are supposed to go to the Southern Women's Exposition. I can't disappoint my best friend. Maybe another time." Inwardly, she smiled. A lonely widower, Arnie needed a wife for many reasons, none of which suited her. She'd been down the matrimonial road before, and it had been an unpleasant experience. She preferred to keep their relationship on a friendship level, although Arnie had other ideas.

"You're a tough nut to crack, you know that?" Arnie said, his dark brown eyes gleaming.

She grinned, her mood lightening. "I don't know why you keep trying."

"I like the challenge. So what's it going to take to get you interested, huh?"

"Just stay as sweet as you are."

"Come on, I know we'd hit it off if you'd give me a chance."

"Sometimes just being friends is more important."

"You've got a lot of friends. Look," he said, flexing his muscles, "don't I have sex appeal?"

She raised an eyebrow. "Sure you do, pal, but that's not the issue here."

"Then what is? Wait, I've got it. You don't like my hairstyle."

"Well, now that you mention it," Marla began, pretending to study his receding hairline.

He glanced at the waitress bustling between tables. "I should get back to work." Scraping his chair back, he stood, giving her a wry grin. "Let me know if you change your mind."

She smiled in response, nodding. A few minutes later,

she was walking outside. The shopping strip was a bustling center, unlike many others with empty storefronts. Her clientele mainly consisted of young professionals, who provided a brisk business. Squeezed between Fort Lauderdale to the east and the Everglades far to the west, Palm Haven's prime location guaranteed success.

Marla was proud of her reputation, one she'd struggled to earn after the tragic incident in her past. It hadn't been an easy choice to settle near the place where the accident happened. Too many reminders still haunted her, but she'd learned to use them as a force for good. Viewed as an active, helpful member of the community, she'd reached a tentative peace with herself. Customers appreciated her sensitivity, and many had become good friends.

She veered toward her Toyota Camry, its white color being the most popular choice in sunny south Florida. Reflects the heat, said the salesman, like all the white-tile roofs. Black was the other common choice, in her mind representing funerals of so many senior citizens. Now Bertha would be among them.

Heat from the car's interior slammed her face as she slid into the driver's seat. Gripping her keys, she started the engine. A refreshing blast of air-conditioning cooled her cheeks. Though late May, humidity hung heavily in the air.

Heaviness burdened her heart as well as she considered her next move. Now what? To her knowledge, Bertha Kravitz still kept that damned envelope in her mansion. Marla had no doubt that if the cops found it, they'd accuse her of having a motive for murder if this did turn out to be a homicide case. Her best bet would be to retrieve it before they searched the Kravitz house. *At least*

Bertha can't use it to blackmail me any longer, she thought with grim satisfaction.

Switching gears, she backed out of the parking space. She'd been to Mrs. Kravitz's stately home on the Intracoastal Waterway once before, an occasion she'd never forget. This was her chance finally to bury the mistake she'd made years ago. Survival instincts, honed through past traumas, took precedence over any attacks of conscience that might afflict her.

Gritting her teeth, she pulled onto the main road and headed east.

2

Marla drove slowly past the imposing two-story Mediterranean-style house, her gaze sweeping the red barrel-tile roof and stucco exterior. At the upper level, a balcony jutted outward, enhanced by iron grillwork. Brick red shutters flanked jalousie windows, their vacant exteriors like eyes on a mannequin. The light paint applied to the rest of the house reminded her of the gray peppering Detective Vail's black hair, and that dire thought increased her heart rate. She'd better complete her business quickly and move on.

Cruising down the street, she was relieved to note an absence of parked cars in the driveway. At least the police hadn't arrived yet. Tropical foliage graced the grounds, marred by a standard-issue mailbox on a post by the roadway. Rounding a bend, she caught a glimpse of the pool with a chickee hut in back facing the Intracoastal Waterway.

She'd remembered the directions pretty well considering how long it had been since her first visit. The details of that interview were vividly imprinted on her mind, like the image of Mrs. Kravitz in the shampoo chair. Now the old woman wouldn't plague her any longer with the shame of her past. A sense of liberation lifted her spirits, but it was quickly replaced by guilt. She shouldn't be so glad her wealthy customer was dead, even if it meant one less piece of emotional baggage to lug around.

Shaking off her morbid thoughts, she decided it would be smart to park her vehicle around the next corner. Turning the bend, she pulled onto a grassy swale and switched off the ignition. Sweat trickled down her chest as soon as she stepped outside, where moisture thickened the air. That line of perspiration beading her lip wasn't from the humidity, though.

You've got chutzpah, *girl,* she told herself. *Go to it and then get out of here.* She was inviting trouble by her foolhardy actions, but what other choice did she have? She had to get hold of that envelope.

Several moments later, she rang the front doorbell. Maybe Mrs. Kravitz's son was home, although she believed he had his own apartment. Still, it was worth a try. She'd make her request, pray that he granted it without question, and leave.

Her hopes were dashed when no one responded. She considered twisting the doorknob, but if the house was wired, she might trip an alarm. She'd look for another means of entry.

Prowling around the side of the house, she searched for an open window without protective screening. Nothing. Maybe a patio door was ajar. Her shoes crunched on dry grass as she edged toward the rear. *Mrs. Kravitz should have turned on the sprinklers more often,* she thought irrelevantly. Both screen doors were locked, and the other side of the house was just as secure. Now what? She couldn't take the risk of breaking in. She'd just have to find another way to get the envelope.

The sound of a car engine threw Marla into a panic. Someone was pulling into the driveway! Keeping close to a sidewall, she peered around a fragrant gardenia bush. Her blood chilled when she observed a beige-and-black police car. Aware of how bad it would look if she were spotted, she changed direction.

Her thoughts raced as she furtively made her way through various neighbors' yards toward her car. Attending the funeral would be the best way to meet the old lady's relatives. After expressing condolences, she'd casually mention that Mrs. Kravitz kept an envelope addressed to her, an important document that she needed returned. Hopefully someone would agree to find it for her. Today's loss was merely a temporary setback.

Reassuring herself that all would be well, she slid into the driver's seat of the Toyota, shut the door, and started the engine. Her heart still pumping vigorously from a mixture of anticipation and fear, she shifted gears and headed out of the ritzy development. Passing by the police car was her most harrowing moment. She scrunched down in her seat, hoping they didn't already have a fix on the make of her car.

Twenty minutes later, she turned into the entrance of Green Hills, a prestigious subdivision west of Pine Island Road. After driving by the cascading rock waterfall that was meant to impress visitors, she wound through a maze of streets toward her town house. Using the automatic opener, she pulled directly into the garage. At last! Now she'd be able to relax.

Excited barking sounded as she emerged from her car. Spooks would be a comforting presence. At least poodles didn't ask questions.

"Marla! What are you doing home this early? You sick or something?" her neighbor's gravelly voice called from outside.

Marla rolled her eyes. *So much for my peace and quiet.* Strolling into the sunshine, she nodded to the elderly man who was occupied at a worktable in his driveway. A former carpenter, he took on small jobs to keep busy. A naval cap sat at a jaunty angle on his head of sparse white hair, but it didn't provide much protection from the scorching sun. His leathery skin showed the effects of too much exposure to damaging rays.

"One of my customers took ill this morning at the salon," she explained with a tired smile. "It was quite a scene."

"You look frazzled." Putting down his drill, he swaggered over. His lined face crinkled into a grin. "I've got just the thing to cheer you." Reaching into a back pocket, he yanked out a scrap of paper.

"Oh, joy." Marla wasn't in the mood to hear one of his limericks. Moss Cantor dreamed of fame as a poet and kept adding verses to an increasing volume of pages in his manuscript. Not being an English buff, she had no idea if his work had the proper cadence, not that it mattered. Moss kept himself entertained, and that made the project worthy in itself.

He read in a loud, steady voice:

> There was a man who lived in Walloon
> Who liked to stop in every saloon
> One day he met a tall fellow

Who dared to call him yellow
Whereupon he deflated fast as a
    balloon

Marla couldn't suppress a grin of pleasure. "That's very good, Moss. I like it."

His expression brightened. "Then listen to this next one I've been working on."

"Not now," she cut in quickly. "I've got to go inside. Tell me later when it's finished."

His blue eyes darkened with concern. "You'd better get some rest, mate. You know you can count on Emma and me if you need anything." Tugging on his beard as though for emphasis, he hovered solicitously.

"Thanks, but I'll be all right."

Breathing a sigh of relief to finally be alone, she rushed inside the house. After letting Spooks out to the fenced backyard, she strode into her study. Ignoring the pile of mail on her desk, she picked up the phone. *Business first,* she told herself. She punched in the number for her salon's janitorial service.

"Tomas?" she said when his accented voice answered. "Who was on duty last night? One of your boys left the back door unlocked at my salon. You may have heard what's happened today, and I'm pretty upset."

"*Sí,* I get a call from the cops already. Pete and Carlos did your place. Pete says Carlos was the one who locked up. They finished by midnight and went on to their next job. I try to reach Carlos, but he lives on a boat. I have to leave message with dockmaster."

"I see. Well, if he comes in to work tonight, I hope you'll reprimand him for being so careless."

"I will talk to him, miss."

"Send someone else next time, okay?" She hung up, disgusted. She had enough problems without worrying about a sloppy cleaning crew.

She'd just changed into shorts and let Spooks back inside when the phone rang. Snatching up the receiver, she wondered who'd be calling. "Hello," she answered, half-fearing it was Detective Vail with a new slate of questions.

"Marla, dear," crooned her mother, "how are you? Don't forget you're coming to dinner on Sunday. Uncle Moishe will be in town."

"I don't know if I'll be able to make it."

"What do you mean?" Anita demanded. "Of course you'll come! Your cousins will be here."

As far as Marla was concerned, that was reason enough to stay away. Something warm and moist nudged her hand. Glancing down, she smiled at Spooks, who gave her an imploring look. She scratched behind the poodle's ears, gratified when he arched his head in response. His creamy white hair felt fluffy and soft as she stroked his neck.

"Ma, let me tell you what happened today," she said, anxious to share her tale.

"Sorry, I've got to run. I'm late for the Hadassah luncheon. You can still come if you want; I'll pick you up."

She heard the hopeful note in her mother's voice. "No way."

"You should get involved, you know, Marla. It's for a worthwhile cause."

"That's your opinion."

"Suit yourself. I'll talk to you later."

Marla heard the click and hung up, exasperated. Spooks, having her full attention, flipped onto his back and lay with his legs bent while she patted his belly. If only her mother would get off her case about religious groups. Marla had plenty of projects she supported; they just weren't the same as Anita's.

Fierce stomach rumblings propelled her into the kitchen, where she fixed herself a bagel with nova and cream cheese and a cup of hot tea. Just as she finished eating, another phone call disrupted the afternoon.

"Hello," she barked into the receiver. What now?

"It's Tally," said her best friend. "What's going on at your place? I saw the commotion on my way to work. I stopped off, but a cop told me you'd already left. This is the first chance I've had to call you."

Marla's shoulders sagged. "Oh God, Tally. Mrs. Kravitz croaked in the middle of a perm!"

A brief moment of silence met her words. "What did you do, use a lethal solution?" Mirth-filled chuckles followed. "Sorry, I know how much you disliked the old biddy. Tell me what happened."

Hearing her friend's voice cracked her reserve. Briefly, she related the sequence of events.

"How awful! You must be wiped out."

"I'm doing okay, except I can't help feeling it was my fault."

"Marla, stop with the guilt trip. You've been there before." Tally's voice sharpened, and Marla cringed. She didn't want to hear what came next. "Mrs. Kravitz's unfortunate demise had nothing to do with a two-year-old toddler. You were nineteen when Tammy drowned in that pool. I thought you'd finally put her to rest. Hold on a minute, will you?"

Tally spoke aside to one of her clerks at Dressed To Kill. As owner of the women's fashion boutique, she often

referred customers to Marla and vice versa. "Look, why
don't you come over here? You shouldn't be alone,"
Tally urged her.

"That's okay. I need some time to think. I'll call you
later."

As soon as she hung up, the phone rang again. It didn't
stop for the next few hours. Apparently the story about
a woman taking ill in her salon had spread, and everyone
she knew was trying to reach her. Tired of repeating her
story, she turned on the answering machine and screened
calls for the rest of the day. That night, she retired early,
feeling emotionally drained.

Freshly alert in the morning, she turned on the TV
while getting dressed in her bedroom. Buttoning the top
to her pale yellow shorts outfit, she focused her attention
on the screen where a view of her salon was on the air.
I timed this just right, she thought sardonically, wondering
how much news coverage she'd missed already. Spooks
flopped at her feet, licking her ankle, while she stared,
transfixed.

"The victim was poisoned," said the news anchor, a
deadpan-faced man in a dapper suit. "The police won't
release any further details except to say they're pursuing
an investigation."

Poisoned! Marla sank onto her bed, stunned. *Dear Lord,
what does this mean?* Before she could think, the phone
jarred her senses.

"Why didn't you tell me about this yesterday?" her
mother demanded without so much as a friendly
greeting.

"I tried, Ma. You were in a hurry." The doorbell
sounded, making her grimace in annoyance. "Sorry, I've

got to go. Someone's at the door." *God, this promises to be a long day.*

"Spooks! Get back!" she ordered as the dog leapt against the front door in a barking frenzy. Swinging it open, she stared at her caller.

"May I come in?" Detective Vail asked, marching inside without waiting for a reply. He wore a lightweight suit in a medium wheat color with a striped tie, a nondescript outfit that would let him blend in with the crowd. His hair, gelled and coiffed, was properly styled for the conservative image he tried to project. But his purposeful stride, gray eyes glinting with determination, gave him away as a man used to command.

He halted in the foyer, his narrowed gaze sweeping the living room. She took the opportunity to study his profile, noting the stubborn thrust of his jaw. He looked like a man who focused on his job without allowing any distractions.

"I hope you don't mind the intrusion, but I have a few more questions," he said, his gaze leisurely roaming her body and settling on her bare legs. She thought she saw mild interest flickering behind his expression, but then it was gone. Her imagination must be on overdrive.

"Have a seat," she offered, graciously gesturing toward the living room. Planting herself in an armchair, she crossed her ankles self-consciously and waited for his first move.

"Are you familiar with Mrs. Kravitz's acquaintances?" he asked, leaning casually back in an upholstered love seat.

"She was quite chatty with some of our customers at the salon." Marla described a few of the ladies, most of whom considered themselves buddies when Bertha

Kravitz was present and who gossiped about her when she wasn't there.

"Would anyone have reason to bear a grudge against her?"

Marla shrugged. "She was well respected in the business community, but on a personal level, most people disliked her."

"What about her relatives?"

"She has a son. I don't know what he does for a living, but she used to speak disparagingly about him. She always bragged about her niece."

"Would you say she favored the niece over her son?"

"Why are you asking me these questions?"

"Women confide in their hairdressers."

She appreciated his understanding of her occupation. "The news report gave poisoning as the cause of death. Isn't it possible Bertha ingested a toxic substance before coming to the salon, and it just took effect while she was there?"

His eyes narrowed, but not before she'd noticed their remarkable shade of smoky gray. "Traces of cyanide were found in the powdered creamer jar," he said, watching her reaction.

Marla gasped. She hadn't truly wanted to believe Bertha had drunk a cup of poisoned coffee, one that she'd prepared. Did Vail suspect her of doing the deed? Who else might have contaminated the supplies, and why? "Have you contacted the cleaning crew yet? Carlos left the back door unlocked."

"Carlos didn't show up for work last night, and his boat isn't in dock," Vail said, his face impassive. "We're trying to reach him."

"Anyone could have sneaked into my salon and doctored the creamer," she remarked. Thank God it wasn't in the coffee. She might have drunk a cup herself if she hadn't been so busy!

"Who else knew about her hair appointment besides your staff?"

Marla shifted in her chair. "Her niece was attending that luncheon with her later, so she might have known. I can't guess who else Bertha told."

Vail seemed to weigh her words. "Mind if I get a drink of water?" he said, a devious smile on his face. He rose, and the room seemed overpowered by his presence.

Following him into the kitchen, Marla saw he wasn't really interested in a beverage. His gaze swept across her counters like a bloodhound chasing its target. He was looking for something in particular, she surmised, irritated that he'd think her simple enough to fall for his ruse.

"I see you have an extensive cookbook collection," he announced, striding to her bookshelf. He pointed to a volume entitled *A Taste of the Tropics.* "Are you into natural plant foods?"

"Not really. I like to experiment with tropical-fruit recipes, but I used to do more gourmet cooking when I was married. I'm divorced," she explained. Preparing meals for herself was a heck of a lot easier than fixing food for a man who demanded a hot meal every night and who refused to eat leftovers. There were a few things she missed about the matrimonial state, but cooking detail was not one of them.

Vail gave her a friendly smile that didn't quite reach his eyes. "Do you like gardening?"

"Nope, I kill anything green that gets near me." Her

eyes narrowed. "Why are you so interested in my hobbies?"

"Another toxic substance was added to the creamer. Monkshood is a poisonous plant. Someone made it into a powder and gave Bertha Kravitz a double whammy."

"Oh, so you think I fixed it in my backyard? Go on, take a look. I've got a lychee tree and some citrus." She thrust her chin forward. "Why do I get the feeling you suspect me of doing away with Mrs. Kravitz?"

He sauntered forward until he was nearly nose to nose with her. "I'm wondering about your relationship with the deceased. A few of your staff members say that you bad-mouthed her."

"We often discuss our customers," she said hastily. "Some of their more annoying traits are common topics. It doesn't mean anything significant."

"You were alone in the shop with the victim. I only have your word for what happened. According to your story, you admit fixing her coffee and handing it to her."

Marla felt a sudden lump obstruct her throat as a nasty image came to mind: her business in ruins as she was hauled off to jail.

"I'm telling the truth," she stated.

"Are you?"

He stared at her so hard and long, she felt her blood drain to her toes. *God, has he found out about the envelope?* "When can we reopen the salon?" she ventured, changing the subject.

"We'll be finished in there sometime tomorrow, so Monday would be fine."

"We're closed Mondays."

"So make it Tuesday." He paused, a crafty look entering his eyes. "By any chance, is your ex-spouse Stanley Kaufman, the attorney?"

A chill crept up her spine. He already knew the answer, which meant he'd been checking up on her. She'd reverted to her maiden name after the divorce. What else had he learned about her background?

"Stan and I were divorced nine years ago." When she was twenty-five. He'd remarried and divorced again in the interval. Now he was on wife number three. "What does that have to do with anything?" she shot back.

"You might consider calling him for legal advice."

"Why, are you going to arrest me?"

"No, ma'am. But you should think about protecting yourself."

From what, pal? Maybe he wasn't going to drag her into the station today, but tomorrow was always a distinct possibility.

Depressed, Marla showed him to the door. Damned if she'd call Stan for anything. He and Kimberly would enjoy seeing her squirm, and she wouldn't give them the satisfaction!

After she was left alone, Marla entered her study and lifted the phone receiver. She called several funeral homes, the numbers for which she'd written down earlier. Her work paid off. Mrs. Kravitz's funeral was scheduled for Sunday afternoon. She would have just enough time to attend before going to Anita's house for dinner. It was imperative she get that envelope before Detective Vail got wind of it, or she'd be sunk for sure! Mrs. Kravitz's relatives were her only hope.

Rosenthal Memorial Gardens, one of the county's older cemeteries, sat squeezed between condo developments in a western suburb of Fort Lauderdale. Bordered by tall black olive trees in a rectangular subdivision, the gardens gave the appearance of an oasis of tranquillity away from the bustle of modern life.

Marla parked in a lot situated to the side of a chapel building where solemn-faced men in dark suits stood ready to direct visitors. She hadn't attended many funerals and didn't feel comfortable in cemeteries. Her annual pilgrimage to Tammy's gravesite was a painful event, but a necessity to her conscience. She also visited her father's resting place each year at Rosh Hashanah. Glancing across the lawn, she wished he were here now to offer his support. She missed him with an aching intensity as she remembered how he'd listened to her hopes and dreams, and later, her despair.

He'd understood when Marla made her career switch, while Anita still tried to push her into becoming a schoolteacher. Unable to face being near children after the accident, Marla had forsaken her two years of college as an education major to become a hairstylist. She'd always liked doing hair, experimenting on her friends much to their delight, but she'd suppressed her true calling because of Anita's lack of support. When Anita gave her a hard time later on, Marla countered that it was her life, not her mother's. That discussion was typical of their bittersweet relationship.

Giving a last nervous tug to her jet-black suit jacket, she approached the polished wooden doors. Memories aside, she'd be glad when this ordeal was over.

Inside, she was directed past a lobby toward a room on the left where the family of the deceased were greeting visitors. She signed a guest book and entered the dimly lit interior. Somber individuals stood about in small clusters, chatting quietly. Remembering how Mrs. Kravitz had described her niece as a petite brunette, Marla spotted her engaged in conversation across the room. Waiting for a lag in dialogue, she tentatively approached.

"Excuse me, are you Wendy Greenfield? I'm Marla Shore, owner of Cut 'N Dye Beauty Salon. Please accept my sincere condolences. I'm so terribly sorry about your aunt."

Half-expecting a rebuff, she was glad when the woman smiled at her.

"It's kind of you to come, Ms. Shore." Wendy's pretty face showed no signs of weeping. Her large brown eyes were outlined in black, a stark contrast to her pale complexion. Ginger-tinted lips gave a hint of color along with a matching blush. Her hairstyle, straight and one length down to her shoulders, was not one Marla would recommend for someone of her small stature. At least she'd chosen a smartly cut black suit trimmed in crisp white for the funeral service.

"Call me Marla. Your aunt has . . . had been my customer for many years. I'll miss her," she said, hoping her lie wasn't evident.

"Won't we all," a man's voice snarled from behind.

"Marla, this is my husband, Zack. Marla owns the hair salon where . . . er . . ." Wendy's voice trailed off.

Marla turned to shake hands with a tall, thin-faced fellow with bushy dark eyebrows that reminded her of an eagle's nest, perched high on his face as the dominant feature. His wide mouth stretched in a sneer as he took her hand. His handshake was limp and moist like a strand of freshly bleached hair.

He looked down at her over his long nose. "Come to send off the old lady?"

"Zack!" Wendy said. "Please show some respect."

"Why should I? Aunty Bertha can't tell us what to do anymore. I hope she was telling the truth about leaving you her fortune."

Wendy's eyes narrowed. "Watch what you say, Zack," she warned. She turned to Marla, giving an apologetic shrug. "You'll have to excuse his behavior. He and Aunty Bertha weren't getting along."

"Where's cousin Todd? Isn't he going to show up for his mother's funeral?" Zack glanced around the room, a skeptical look on his face.

Marla considered mentioning the envelope, but this didn't seem to be an appropriate time. Excusing herself instead, she edged toward the door. A young man rushed inside, nearly colliding with her. He gave her a startled glance and she stared back, wondering why he looked familiar. Dark stubble shadowed the lower half of his face. Dulled blue eyes were set close together above a narrow nose. But it was the cleft in his chin that reminded her of something with an unpleasant association. The guy looked like he'd just rolled out of bed. He was dressed in a loosely tucked-in dress shirt and trousers, mismatched socks, and loafers. Apparently he hadn't thought to put on a tie for the occasion, or else he didn't care.

She watched him greet Wendy and Zack. Was this Mrs. Kravitz's son? That could explain why she felt she knew him. He might have come into the salon when his mother was having her hair done. How sad that none of the relatives showed any signs of grief. Wendy's manner seemed subdued, but she wasn't weepy.

A tall broad-shouldered man with gray hair broke away from a group and strode in her direction. His handsome face was lined with creases, but they added distinction to his even features. That three-piece suit must be warm in the Florida heat, she thought, her gaze assessing his expensive attire.

"You're Marla Shore?" he said, an icy look in his tawny eyes.

She nodded. "And who are you?" she challenged, offended by his curt tone of voice.

"I'm Roy Collins, vice president of Sunshine Publishing. Bertha's business partner," he added. "I heard the circumstances of her death. Be warned, Ms. Shore, that I am considering suing you for neglect. I must say I am surprised you had the nerve to show up here."

Marla's eyes widened. "Whatever are you talking about?"

"You gave her a poisoned cup of coffee, then left her alone. She could have been resuscitated if you'd been with her and noticed she was ill. I won't permit this flagrant lack of responsibility to go unpunished." His eyes narrowed menacingly. "My attorney will be in touch with you."

With a supercilious tilt of his chin, he stalked away and joined the cluster around Wendy and Zack.

Her blood boiling, Marla strolled to a corner and leaned against the wall to observe the proceedings. Watching the interactions of Bertha's relatives, she determined not to let Roy Collins unnerve her. He wouldn't have a leg to stand on in court, she told herself reassuringly, ignoring a pang of doubt.

When the doors to the chapel opened, she marched inside, her spine stiff. She sat through the service with quiet respect. Wendy sniffled in the front row, flanked by her husband and the man Marla assumed was Todd

Kravitz. The rabbi eulogized Bertha for her numerous charitable works and her contribution to the regional publishing scene. She'd started Sunshine Publishing Company from scratch, using funds provided by her banker husband. When he died, she continued to make the business a profitable enterprise. She'd been a shrewd businesswoman, Marla conceded, even if she was ruthless.

A brief gravesite service followed, after which the guests dispersed. Marla's heels sank into the soft ground as she approached Mrs. Kravitz's niece.

"Please let me know if there's anything I can do for you," she offered, squinting against the bright sun.

"It was kind of you to come," Wendy replied. Her eyes were rimmed in red, but her waterproof mascara kept her makeup intact. Marla noticed a tissue clutched in her hand.

"I'd like to talk to you again." Marla wished she could bring up the topic of the envelope now, but other guests were hovering to say their farewells. "Can I call you at a more convenient time?"

"We'll be sitting *shivah* for the next few days at our house. You can stop in if you like. I know my aunt went to your salon often. You can't blame yourself for what happened," she said, patting Marla's shoulder.

Marla smiled at her, grateful that at least one person in the family was friendly. Hope swelled within her that she'd be able to obtain the envelope easily. Then she could put the matter to rest once and for all.

She turned to go, nearly bumping into another woman. "Darlene . . . and Nicole! What are you two doing here?"

"We thought we'd pay our respects," Darlene said, chewing a wad of gum. Garbed in a brown-leather mini-skirt, boots, and a skimpy halter top, she seemed dressed for a picnic instead of a funeral. "Lucille's here, too. We kind of figured you'd need our support."

Marla glanced across the lawn to where Lucille appeared to be arguing with Roy Collins. The reception-ist's shoulders hunched as she punctured the air with animated gestures, a scowl on her face. Collins looked mildly entertained. Recalling that Lucille had worked for him before her present position, Marla wondered at their current relationship.

"We were sitting in the back row," Nicole explained, fingering her flowered silk dress. "How about joining us for a bite to eat? We're driving to the Beverly Hills Cafe from here."

"Thanks, but I'm going to my mother's for dinner. It's a command performance," she said, waggling her eyebrows.

"Too bad. How are you holding up? Any news on when we can go back to work?"

"Detective Vail stopped by my house to ask more ques-tions. He said we're clear for business on Tuesday."

"Aw, heck," Darlene said, shaking her head of wavy blond hair. She pouted her lips, colored a pastel pink shade. "Like I was hoping for a little vacation."

"What did you do all weekend?" Nicole asked Marla. "Have reporters been on your tail?"

"I gave one interview, just to set the record straight. Otherwise, I spent a quiet few days. Tally and I went to the Southern Women's Exposition last evening, and Friday night I went out with Ralph. I'm afraid I wasn't very good company."

Nicole grinned. "Ralph is more interested in your looks than your brains. After all, he works in a *body* shop, doesn't he?" she said, winking.

"You're right. Say, here comes Lucille."

The receptionist was heading in their direction, her narrow hips swaying in a knee-length skirt. She wore a sleeveless blouse, showing off her supple arms. You'd never know her age from that athletic figure, Marla thought with a twinge of envy. Walking the dog was her sole form of exertion. She hated calisthenics and wouldn't be caught dead lifting weights. Besides, doing people's hair all day and listening to their gossip was enough exercise for her. The job required stamina and built character, which was more than she could say for any exercise video.

"How ya doing, honey?" Lucille asked, her cornflower blue eyes warmly sympathetic.

"I'm okay. I didn't realize you and Roy Collins were still communicating. Seems like you were having a disagreement."

"Roy never appreciates me, but that's old news. You coming with us to the restaurant?" She tightened her earring, its screw back having loosened.

"I'm going to my mother's for dinner, but thanks anyway. We're allowed to reopen on Tuesday, so I'll see you then. Bye, Nicole," Marla said, turning to her friend.

Nicole swatted a mosquito buzzing near her face. "Man, the bugs are out early this year. Where's Darlene? I'm ready to leave." Marla glanced around, surprised to note the girl was heading toward a group that included Roy Collins. Striking up a conversation, Darlene assumed a provocative pose, but Collins appeared uninterested. He said something to her and turned to speak to someone else.

"It's just like her to introduce herself to the best-looking man here," Nicole commented. "She's a fool if she thinks he'd be interested in her. He's probably happily married."

"Roy Collins is a confirmed bachelor," Lucille replied, a hint of bitterness in her tone. "Darlene just isn't his type. See, he's sent her away."

Darlene returned to her friends, a sullen look on her face.

"I've got to go," Marla said. "Have a nice dinner. I'll see y'all on Tuesday morning." Slinging the strap of her black-leather handbag over her shoulder, she marched toward the parking lot.

"Ms. Shore?" a man's voice called from behind.

Whirling around, Marla suppressed a gasp of surprise. Todd Kravitz was rapidly bearing down on her, a fierce frown on his face. Her nose wrinkled as she took in his scroungy appearance. *Boy, does he need some of my expertise,* she thought. It looked as though he hadn't shampooed his dark hair in weeks. Or colored it, she noticed, startled. Dirty blond roots were beginning to show. Now that was unusual. She hadn't seen a man color his hair from any shade of blond to ebony. Usually someone with dirty blond hair would go lighter. Adding a note to her mental files, she smiled and extended her hand.

"You're Mrs. Kravitz's son, aren't you?" she said. "I'm so sorry about your mother."

"Thanks." He shook her hand, and a strange sensation shimmied up her spine. Why did his touch feel so familiar? "I need to talk to you about my mother," he muttered. "There's something you should know."

"Oh? Like what?" She scrutinized his face, but his shifty eyes wouldn't allow her to read his thoughts.

"Like who wanted my mother dead." He glanced over his shoulder, his expression furtive. "Can't say more here. Just come and see me this week, and I'll tell you. *He* had every reason to want her out of the way."

3

Marla pulled up in front of the single-family home owned by her mother and parked on the swale, the driveway already being occupied by her cousin's black Mercedes. Many of the homes in the development were similar in design, but it was better than those condos where you couldn't tell one building from the next. Marla couldn't stand to live in a place where you could hear your neighbor's footsteps overhead or you had to climb stairs holding a bundle of groceries. Anita's house suited her active lifestyle. Two bedrooms were sufficient because Marla lived nearby, and her brother had a home in Boca Raton. Anita rarely needed to house visitors.

Speaking of visitors, she'd promised to call on Todd Kravitz after the mourning period passed. Too bad he'd refused to tell her anything further this afternoon. He'd been close-mouthed, giving her sly looks that discomfited her. Caution dictated that she should meet him in a public place, she decided, strolling along the paved walkway toward her mother's house.

"Hi, Ma! I'm here," she called, pushing open the unlocked front door. Anita was in the kitchen directly to her left, arranging a platter of chopped liver and crackers. Ahead in the living room sat her relatives, their boisterous conversation interrupted when she called out a greeting. Anxious to make herself useful, she entered the kitchen to ask if Anita needed help. A mouth-watering aroma of baked brisket and roasted potatoes tantalized her appetite.

"Don't you look nice," Anita said, wiping her hands on a limp dish towel before hugging her daughter. She wore a black-and-white top enhanced by decorative silver discs, a white skirt, and dangling ivory earrings that complemented her short, sleek white hair. Marla's glance dropped to her mother's brightly colored toenails, peeking out from a pair of heeled sandals. Not a day went by that Anita didn't wear red lipstick and nail polish. It gave her confidence, she'd said once, but Marla knew she wasn't the type to cower in the wings while a show was going on. Regardless of how she enhanced her appearance, she drew attention.

"I went to Mrs. Kravitz's funeral today," Marla stated, glad to be in a cheerful atmosphere after the strain of the afternoon.

Anita returned to her preparations, decorating the chopped-liver platter with sprigs of fresh parsley. "She'd been coming to your salon for a long time, hadn't she?"

"Eight years. I met some of her relatives."

"Bertha Kravitz was a pillar of the community. I'll bet the chapel was crowded."

"Yeah, it was. A few of my stylists came, too."

"That was thoughtful of them." She glanced at Marla, studying her as only a mother can scrutinize a child. "Are you all right?"

"Yes, I'm fine." An inner warmth stole upon her, bringing a sense of comfort. In the competitive world of modern society, motherly concern was a gratifying constant. "The police detective came to my house to ask more questions," she said. "He makes me feel guilty even though I didn't do anything wrong."

"You were alone with that woman, weren't you? If I were a homicide investigator, I'd be suspicious of anyone remotely connected to her."

"Exactly. He should be checking out her relatives. They're a strange bunch if you ask me. As if I don't have enough to worry about, Bertha's business partner is threatening to sue me for neglect."

"Boy, have you got *tsuris*," Anita sympathized.

Indeed, and her woes were multiplying. "Tomorrow, I'll make a condolence call on Wendy Greenfield, Mrs. Kravitz's niece. It's the least I can do." She didn't mention the matter of the envelope. Her mother believed she'd earned the money for cosmetology school through regular modeling jobs, and Marla prayed she'd never learn the truth.

"How's your coalition gearing up for water safety week?" Anita said, checking the brisket warming in the oven.

"We're sending flyers to the schools. We've got a TV commercial lined up and a meeting next week with the town council. We're pushing for a law requiring pool enclosures. It's a measure that can save a lot of lives."

Tammy's house didn't have a pool fence; nor was the patio door locked. Just because she'd baby-sat for the family before, Marla shouldn't have assumed the door would be secured each time. She'd been on the telephone taking an important message when Tammy let herself outside. Having been instructed to expect the phone call, she'd thought Tammy was safe. Little did she know the toddler had learned to climb out of her playpen. The parents had blamed her, even though they should have taken better precautions.

Drowning was the number one killer of children four years and younger in Florida. Tragedy had taught her it was a preventable accident. Now she advised others what she'd learned the hard way: Put childproof locks on all exterior doors. Build an enclosure around the pool. Begin swimming lessons as early as possible. And never leave a small child unattended. Saving lives by educating the public gave Marla redemption for the loss she'd caused, but nothing could ever assuage the grief she still carried in her heart.

"Here, see if your cousins need refills," Anita said, thrusting a bucket of ice cubes in her direction. "Say hello to everyone. We'll talk more later."

Glad to be roused from her morose thoughts, Marla joined her relatives. "Uncle Moishe!" she exclaimed, greeting the elderly gentleman seated on the brocade upholstered couch. "Has it really been two years since I visited you in Denver?" Leaning over to kiss his cheek, she clutched the ice bucket to her chest.

His wrinkled face split into a grin. "It's good to see you! I hear you've been having some excitement at your job."

"Did one of your customers really get murdered?" chirped Aunt Selma, a diminutive woman who had always reminded Marla of a parakeet with her beaklike nose and brightly colored clothing. She sat next to Uncle Moishe, her gnarled hands neatly folded in her lap. An untouched lemonade rested on a side table.

"Yes, but I'd rather not talk about it." Making the

rounds of greeting her cousins, she plopped ice cubes into drinks that needed refreshing.

"Tell us the details," demanded Julia, taking a sip of white wine from a Waterford glass. Married to Alan, an accountant, she hadn't worked a day since they were married. Even so, she always looked hassled. Sitting on a plush armchair, she kept crossing and uncrossing her ankles. Her layered, shag-cut dirty blond hair could have used more care, as could her peach lipstick, blurred at the edges. She'd put more effort into choosing her wardrobe, a tailored beige-silk blouse and dark brown slacks.

"There's not much to say," Marla replied, putting down the ice bucket. Clearly, she wasn't going to get away with avoiding the topic. "I wrapped Bertha's hair for a perm, then gave her a cup of coffee. After a couple of sips, she was dead."

"Wasn't she the head of Sunshine Publishing?" asked Alan, glancing at his watch. He checked the time at regular intervals, giving the impression that he compartmentalized his life into prescribed zones. "I seem to recall reading about the company in one of my journals. They were being investigated for tax evasion."

"When was this?" Marla gave him a sharp glance.

Anita strode into the room, bringing the chopped-liver platter and a bowl of pickled herring. "Help yourselves," she said, placing the dishes on a cocktail table. She went to the bar to pour herself a wine cooler.

"The incident occurred some time ago," said Alan, stooping to smear a spoonful of chopped liver onto a wheat cracker. Stuffing it into his mouth, he frowned. "I don't remember hearing anything else about it. Maybe the case was dropped."

Lucille might still have been working there, Marla thought. *This might be worth following up on.*

"How's the beauty business?" crooned Cynthia. Seated beside Julia, she'd maintained her glacial aloofness until this point, buoyed by her husband Bruce, who stood stiffly by her side. The eldest of her cousins, their wealth provided an excuse to look down their schnozzles on the rest of the family. Marla tolerated them only because she liked going to their villa by the sea each year for the Passover seder. Her scornful gaze swept their coiffeurs before she replied. Cynthia's hair was teased so high it reminded her of a beehive, and Bruce's stood on end as though he'd been hit by lightning.

"Business is fine, thanks," she retorted. "Maybe you'd like to stop in at the salon and update your style. Besides, you could use a new color rinse to get rid of those brassy tones."

"How's your love life?" Julia probed.

Marla bristled. "I'm seeing a few guys, no one serious." *Not that it's any concern of yours.* "How about yourself, sweetie? Now that tax season is over, are you and hubby getting reacquainted?"

Julia ignored her barb. "I understand Stanley remarried." Her singsong voice told Marla what a fool she'd been to let such a prize go.

"Yes, he did. Kimberly is a real gem." She didn't bother to hide her sarcasm. Living in a six-bedroom mansion at exclusive Mangrove Estates wasn't good enough for Stan's new wife. Kimberly insisted a house on the ocean would be more fulfilling.

In order to finance this dream house, Stan had been nagging Marla to sell their jointly owned property, which generated steady rental income. The divorce settlement had given her funds to establish the salon, but that money was gone. Now she needed the extra income to maintain her lifestyle.

Hopefully she wouldn't have to call Stan for legal advice as Detective Vail had suggested, because she knew he'd take advantage of her. She'd never sell her share of their property, not under any circumstances.

"I warned you to hold on to Stan," said Anita, wagging her finger. "He was a good catch. Now look at you, Marla Shorstein! You have to work for a living, and none of the men you date are Jewish."

"I like my work, Ma, and I changed my last name to Shore if you'll recall. So what if my dates aren't Jewish? Neither are my best friends for that matter."

"There's no one closer than one of your own kind."

"Sorry, but my values are different. And excuse me, but who I choose to be my friend is my decision. I don't fit in with Stan's crowd, which is where you'd like me to be."

Stuffing a cracker with chopped liver into her mouth, she chomped resentfully. Anita implied that she needed a Jewish man to make her life worthwhile. Marrying Stan had been a mistake, although at the time it seemed like the right thing to do. She'd learned that following other people's well-meant advice often turned out to be a bad choice.

Aunt Selma wobbled over and placed a hand on her arm. "You're out of sorts by all that's happened," she warbled. "Well, you just ignore these *yentas* and come with me, *bubula.*" Under her aunt's kind tutelage, Marla took her seat at the dining-room table. Her mouth watered at the presentation of gefilte fish and red horseradish. At least she could count on a good meal when she visited her mother.

For the duration of dinner, she listened to family gossip. Her mind couldn't concentrate on what anyone was saying. Instead, she thought about tomorrow and what she'd say to Wendy Greenfield when she called upon her.

The Greenfields lived in Jacaranda, a pleasant suburban enclave of Plantation, which used to be the upscale neighborhood until people moved to Weston or Coral Springs to maintain their status. Driving the streets was similar to being at a car show: Mercedeses, Lexuses, and Jaguars were the norm. Live-in domestic help went along with the ride, as did designer labels. Marla preferred to think her tastes were simple but classier.

She pulled to a stop at a sprawling house with a mixed stone-and-stucco exterior. No barrel-tile roof here. The sloping roof consisted of traditional white tiles, coated with mildew. A yellow fire hydrant, paint rusted from well water, sat on the swale. Her gaze swept the sabal palms, red hibiscus bushes, and spiky ground-cover plants that complemented the freshly cut lawn. The estate appeared to be well maintained, although it could use a roof cleaning and a coat of sealant on the driveway.

Her Toyota was the only vehicle parked in the circular driveway. Marla assumed that meant the stream of visitors had let up for the moment. Her heartbeat accelerated; it would be a lucky break if Wendy was alone.

Warm, humid air scented with a spiced fragrance filled her nostrils as she stepped from her car. Her white blouse stuck to her back, but there wasn't much she could do about it. Sweat came with the territory in south Florida. After smoothing down her skirt, she reached inside the car and grabbed the box of cookies she'd picked up at a local bakery. Hopefully this visit would yield results.

Undaunted by ferocious barking coming from the

house, she locked the car door and strode forward with an eager step.

"Marla! How kind of you to come," said Wendy, greeting her with a friendly smile. For someone in mourning, she didn't exhibit any signs of grief. Marla's glance raked over her casual attire. Make that casually expensive, she amended. Wendy wore a navy-silk shorts outfit which went well with her petite figure. Low-heeled pumps were dressy enough for company but comfortable for the feet. Marla liked the way she'd fixed her hair, a short wavy style that framed her face.

As she stepped inside, two golden retrievers bounded at her like attention-starved children. They must have smelled Spooks because they slobbered all over her. Grinning at their antics, she thrust the bakery box at Wendy. "Here, I brought this for you." She bent to scratch one of the dogs behind the ears.

"Thanks!" Wendy said. "Lolly and Dancer, sit!" Whining, the dogs obeyed while Marla surveyed the living room. A vision of blue overwhelmed her senses. The Berber carpet, draperies, and even the knickknacks in a curio cabinet featured pastel blue.

Wendy led her through a spacious kitchen—with a blue-porcelain sink—toward a family room facing a screened-in pool at the rear of the house. She took a seat on an ivory-leather sofa and waited while Wendy fixed her an iced tea. The dogs trailed after their mistress like two silent shadows.

Wendy returned with her drink, then plopped into a chair opposite Marla. "You're probably surprised that I'm not wearing black," she said. "I don't believe in that custom."

What do you believe in, pal? Your aunt's money? "Bertha

was very fond of you," she remarked. It was truthful
enough; the old lady used to brag about her niece.

A wistful expression captured Wendy's face. "She
always wished she'd had a daughter. I'm very grateful to
her. Aunty Bertha helped me out a lot, at least until I
married Zack. She was ecstatic when I told her I was
pregnant. Now she won't be here when the baby is born."

Marla's eyebrows shot up. "You don't look . . . I mean,
you're so slim." Her cheeks warmed with embarrassment.

Wendy chuckled. "I'm only three months along." One
of the golden-haired dogs nudged her hand and she
petted the soft fur on top of its head. "Zack is worried
about the time off I'll have to take from work."

"Oh. For some reason, I thought you stayed home."
A foolish grin curved her mouth. "What kind of work
do you do?"

"I'm a physical therapist. Don't get me wrong. Zack
wants me to stay home to care for the baby, but we need
the income. Especially when—" She bit her lip, stopping.

"Go on."

"It's nothing."

Marla considered what to say next. She could try to
draw Wendy out, or she could address the urgent matter
that had brought her there. Her own needs took precedence, she finally decided.

"Forgive me for changing the subject, but your aunt
had an item of mine she planned to return: a manila
envelope addressed with my name. If you come across it
when you sort through her things, I'd appreciate it if
you'd give me a call. It's urgent that I retrieve this as
soon as possible."

Wendy gave her a curious glance. "I'm planning to go
to her place on Friday, after the *shivah* period is over.

Maybe you'd like to meet me there so you can look for yourself."

"Sure, what time?"

"Let's say one o'clock." Wendy petted one of the dogs, the other eyeing her jealously while prowling the room. "Todd didn't get along with Aunty Bertha, you know," she blurted.

"Oh? How's that?"

Wendy lifted her eyes, meeting Marla's assessing gaze. "She didn't approve of his lifestyle, because he doesn't have a regular job. He's sort of a drifter if you know what I mean. Aunty Bertha didn't give him a cent, but he has enough money to pay the living expenses for that ratty apartment he keeps. I've always wondered where he gets the funds. Maybe Aunty Bertha found out and—" She sucked in a breath, her face coloring.

"Found out what?"

"You know, that he's doing jobs that are less than ethical . . . or legal."

"So?" Marla gaped at her, shocked by what Wendy had left unsaid. "You think he might have killed his own mother to silence her?"

"I'm not saying that!"

Then what are you saying? She gritted her teeth in frustration. "Have the police been to see you yet?"

Wendy nodded, a glum expression overtaking her. "Detective Vail was here. He said he'd spoken to you. I didn't say anything against Todd, but you might want to mention the possibilities to him."

Now she got it. Wendy didn't want to implicate Todd herself. She wanted Marla to do the dirty work for her. Her estimation of Mrs. Kravitz's niece fell a notch.

"At the funeral, your husband Zack seemed annoyed with your aunt."

Wendy rose abruptly. "Zack respected Aunty Bertha," she snapped. "They didn't always see things eye to eye but that doesn't mean anything."

"What line of work is he in?"

"He's a financial advisor." Wendy paced the room, hands clasped behind her back. Bored, the dogs settled by a large potted palm to lazily watch the proceedings.

"You said Zack was upset because you'll have to take maternity leave. Does that mean his business isn't as prosperous as you'd like?" Marla persisted, hoping to learn more about their situation.

Wendy shot her a worried glance. "He's doing fine," she retorted, but her voice wavered.

"Is it true that Bertha's will favors you as her heir?"

"Really, Marla, is that any concern of yours? I mentioned Todd to you because I felt you would understand. Now please don't think me rude, but it's been a tiring day. We can talk more on Friday." Her eyes flashing indignantly, she gestured toward the front door.

Marla understood she was being dismissed. Rising, she said good-bye, promising herself to interview Zack at a later date. Wendy had raised some interesting issues, but she wasn't telling the whole story.

Heading for her car, she contemplated what was bothering her the most. Wendy hadn't admitted they needed money, but she'd gotten that impression. The upkeep for their house must require a lot of income, not to mention a baby on the way. If Zack's business wasn't doing well, and Wendy was the heiress to Mrs. Kravitz's estate—how far would her husband go to secure their future?

4

"Marla, are you able to fit Pat Williams in today?" asked Lucille, holding the telephone receiver to her ear.

Marla glanced toward the receptionist's desk, a hairbrush poised in her hand. "I'm booked solid, so I won't have time. My two o'clock is due to arrive soon, and I've already squeezed in Ginger Blackstone. I won't finish until after six. Maybe someone else is free to take her."

"I can do the lady at four," Giorgio piped in. Her only male stylist, his dark handsome face and svelte voice were a boon to business. Women flocked to him like conditioner to hair. Unfortunately for them, he was gay.

"Thanks, pal!" she called, waving in acknowledgment. Ever since they'd come to work that morning, appointments and walk-ins cluttered the schedule. Lucille had been right in guessing that the busybodies in town would congregate at the murder scene. Considering the benefits, it didn't bother her as much as she'd thought it might. The increase in business refilled her coffers. So if her business hadn't suffered, why worry?

Because Detective Vail suspects you of having poisoned Bertha's coffee. And if you didn't do it, who did?

Picking used end papers off a set of perm rods, she wondered if someone on her staff were guilty. Everyone had disliked Bertha Kravitz, but to her knowledge, no one had reason to kill her. That left one other alternative: The murderer had entered through the unlocked back door.

If Carlos were found, he'd be able to put that matter to rest. Possibly one of Bertha's relations or a business associate had paid him to leave the door unsecured. If that were true, then the guilty party must have known about Bertha's hair appointment. Or, the killer was merely creating an opportunity to poison the creamer without knowing when Bertha would come into the salon next.

Discarding the papers in her hand, Marla shook her head. The first option presented a more likely scenario. Otherwise, Bertha's time of death would be left to chance. Either way, the perp had to have been aware Marla kept a jar of powdered creamer reserved for the old woman. Since Bertha had bragged about her preferential treatment, that could be anyone.

Detective Vail's job was to figure that out, Marla told herself, but she was afraid he'd overlook an important fact by focusing his suspicions on her. It wouldn't hurt if she checked out a few things herself. If she learned anything significant, she'd tell him. Arnie's warning rang in her ears, but she ignored it. The need to preserve her reputation foremost in her mind, she determined to do whatever was necessary to help uncover the murderer.

And speaking of Arnie, maybe he'd heard some relevant gossip. She'd stop in at the deli when she had a chance to schmooze and pick his brains. In the meantime, she had a few questions to ask Lucille.

Approaching the receptionist, she smiled evenly. "I'd like to talk to you in private. Let's go into the storeroom so we won't be overheard."

"Sure, honey." Wearing a puzzled frown, Lucille rose from her chair, smoothing down her pleated shirtwaist dress.

Marla headed toward the rear. Inside the back room, she scanned the shelves stocked with bottled solutions. A new supply order was supposed to arrive that day. Her nose detected a familiar chemical scent, which she sniffed appreciatively. In her mind that pungent odor represented the salon, and she missed it on days off. *Irrelevant,* she told herself. *Get to the business at hand.*

Her stomach rumbled, delaying her objective. Moving forward, she rummaged in the small refrigerator for the container of cappuccino yogurt she'd brought in earlier.

Lucille, standing just inside the doorway, folded her arms across her chest. "What did you want to talk to me about?"

Marla tore off the top and dug into her snack, using a plastic spoon. A mound of yogurt slid down her throat, cool and slick. "I heard that Sunshine Publishing was involved in a tax-evasion case," she said between mouthfuls. "Do you remember anything about it from when you were working there?"

Lucille's expression clouded. "A rival was trying to discredit us. The case was dropped after the records were examined."

"When did this happen?"

"Oh, I'd say a good ten years ago."

"You quit working for them just before you came here, isn't that right? Why did you leave?" Lucille had given personal reasons as her explanation, and Marla hadn't delved deeper because she'd needed a receptionist. In view of Bertha's death, she felt compelled to ask now for more details.

Lucille stiffened her spine. "Roy was acting in a manner detrimental to the company. When I told Bertha, she didn't believe me. I was asked to leave."

So she hadn't left the company willingly. "What were you speaking to Roy about at the funeral?"

"I just asked him how things were on the job. He wasn't in a talkative mood, at least not to me." Her eyes narrowed. "Why are you so interested? I wasn't asking for my old position back, if that's what is worrying you."

"No, that's not it. I've been trying to figure out who'd benefit from Bertha Kravitz's death."

"Her niece will get most of her money. I'd guess the business goes to Roy."

"What about Todd? What does he get now that she's gone?"

Lucille raised an eyebrow. "He's a wily one. There's more than meets the eye where he's concerned."

Darlene rushed into the room, forestalling any further questions Marla might have asked.

"God, I'm so thirsty I could croak!" the girl exclaimed. Grabbing a soda can from the refrigerator, she popped the lid. After gulping down a few hasty swallows, she surveyed the others. "Hey, did I tell you about my hot date this weekend? Like I met Jules at the beach, and we went to one of the clubs on the Strip. Does that guy know how to move!"

Lucille pursed her lips. "Did you drive your new car? He must have thought you were rich to have a Chevy Corvette. I can't help wondering where you got the money to finance it."

"You're just jealous," Darlene sneered. "Maybe next time you'll come along and meet someone, too."

"No, thanks!"

Darlene gestured at Marla. "I think she's still carrying a torch for that guy who turned his back on her years ago. Like she needs to get out on the social scene once in a while."

"It's not safe to pick up men on the street," Lucille countered.

"Oh, yeah?" Darlene gave her a scorching look. "Marla has a good time with the guys she meets. Like loosen up, and you'll be happier." Peeking into the salon, she grimaced. "Elsie is ready for her rinse."

"All Darlene cares about is men." Lucille sniffed when the girl had left to tend her customer. "She should be more concerned about her unhealthful habits. If you ask me, those diet sodas are addictive." She smiled at Marla, her lined face creasing beside her eyes. "By the by, I made a new herbal tea with hibiscus blossoms from my yard. Want to try some? I'll bring it in tomorrow."

"No, thanks. Speaking of addictions, mine is to caffeine. I need another cup of coffee." After tossing her empty yogurt container into the trash, Marla rinsed out a mug and helped herself from the spare coffeemaker she'd bought for the staff.

"When is the new shampoo chair due in?" Lucille queried. "It's a good thing you got rid of *that* one before today."

"Tell me about it. The new chair is being delivered on Friday. I can't wait."

"Good. We wouldn't want—"

"Marla, your two o'clock is here," Giorgio shouted from the salon, interrupting Lucille's reply.

"Thanks!" Marla called. "Never a moment's rest, is there?" she said to Lucille. "Let's get back to work."

Scurrying out, she spied her customer waiting by the reception desk. "How are you, Jess? Go ahead and get shampooed. I'll wait for you here."

While the woman was gone, Marla sipped the steaming brew in her mug. Snatches of conversation reached her ears. Gossip centered on Bertha Kravitz, but she'd expected no less.

"The news didn't surprise me in the least," snapped Doris Howard, sitting at Nicole's station beside Marla. "We used to be quite close, you know, but I never liked her. Bertha had a grating personality."

The woman getting a trim beside her replied, "We were active in the garden club together. Bertha raised a lot of money for the conservatory plus she was a major contributor. But I couldn't stand to be on the same committee with her. What a viper!"

Doris lowered her voice so Marla had to strain to hear. "I know what you mean. She tried to get me to go on a cruise with her. She wouldn't take no for an answer and made it seem like I was wrong for refusing."

The other woman gave a vigorous nod. "She pushed herself on me, too. Anything you said to her, she made a sarcastic remark in return. Do you know she wouldn't park in an underground garage? I picked her up to go to the mall, and even if it was raining, we'd have to park outside because she was afraid of getting stuck in those narrow spaces."

"Everyone thought she was such a saint, but we know better, don't we?" smirked Doris. "If you ask me, she got what she deserved. Probably stepped on someone's toes."

Nicole slipped Marla a sidelong glance as she gelled Doris's hair. "What's your theory about who wanted her out of the picture?" the stylist asked.

Doris narrowed her eyes. "Maybe one of the people who worked for her at that publishing company. She had a reputation for ruthlessness."

Marla's client returned, making her abandon the listening post. Too bad. It was just getting juicy.

Jess's raven hair glistened with moisture. "You look tired," she said, giving Marla a keen glance.

"It's been a long day." Without elaborating, Marla flung a black plastic cape over Jess's shoulders after she took a seat. "What are we going to do with your hair?" Scrunching and lifting several strands, she noted some remaining body from an earlier perm. "How about if I angle it around your face?"

"Sorry, not this time!" Jess laughed. It was a standing joke that Marla kept trying to change her style. "It's a little heavy on top, but I'd like to keep as much length as possible. My gray is beginning to bother me, especially in front. I'm ready to do something about it."

Marla played with her hair a moment longer while examining Jess's profile. "Let's get another trim out of that perm. We'll tackle those signs of aging at your next visit. Do you want to use semipermanent or permanent color?"

"What's the difference?"

Selecting a pair of shears, Marla began cutting. "The semipermanent will blend your gray but won't cover it completely. Gradually, the color wears off by itself. Permanent color actually changes the color of your gray hairs. It stays until it's cut out, but you'll need to touch up your roots every six weeks. You may want to start with the semipermanent to see the effect."

"Okay, I'll make an appointment."

"How'd your bathroom turn out? Last time you were here, you'd mentioned new tile."

Jess smiled. "It's great. The new flooring brightens the whole place. Now I'm refurbishing the bookshelves in our family room. They're such a dark stain, and the wood is warped."

"I'll tell you what's warped!" exclaimed Giorgio from across the room. Startled, Marla shot him a glance. She hadn't realized he'd been eavesdropping. His previous customer had left and apparently he was waiting for his next appointment. "That lady who was just here, she told me she saw Mrs. Kravitz's son cruising down the boulevard driving his mother's Cadillac. Can you imagine? He didn't even wait for the old lady to grow cold before taking her car."

"That reminds me," Marla said, snipping furiously. "Does anyone recall Todd Kravitz coming into the salon? He seemed so familiar when I met him at the funeral."

At the next station, Nicole shook her head. "I'd remember his looks if I'd seen him before. Man, could he use a good stylist. What a slimeball!"

Marla almost blurted out that she intended to meet him later in the week but held her tongue. Talk got around in a salon, and it might reach the wrong person's ears.

"That's perfect," Jess said, studying herself in the mirror when Marla was done. She always gave a compliment, unlike other women who *kvetched* about how their hair was cut too short or their white hairs were exposed. "So tell me, what happened to Bertha Kravitz? She's the talk of the town."

Marla groaned inwardly. She'd repeated the story so many times she could hear it in her sleep. "I wrapped Bertha's perm and gave her a cup of coffee," she said, seeing no way to avoid the story. "After a couple of sips, she was dead."

"Wow, and the cops said she was poisoned?"

"Right." She untied Jess's cape and used the dryer to blow stray hairs from her neckline, drowning out the possibility of any further conversation.

To her relief, Jess let it go at that and departed just as her next customer showed up. Kept busy for the next couple of hours, Marla fielded questions and comments with a finesse she hadn't known she possessed. Her cool reserve wavered when Detective Vail marched through the door, but she told herself his visit was just routine. At least he didn't flaunt his status as a police officer. His navy sportcoat and red-and-blue-striped tie could have belonged to any businessman. Her glance swept his peppery hair brushed back from a wide forehead then settled on his craggy face.

"Good afternoon, Detective Vail," she said evenly as he approached. "What can I do for you?"

"I have a few more questions to ask, if you don't mind." He smiled in a manner that reminded her of a wolf about to devour its prey.

"Fire away." She looked him directly in the eye, showing him she wasn't fooled by his supposedly friendly demeanor.

"Where did you go after I dropped you off here on Thursday?"

"I kibitzed with Arnie in the bagel shop, then I went home."

"Directly home?"

Oh God, was I spotted cruising by Mrs. Kravitz's house? Or worse, prowling around the grounds? Thinking fast, she delivered a glib reply. "Actually, I went for a drive. I was nervous and upset. I didn't want to go home right away."

"A car like yours was seen in Bertha Kravitz's neighborhood."

So it was possible she hadn't been personally identified. "I drove by her house. I couldn't help feeling sorry for the old lady, and I'd remembered where she lived. I went to her home once to do her hair before a party," she lied.

"Umm." Vail didn't look convinced. "I'll just meander around and talk to your employees. Don't let me keep you from your work."

"Sure," she gritted.

The next hour crawled by as she felt his eyes on her constantly. When would the man leave? His presence distracted her so she couldn't think straight. Glancing at him when his attention was diverted, she felt struck by the aura of power that accompanied him. Even her staff responded deferentially when he addressed them. Arrogance showed in the firm thrust of his jaw and the wide set of his shoulders. But even more imposing was that observant, piercing gaze that he tried to hide behind an amiable exterior. Clearly he presented a challenge, Marla decided, intrigued despite her sense of caution.

When she was between customers again, he strolled toward her. "How well do you screen your employees?" he asked in a low tone so no one else could overhear. His deep voice had a smoky quality she hadn't noticed before, and her cheeks warmed in response. Disconcerted by her reaction, she brushed a strand of hair off her face.

"I interview prospective staff members and verify licenses, but turnover is high in this business."

"You don't do a background check of any sort?"

"That would be a waste of effort. As long as my people show up on time, are personable, and do their jobs, why ask for more? Finding good workers is difficult enough without being overly selective."

"Darlene's home address doesn't check out. Either she's given you false information, or your records are inaccurate."

"Really? Darlene, can you come here for a minute, please?" When the stylist approached, Marla said: "Detective Vail claims your home address isn't valid. I'm sure you have a reasonable explanation."

Darlene's jaw worked a piece of gum as she met Vail's gaze defiantly. "Like I moved in with a friend and forgot to tell Marla. It's no big deal."

"What friend?" Vail demanded.

"You need his address? So I'll write it down for you." She hastened to the front desk, where Lucille, who'd been watching, gave her a blank piece of paper. Darlene scribbled the information, then handed it to the detective.

"Is there anything else?" Marla asked Vail, a smug smile on her face.

"Yes, one more thing," he said, his sly look making her

feel like an animal caught in a trap. "Over the weekend, I checked through your computer files which, if you recall, you gave me permission to do."

"That's right."

"I'm wondering why you didn't charge Mrs. Kravitz a dime in the eight years she'd been coming to the salon. The deceased never paid a cent for a single appointment. Can you explain, Miss Shore?"

"I owed Bertha some money," Marla said, her heart racing. "Instead of payments, she wanted free hair appointments."

"For eight years?" he scoffed.

"She gave me a loan to pay for beauty school. My parents didn't approve of my career choice, so I was forced to secure my own funding." Hopefully he'd believe her story.

"You said you'd met the deceased at a charitable event."

Marla lifted her chin. "That's right. I was a volunteer at a fund-raiser she chaired and was introduced to her. I made a gauche comment about her hair and how much better she'd look with a different style. She wanted to see if I could deliver what I promised. The rest is history."

"Was this loan money deposited in a bank?"

"She paid my tuition directly."

"How much of the loan remains unpaid?"

She shifted her feet. "The salon has done well, and I reimbursed her in full with interest. I've been doing her hair these last few years as a favor, feeling I owe her a debt of gratitude." Afraid he'd ask to see her canceled checks, she groped for a change of subject. "By the way, did you ever get hold of Carlos?" she asked, smiling sweetly.

"His boat is missing, and he hasn't shown up for work," Vail said in a gruff tone.

"I hope nothing has happened to him. He'll confirm that he left the back door unlocked. Did you find anyone's prints on the doorknob that don't belong there?"

Vail's mouth lifted at the corners. "Maybe."

Obviously he wasn't going to confide in her. Well, forget telling him what she'd learned so far by talking to Bertha's relatives. "There's Elanna!" she exclaimed, spotting her next customer walking in. "You'll have to excuse me. I need to get back to work."

"One more thing." His glance dropped, his heavy-lidded eyes making a lazy perusal of her body that brought a flush to her cheeks. "Maybe we can have coffee together later this week."

Marla's jaw dropped. Was he serious? Or was this a line to throw her off guard, perhaps a new way of cross-examining murder suspects by pretending a personal interest in them? "W-why, ask me later, Lieutenant," she stuttered.

"Dalton. My name is Dalton."

5

"Detective Vail makes me uneasy," Marla said. Huddled in a booth at the Mason Jar, a local steak restaurant, she dug into her house salad and conversation with equal fervor. Tally sat across from her, an expression of rapt interest on her face. Marla had filled her in on events since the weekend.

"I don't understand," Tally said, her perceptive blue eyes noting Marla's troubled expression.

"Vail ... Dalton ... makes me feel guilty," she explained, his given name sounding awkward. She preferred his formal title while the case remained unsolved. To hide her discomfort, she took a bite of mixed greens dribbled with raspberry vinaigrette.

Despite being vigilant about her diet, Tally indulged in a Caesar salad. She looked great in a leopard silk blouse and flowing raven trousers, while on Marla the outfit would swim. Broad-shouldered with wavy blond hair, Tally displayed her tall stature with a flamboyant flair. Marla preferred her own denim skirt and sky-blue sweater, but then she was a conservative dresser. Luckily, she didn't gain weight as easily as Tally.

"Sounds to me like you're attracted to the man." Tally's eyes twinkled playfully.

"How can I like someone who suspects me of being a murderess?"

"You've described him as a tall, dark, and ruggedly handsome detective who fights for justice. If you ask me, that's akin to hero worship."

Marla snorted. "Not in my case. He's trying to pin a homicide on me; I know it. It's clear his interest is merely a ploy to get me to confess."

"Then you'll just have to accept his offer to find out what he really wants, won't you?"

"Yeah, we'll go to Arnie's Bagel Busters for coffee. At least he's a friend I can trust."

"I like Arnie. He'd be more than a friend if you gave him a chance." Tally's face sobered. "Who do you suspect so far?"

Marla put down her fork. "Wendy's husband, Zack, may be having financial difficulties. He's worried about Wendy taking time off from her job when she has the baby, and she did act evasive when I asked about his business. Maybe he views her inheritance as a saving grace."

"Is there any way to check on his work status?"

"Wendy didn't say whether he's an independent consultant or if he works for someone else. I'll ask Todd when I meet him tomorrow night."

"Holy smokes, you're not wasting any time. Shall I come with you?"

"No, thanks. We're meeting at Scudders at nine o'clock. Plenty of other people will be strolling the Strip by then. Besides, Todd expects me to come alone, and I don't want to scare him off."

"Why talk to you and not the cops?"

"Who knows? He's such a scumbag, Wendy might be right about him."

"You mean about earning money illegally? That could give him a motive if his mother learned about it." Tally signaled to the waiter to remove their empty salad plates. "What about her business partner? Didn't you say he was pulling some shenanigans on the company?"

"My cousin's husband hinted at a tax-evasion scheme, but Lucille said it was nothing. She mentioned Roy had been acting against the company in some manner, but she didn't explain. I'll ask Lance to examine the company's records. He's a whiz at accessing data."

Tally winked. "Especially when you're leaning over his shoulder. Hey, do you think Lucille resented Bertha for firing her?"

"She didn't seem angry about it. You'd think she'd be more upset by Roy since his wrongdoing led to her dismissal, but I got the impression she likes him."

"You're kidding? I thought she'd sworn off men."

"She spoke to him at the funeral. Afterward, when Darlene tried to get his attention, Lucille seemed glad he turned her away."

"Maybe you should talk to Roy to sound out his views. Although I'm not entirely clear why you feel the need to do all this legwork. Isn't that Vail's job?"

"Of course it is, but Bertha died in my salon. I feel it's my responsibility to learn what happened."

"Why?" Tally persisted.

Marla stumbled for an answer. *Because her death was my fault. I should have been more vigilant. Like with Tammy . . .*

"I was alone with her. I don't want anyone thinking I poisoned her coffee."

Tally's eyes narrowed shrewdly. "Vail's really spooked you, hasn't he? Or are you blaming yourself, Marla?"

The waiter swept by carrying a tray laden with aromatic dishes, distracting their attention. Marla's mouth watered, but the meals went to a rowdy group of businessmen who'd already whetted their appetite with large quantities of beer.

"Hey!" Tally called. "We were seated before them."

The waiter, a harried young man whose limp hair tumbled onto his brow, stopped by their table. "I'll check on your orders, ma'am."

"I'd like a glass of burgundy," Marla requested, needing to relieve the tension knotting her brow. She could think more clearly if so many possibilities weren't clouding her brain. Then again, maybe it was better not to think at all.

"You're upset," Tally said, wagging a finger.

"Of course I'm upset." She leveled a steady gaze on her friend. "Do you know what Vail suggested? He said I should contact Stan for legal counsel."

"Dear Lord." Tally raised her eyes heavenward. "Just what you need. Look, do me a favor and be careful when you talk to Todd. You don't want to invite any more trouble."

Marla remembered the odd feeling of recognition she'd had when their hands touched at the funeral, and a shiver ran up her spine. "Roy Collins could be a pain," she said, pushing aside her doubts about Todd. "If he decides to sue me for negligence, I'll have to notify the carrier for my liability policy. If they won't cover this situation, I'll be forced to call Stan."

Tally grimaced. "I'm surprised he hasn't come running

to you already to gloat. He must have seen the shots of your salon on TV.''

''He'll drop by when it's to his advantage.'' The waiter returned with steaming-hot plates and her glass of wine. ''Don't you want a drink?'' she asked Tally.

Tally shook her head, waves of blond hair brushing her face. She wore a loose, easily manageable style that Marla trimmed for her every six weeks. ''My weight is up by two pounds. Alcohol adds too many calories.'' She examined her plate, squinting. ''This piece of chicken is undercooked,'' she told the waiter. ''Look, see this red juice?'' She prodded the meat with her knife. ''It needs to go back on the grill for a few more minutes. See that it's done properly this time, will you?''

After he left for the kitchen, Tally leaned forward. ''I stopped by the new Trim 'N Slim sport place. It costs seven hundred fifty to join, then thirty a month. Want to go with me?''

Marla tasted her grilled salmon with dill sauce. A warm buttery slice slid down her throat. ''You know I hate exercise classes.''

''Never mind the classes. We can use the machines. I'll meet you after work three times a week.''

''Not me, thanks.'' Stirring a generous dollop of sour cream and chives into her baked potato, she mixed it in with her fork.

''You think you're eating diet food with that fish, but look at the oil running off the dill sauce. And all those high-fat toppings you put on your potato, plus the wine, and your roll with butter—''

''That's enough!'' She wanted to enjoy her meal, not feel guilty over it.

The waiter returned, putting Tally's plate in front of

her for inspection. She nodded and picked up her fork. After a few bites where she rolled her eyes appreciatively, she said: "I just got in the perfect outfit for your size."

"Is that right?" Marla let a gleam of interest spark in her eyes. "I hope it's that pearl gray jumpsuit you showed me in the catalog. I didn't think it would be available so soon."

"I got a shipment yesterday and put it aside for you."

"When can I stop in?"

"You tell me. You're the busy one these days. Better come before Friday afternoon, though. Ken will be home, so I'm leaving early."

At the mention of her husband's name, a frown creased her forehead. Tally bent her head, supposedly intent on eating her dinner.

"What's wrong?" Marla asked, concerned. It wasn't like Tally to stop talking. She could usually hold up her end of a conversation for an entire meal.

Tally played with her parsley-sprinkled potatoes. "Ken has been acting strange since his last trip."

"How so?"

"More distant, like he doesn't want to spend time with me."

Marla didn't like the sound of this. Tally and Ken never had any trouble before. Married for ten years, their relationship reminded her of a meandering stream: just a few rocks in the way but easily bypassed. She hoped nothing serious was happening.

Tally's lashes shaded her downcast eyes. "He runs off to play golf on Sundays and doesn't ask me to join him. He barely talks to me when he's home. I'm afraid . . . maybe he's found someone else."

Marla heard the strain in her voice and felt a rush of

sympathy. "Ken doesn't strike me as the wandering type. Have you any evidence that he's interested in another woman?" She knew the score, having been through it herself with Stan.

"No, but I'm too embarrassed to call up his golf buddies and ask if he's there."

"So come up with an excuse. Peace of mind is worth it." She thought a minute, searching for a plausible explanation. "Could it be something at work is bothering him?"

"Ken just got promoted to regional director of disaster claims. It means he's away more often. If anything, he seems to look forward to these trips . . . and to not being with me."

Tally looked so disconsolate, Marla wanted to hug her. Surely she was misinterpreting her husband's reactions.

"Ken loves you," she said reassuringly, believing her own words. "Maybe if you talk to him—"

"I've tried to ask him what's wrong," Tally said, lifting her eyes. "He says I'm imagining things, then he gets close-mouthed. What should I do, Marla?"

She swallowed. "Look for evidence to back up your suspicions. Review the payments in your joint checking account, and see if there are checks made out to someone you don't know. Examine your phone bills and credit-card receipts." Hesitating, she cleared her throat. "I hope you've protected the income from your boutique." *Not that it's any business of mine, but I care about you.*

Tally's lip curled. "Don't worry, the income goes into my private savings account, and I manage the bookkeeping myself. I've always believed women should be self-sufficient regarding finances. Besides, I'm not going to give up without a fight."

"Uh-oh. Sounds like you're planning something wicked."

"You'll see."

"Tell me!"

"Sorry, I can't give away the details."

Marla decided not to pressure her. Instead, she drained her wineglass, feeling slightly woozy. When the waiter handed them each a dessert menu, she was sorely tempted to order a decadent sweet. Just for tonight, because she had so much on her mind. The extra calories would fuel her brain cells. Besides, tomorrow was time enough to tighten her belt.

"So what are you going to do if Todd Kravitz doesn't offer any useful information?" Tally said, switching topics with gusto. If there was one quality Marla admired in her, resiliency stood out. Tally rarely let anything dampen her high spirits.

"I'm going to see Wendy later in the week," she said, deliberately not mentioning why. No one else knew about that envelope, and she hoped to keep it secret. Her disgraceful act had been too shameful to confide even to her high-school friend.

"If Todd can't tell you where Zack works, Wendy might cooperate if you've got information to throw back at her," Tally offered. She eyed the dessert menu but just ordered an espresso.

"Like what?"

Tally lifted an eyebrow. "You'll think of something. You've got to play these people like musical instruments. Either they blend in with harmony, or you can use discord to make them talk."

"You may have a point," Marla conceded.

"If you think one of them paid Carlos to unlock the

back door at your salon, then find out where everyone
was that night. Also, who else besides Wendy knew Mrs.
Kravitz had an early hair appointment?''

"Good questions.''

"So they are, although I don't know why I'm helping
you. In my opinion, you should leave this stuff to Detective
Vail." Tally's face broke into a smile. "You can be very
stubborn when you set your mind to do something, and
I know you won't leave well enough alone. Just be careful,
and stop blaming yourself for what happened.''

Marla opened her mouth for a retort but the waiter
returned with their orders. *Gosh, that slice of brownie pie is
big enough for two! And look at that mound of whipped cream
dribbled with fudge.* She'd never be able to finish it.

"You've got to help me!" she pleaded, shoving the
plate forward. "Here, have some. This is too much!''

Tally laughed, dipping her spoon into the treat. "This
isn't my week for desserts, but you've forced me. Umm,
it's so-o-o good!''

Small talk occupied the time until the bill came. As
they walked to the exit, Tally turned to her.

"Call me tomorrow after your meeting with Todd. I
want to know you got home safely.''

"All right, if you promise to keep me informed about
you and Ken. I really don't think he could be involved
with someone else, Tally. He's always been so devoted to
you.''

"Not these days." She hugged Marla, and they went
their separate ways in the parking lot.

A heavy stillness, dominated by the rich smell of rotting
vegetation, hung in the night air. In the distance, a flash
of lightning ripped the skies, illuminating clouds sodden
with moisture. Storms heralded the approach of summer

hurricanes, even though the official season didn't start until June.

Driving home before the rain came, she pondered her conversation with Tally. How drastically her life had changed since last week. Obstacles blocked her path where before there were none, but at least she didn't have to face them alone. Friends like Arnie and Tally were ready to pitch in, as was Lance. Tonight wouldn't be too soon to call him.

The neighborhood was quiet as she pulled into her garage. She got her mail and turned to go inside when her eye caught on a return address. Galloway and Myers, Attorneys-At-Law. Oh, no.

Her stomach constricted as she tore open the envelope in her brightly lit kitchen. Quickly, she scanned the letter embossed with the firm's name as though the paper itself could intimidate the recipient. Roy Collins, on behalf of Sunshine Publishing, intended to sue for the amount of $250,000 owing to the loss of publisher and president, Bertha Kravitz, who died on the premises of Cut 'N Dye Beauty Salon because of the negligence of said owner, Marla Shore.

Damnation! Marla slammed the paper down on the counter and paced the kitchen, her blood boiling. How dare the man accuse her of neglect! Who knew Bertha would consume poison in the brief time she was gone? She'd only wanted to get some clean towels from the storeroom. She hadn't been the one who'd added cyanide to the powdered creamer. Someone else who'd known Bertha had a hair appointment that morning had done it . . . maybe even another customer. She hadn't considered that idea before because a relative or close business associate was a more likely suspect.

Her eyes narrowed, and she skidded to a halt. Maybe it was Roy Collins. This lawsuit could be his attempt at a cover-up. Wendy might get her aunt's fortune, but who gained control of the company? Did Bertha's partnership with Roy include right of survivorship?

Dashing to a phone, she picked up the receiver and dialed Lance's number.

"Hi, pal," she said when his deep voice answered. "You busy? I've got to talk to you."

"Sure, come on over," he crooned. "I've been wanting to show you some cool new web sites."

Right, pal. Like I don't know what you mean. "Let me buy you a drink at Tulario's instead," she replied, her stomach heaving at the thought of ingesting anything else. In her current mood, she'd be able to tolerate the lounge in the Italian restaurant. Small tables allowed for quiet conversation, and lighting was dim.

After Lance agreed to meet her, she raced into the bathroom, sparing a few minutes to freshen up. This was proving to be a very long day. As she powdered her nose, she glanced critically at the dark circles under her eyes and the pallor of her complexion. If she didn't take better care of herself, she'd get sick, and then who would prove her innocence?

Stuffing the attorneys' letter into her purse, she slammed out of the house, hoping the noise wouldn't rouse Moss next door. She wasn't in a tolerant mood, so she was grateful when Lance's friendly smile put her at ease. A small circular table with a votive candle divided them where they sat in the restaurant lounge. Marla took a slow sip of her Diet Coke, leisurely studying her companion. Lance's doughy complexion indicated he spent little time outdoors in the tropical sun. Owlish eyes the color of acorns seemed suited to a man who gazed at a computer screen all day as a systems analyst. His broad nose stood out like a beacon, proclaiming his distinctiveness, but it was his bushy mass of mud brown hair that made her chuckle. Running a comb through the dirty strands must be the last thing on his mind, but then so was ironing his rumpled plaid shirt.

She filled him in on events, then pulled out the letter from Roy Collins's attorney. "Here, read this." She thrust it forward, and he took it avariciously, eager for any intellectual challenge.

"Wow, what a bummer. How do you want me to help?"

She leaned forward, grimacing as the smell of cigarette smoke drifted into her nostrils. "Find out everything you can about Sunshine Publishing. Look into that tax-evasion deal and see if it's valid. I can use whatever I learn about Roy Collins."

He handed her back the letter. "I'll search my databases. Why don't you come over and watch me pick on this dude?"

"No, thanks. You'll work better without distractions. What kind of information will you be able to get?" she asked, curious. Her knowledge of the Net didn't extend much beyond basic search functions and E-mail.

He smiled enigmatically. "Court records, tax reports, bank accounts, you name it. I'll get something for you. This guy sounds like a real skunk."

She pushed away her empty glass. "What if I'm wrong? Maybe we won't find anything to discredit him, and I'll be stuck. I just wish I knew a good lawyer other than Stan."

"You don't want to call him yet, and hold off on notifying your insurance company, too. Wait and see what I come up with first.''

She looked into his sympathetic brown eyes and felt a rush of warmth. ''You know, if you help me get out of this, I just may come over and see your blasted web sites.''

In a better mood, she went home. After tossing her purse onto the kitchen counter, she trotted into her office to check for messages on the answering machine. Sure enough, the light was flashing. Five calls. One of these days she'd get caller ID so she could tell right away who'd phoned. Hoping she hadn't missed an important call, she pushed the play button.

''Hi, Marla. Just checking to see if everything is okay,'' said Anita's familiar voice. Marla bit her lip. She'd forgotten to call her mother earlier to tell her what a good dinner she'd had there on Sunday. Well, that could wait until tomorrow.

She ran through the other calls which were brief messages from concerned friends. Nicole, Ralph, and—

Her heart stopped. Oh, no. Why did his grating voice have to disturb her peace?

Stan had called twice. Damn him. Now she knew he'd be on her back, taking advantage of her vulnerability. If only she didn't feel such a surge of anger in his presence, she could confront him with impunity.

Giving in to her fatigue, she took a shower after Spooks had his evening run into the backyard. She had just slipped into her nightshirt, the new one from Victoria's Secret she'd splurged on last week, when the phone rang.

''Hello.'' She picked her damp towel off the carpet and tossed it into the bathroom.

''Marla Shore?'' said a muffled voice.

''Yep, that's me.'' A frown creased her forehead. She

didn't recognize the voice, nor was she sure of the caller's gender.

"I have a suggestion for you," rasped the person on the other end of the line. "Mind your own business, unless you want your next cup of coffee to be your last."

Click. The dial tone buzzed, but Marla stood riveted with the receiver to her ear.

6

Trace the call. Quick, before it's too late.

Cursing herself for not having caller ID, she replaced the receiver in its cradle and searched her mind for the correct code. What did you dial when you wanted to retrace the last call? Damn, she couldn't remember.

Rummaging through a pile of papers on her desk, she gave a cry of triumph when she spotted the information sheet she'd saved from the phone company. There it was—Call Return. Dial *69 to automatically trace the last number that called you. A one-time charge of seventy-five cents meant you didn't need to subscribe to the service to use it. Pressing the numeral 1 would even return the call for you.

Her trembling fingers punched in the code and she heard a voice announcing a phone number along with the date and time of the last call. She scribbled down the info then pushed the number 1 on her touchpad. The phone rang, but no one answered. Right, what else did she expect? Most likely, the number reached a pay phone.

But just in case information was available, she'd ask Lance to check on it for her. Maybe she'd even tell Detective Vail that she had been threatened. But would he believe her? He might conclude she was trying to put him off her trail. Better to go through Lance, who was more sympathetic, Marla decided.

As she got ready for bed, anger filled her veins. It wasn't enough that a woman had been murdered in her salon and police suspicion should fall upon her. Now she was being personally threatened. It only tightened her resolve to bring the killer to justice. Her sense of responsibility for Bertha's demise might have given her reason to get involved in the first place, but now things had taken a new turn. No one messed with her without paying the price.

"So did you notify Lance?" Nicole asked at work early the next day. Marla, having a break between customers, joined the tall young stylist in the storeroom for a cup of coffee and a private schmooze.

"Yep. He didn't appreciate my waking him up either. Said he'd contact me later once he traced the call." She pulled at her long skirt, feeling fidgety. That nasty message had put her on edge more than she'd realized.

"You're sure you can't identify the voice?" Nicole's brown eyes penetrated hers.

Marla shook her head. "I couldn't even tell if it was a man or a woman."

"I don't like this, Marla. You could be in danger. Aren't you going to tell Detective Vail?"

"No, I won't say anything unless I have some solid information to give him."

"What about Stan? Maybe you should give him a call. He might be able to offer some good advice."

"Like what? Who to hire as a criminal defense attorney? No, thanks, I'll never give him the satisfaction!" She shifted her feet. "I'll bet he's planning to force me into selling our property. He must have heard the news about Bertha Kravitz by now. If he knew about that letter from Roy Collins, he'd be breathing down my neck trying to coerce me into signing papers."

"Much as you hate the idea, Marla, you might have to call him if your insurance company won't handle this lawsuit. Stan is tough as nails, and you'll need someone like him against Roy Collins from the sound of it."

"Hey, whattya guys talking about?" interrupted Darlene, sauntering into the storeroom. "Like I heard Roy's name mentioned."

"Since when do you have such sharp ears?" Marla snapped.

Tension frayed her nerves because she couldn't face a confrontation with Stan just now. Hopefully, Lance would give her the scoop on Sunshine Publishing and any shady deals on Roy's part so she'd have something substantial to use for a counterattack. She didn't need Stan, not yet.

Darlene lifted her chin. "I'm just curious about what's going on, that's all."

"Well, Collins is trying to sue me for neglect regarding Bertha's death," Marla explained, feeling chagrined at herself for being unduly harsh.

"Oh, yeah?" A look of sympathy came over Darlene's face. "That's a real bummer. So what are you gonna do about it?"

Marla bit her lower lip, hesitating. She didn't want to reveal Lance's involvement.

Nicole put a hand on Marla's shoulder. "She has a friend who can help her."

"Is that so? Someone I know?" Darlene persisted.

"I may have to call Stan," Marla said hastily.

Darlene thrust out her bosom which spilled from her low-cut tank top. "Huh! What's he gonna do? Bring a countersuit?"

"Why do you care?" Marla retorted.

Darlene gave a vaporous smile. "Just want to make sure you're doing okay. Someone's got to keep an eye on you, see? For your own welfare."

"How kind," Marla murmured, puzzled by her last remark.

"Ladies, here come your next appointments," Lucille's voice yelled from the outer realm.

Striding into the salon, Marla greeted her customer and directed her to the shampoo bowl. Nicole did the same, while Darlene went to fix her nails at a vacant manicure station.

"I don't think you should reveal so much to Darlene," hissed Nicole. Her ebony hair swung at her back in a low ponytail as she straightened a row of shears. "Something is strange about her. She takes too much interest in that Roy Collins."

"I agree." She risked a glance in Darlene's direction. The miniskirted girl was filing a nail, an insipid look on her pretty face. It seemed inconceivable that she'd possess an ounce of cunning. "I can't put my finger on it, though. Why would she want to get involved?"

Nicole turned her attention to the woman walking in

her direction with soggy hair. "I don't know, Marla, but heed my warning. That girl is trouble."

Marla wiped any further musings from her mind. Tiffany, her next customer, finished her hair wash and was trotting over at a fast clip.

"I'm in a hurry," she gushed, sweeping into the chair Marla indicated. "Gotta run to a Roadkill Society meeting."

As Tiffany was barely five feet tall, her head was too low for Marla to work on comfortably. Marla raised the chair level before draping a cape around the young woman's shoulders.

"Do you know how many animals are killed needlessly each year?" Tiffany said, eyes flashing indignantly. "Hundreds! We can save them by educating drivers."

"How are we doing your hair today?" Marla interrupted, touching the damp strands.

"I'd like the sides more angled." Her sharp gaze darted over other customers. "People let their pets out without any restraint. That's a big mistake," she said in a biting tone. "The animal runs into the street and *boom*—dead meat. Think of the unborn litters that never have a chance. It's a preventable tragedy!"

I can think of worse things, like children drowning in backyard swimming pools. That's where public education can save lives.

Her fingers moving automatically, Marla's mind wandered back to her conversation with Nicole. The stylist's warning popped into her head like a raised flag. What if an outsider hadn't poisoned the creamer? What if it were one of her staff members, like Darlene? So Carlos had left the back door unlocked. That could have been an honest mistake.

Frowning, she reviewed events of the fatal morning. She could have sworn the creamer jar had been at least a quarter full the last time she'd used it, but on this occasion, there was only enough to flavor one cup of coffee. She didn't have another in stock, either. Who could have used this knowledge against her? Who might have emptied the creamer jar so she had to use the last poisoned spoonful? Following this train of thought, she figured it had to be someone who'd known Bertha Kravitz was coming in that morning. Otherwise, Marla might have noticed the depleted creamer supply and bought another jar to keep in reserve. Anyone, including customers, had access to the storeroom, but not everyone knew her appointment schedule.

As soon as her last appointment departed, she gathered her belongings. "I'm leaving," she announced, inspecting her workstation with satisfaction. She'd tidied up and had no further obligations. "Lucille, you'll lock up, won't you? I'd appreciate it."

"Got a date?" the receptionist asked, smiling.

"You might say that." Tonight was her meeting with Todd, but she wasn't about to let Lucille in on her plans. She wanted to gather her thoughts before the interview.

Unfortunately, when she arrived home, chores took up most of her time. After gulping down a hasty dinner, she leashed Spooks for his evening walk and exited into the humid air.

They were returning around the bend in view of her town house when she spotted a familiar male figure pacing her front sidewalk. Her heart sank as she regarded his set jaw and cool hazel eyes. Stan looked every inch the distinguished attorney with his pin-striped charcoal suit and polished dress shoes. Even his dark hair, slicked back from a wide forehead, reflected his harsh self-discipline in that not a single strand lifted in the slight evening breeze.

A sickening weight settled in Marla's stomach as she approached. Spooks yipped furiously, straining her wrist as he sought to charge at the intruder. She yanked on his leash, muttering an expletive under her breath.

"Hi, Marla." Stan stalked directly into her path. "I've been trying to contact you. We need to talk."

Marla stiffened. It didn't matter that the blazing Florida sun left her feeling like a limp dishrag even though she'd changed into shorts and a T-shirt. Stan's presence affected her like a splash of ice water.

"There's nothing we have to say to each other," she said, restraining Spooks from jumping on his leg. Her glance noted the absence of a vehicle in her driveway. "Where's your car?"

"Kimberly dropped me off. She had to go to Eckerd's and then she'll be back."

"Oh, joy." Unwilling to let him inside the town house, she paused beside a bed of colorful impatiens. Gazing directly into his hard, resolute eyes, she challenged him with her own determined stare. "So what do you want this time?" she sneered. *As if I don't know.* Having given up on attacking her ex-spouse, Spooks settled for sniffing the grass near her feet.

"I was hoping you'd decided to sell our rental property. It would be a good move considering your circumstances. A good move," he added in his irritating manner of repeating phrases for emphasis.

Ignoring an itch on her ankle, Marla quirked an eyebrow. "Oh? What do you mean?"

He glowered at her, which was difficult considering the sun was shining directly on his face. Marla had purposely taken advantage of the shadier position. "You must be losing business because of that woman's murder. Selling our building will land us lots of capital. *Lots*, Marla. We can both use it."

"What do you know about the murder?" she demanded. For an instant, the absurd notion swept her mind that he'd committed the crime in order to force her into selling. Apparently he was unaware that business had swelled as a result.

"I heard on the news that the woman was poisoned. Aren't people afraid to come to the salon now?"

She smirked. "Quite the opposite. Business has never been better. Disappointed?"

His scowl grew fierce. She stood firm, refusing to back away like she'd done during their marriage. He'd never been physically violent, but his verbal abuse had been more than enough. *You can handle it. He can't hurt you now.* Memories flooded her: belittling remarks he'd thrown at her, scornful comments made in front of his friends. Humiliation had been her constant companion. Thank God she'd come to her senses, but the bastard still tried to push her under whenever the opportunity arose.

"That woman died in your salon," he told her, peering down his arrogant nose. "Her relatives have a good case if they decide to sue. You should be covering your tail."

"How? By hiring you?" Restless to move on, Spooks pulled on the leash. She restrained him with a sharp command.

"You need me, Marla. Don't think you can handle this alone. You've always needed me, even though you won't admit it." His sweeping gesture encompassed her street. "Look at this place. It's a comedown from what we had together. A comedown. And you, still single, unable to establish a stable relationship—"

"Go to hell," she snarled, unable to help herself. Gripping Spook's leash with tight knuckles, she strode toward her front door.

A strong grip clamped on her shoulder, bringing her to a sudden halt. Stan spun her around, towering over her by a good six inches.

"Don't touch me!" she yelled, jerking free.

His eyes narrowed to slits. "Listen to me! I intend to sell that property. You *will* cooperate. I'll have my assistant run the papers over for you to sign."

"Don't tell me what to do, Stan. I'm not your doormat anymore. I will not sell my share of the property, understand?"

"You'd better do as I say." His fists clenched at his sides.

"Or what? You'll sue me?" She laughed aloud. "Get lost, pal. I'm outta here."

"You'll be sorry!" he hollered, as she rushed inside her house.

"I've got enough problems," she muttered, slamming the dead bolt in place. Stooping, she released Spooks from his leash. "Not you, precious. You're my comfort." Lifting his small body, she hugged him close to her chest. His soft form warmed her heart as he licked her chin. Ironic, wasn't it, that her dog cared more about her than her former husband? But Stan had never cared about anyone except himself.

Depressed, she threw off her shoes and plopped down on the living-room sofa, still cuddling Spooks. He snuggled close, bringing her a fleeting sense of security as she scratched behind his ears. It disappeared rapidly when she recalled Stan's parting words. Great, more trouble. Just what she needed.

How could she have fallen in love with a man like him? Undoubtedly, it was the Cinderella story revisited. Lowly hairstylist wooed by rich, powerful lawyer. Never mind that she was emotionally vulnerable after Tammy's accident. How could she resist when her mother had erupted in raptures at the prospect of a marriage between Marla and a nice Jewish man? Stan's parents had been just as thrilled by the match. With so many intermarriages occurring these days, they were excited he hadn't chosen a *shikseh*, and they showered Marla with attention.

Marla never understood what Stan saw in her until later when things began to unravel. Then she realized he got his kicks out of power plays. He didn't want her to work, to go out with friends, much less to think for herself. The man lived to dominate her. Joining the coalition to help prevent child drownings had given her a purpose. It also gave her the boost of confidence she'd needed to counter Stan's negative influence on her self-esteem. Without Tally's support, she might not have made it through the divorce. Tally came up with the suggestion that Marla use her divorce settlement to buy a salon. It would give her a sense of self-worth which she sorely lacked. Establishing the business had been her salvation. Now Marla reveled in her freedom. No longer did she have to live up to someone else's standards. The prospect of not having children didn't deter her from remaining single. Too much pain could come from that direction, and she preferred for things to stay stable. Oh yes, things were rolling along just as smooth as fudge.

That is, until Bertha Kravitz died in her salon and Roy Collins menaced her and Stan compounded her anxiety with his nasty remarks. What else could go wrong? Don't forget Detective Vail and the envelope! If he discovered its contents, she might end up in jail. Her blood chilled as grim images came to mind: being forced to undergo a body search; finding herself locked in a cell with hardened criminals; days passing with boredom as her only companion. Lord save her.

If only Todd Kravitz would shed some light on his mother's murder, she'd have a new lead to follow. Rising, she plodded into the bedroom to get ready for their meeting. Her assignation took on a higher priority when Lance phoned with his report. As she'd suspected, the threatening call had been made from a pay phone. No scoop there. Praying that her encounter with Todd would be more fruitful, she quickly showered and dressed. At eight-thirty, she grabbed her purse, said good-bye to Spooks, and fled her town house.

Scudders was nestled across the street from the beach between a swimwear shop and a tacky souvenir place selling orange-blossom perfume, T-shirts with crass Floridian emblems, and plastic alligators. You could tell it was a singles hangout by the rock music blaring from the open doorway and the cluster of young groupies wearing jewelry on unusual body parts, like that guy with the nose ring and an earring on his lip.

Marla pushed her way inside, wrinkling her nose at the assault of smoke and beer fumes. Through the dim haze, she squinted, attempting to locate Todd Kravitz. Gyrating bodies on a center dance floor made it difficult to see into the dark corners beyond. Scanning the crowded bar to the left, she didn't catch sight of him.

Someone touched her arm, startling her. She glanced

at the young man with yellow teeth who hovered nearby and suppressed a moue of disappointment. Darn, was Todd even going to show up? Maybe she should walk around to the rear and see if he was situated behind the dance floor. Belatedly, she realized the man was saying something to her, but the din made it hard to hear.

"Excuse me?" she said.

"You wanna dance, luv?" Yellow Teeth leaned closer, sending her a waft of foul breath. His bulging eyes trailed down her sleeveless navy knit dress, making her wish she hadn't chosen an outfit with such a short skirt and snug fit.

She took a step backward. "I'm waiting for someone, thanks."

"So what? I'll keep you busy in the meantime." He grabbed her hand, pulling her toward the dance floor just as the four-piece band started playing a slow number.

Annoyed, Marla wrestled out of his grasp. "Bug off, pal."

The man's pockmarked features reddened with fury. "Hey, nobody talks to Hawkeye like that."

Craning her neck, Marla spotted Todd at a table in the back. Figures he'd pick the darkest corner.

"Sorry, my date is here," she said, feeling a rush of relief. Leaving Hawkeye glowering after her, she headed toward Todd. Seated at a burl wood table, he was clutching a beer bottle and staring at a flickering votive candle. Without waiting for an invitation, she slid onto the cushioned rattan seat opposite him.

"Didn't you see me come in?" she asked.

"Nope." His bleary blue eyes regarded her with disinterest.

"I thought you'd be waiting up front." *No wonder you're*

hiding in the corner, pal. You look like you just crawled out of bed. Her scornful glance absorbed his unkempt appearance. His colored black hair, lighter roots showing, hung like strands on a wet mop framing a face that badly needed a shave. Rumpled clothes bearing old coffee stains indicated he was overdue to visit a laundromat. And the way he slouched in his chair told her this wasn't his first drink for the night, nor would it be his last.

"You didn't bring anyone else, did you?" he muttered.

"No, I came alone."

His gaze shifted to her bosom, half-exposed by her low-cut bodice, and a spark of interest ignited his eyes. Clearly he wasn't interested in the mother-of-pearl choker that matched her earrings. A lazy smile curved his mouth, sending a jolt of recognition through her.

"I always thought you were a classy dame," he said. "You and me . . . we'd be a hot number."

"I don't think so!" She shuddered at the images that came to mind. "What do you mean, 'you always thought'? Did we meet somewhere other than at your mother's funeral?"

He leered at her, making her skin crawl. "You really haven't got a clue, do you? Yo, get the lady a drink," he yelled to a passing waitress.

Marla ordered a bushwacker, in the mood for the coffee flavored beverage with its generous blend of liqueurs and cream. At least she'd get something good from this evening, if only a drink. She was wondering how to proceed when a warm hand touched her thigh. Shocked, she jerked away.

Todd scraped his chair closer. "You want me to talk, you'd better be nice, babe."

His hand snaked back under the table, stroking her

inner thigh with a determined persistence. An unpleasant feeling invaded her senses, making her want to scream. Why did his touch seem so familiar and yet so distasteful? Had they dated before, so long ago she couldn't remember? Narrowing her eyes, she studied him, wondering how he had looked before he'd dyed his hair and lost years to a decadent lifestyle.

Her drink came and she took a long swallow to quell her uneasiness. "What did you want to tell me about your mother?" she snapped, hoping to get this over with as soon as possible. "You said you knew who wanted her dead."

He withdrew his hand, a scowl written across his face. "Zack Greenfield has a lot to gain."

Somehow she wasn't surprised by his revelation. "Why is that, because Wendy will inherit Bertha's money? How do you feel about not being her heir?"

"The old lady cut me out of her will a long time ago."

"You sound resentful."

"She never appreciated my talents, although you could say we were cut from the same mold. My mother was a real bitch." He grinned at her, a sly look in his eyes. "You'd known her for a long time, babe. I'm sure you'd agree."

Marla stared at him. *Dear heaven, does he know about the envelope?* Quickly, she changed the subject.

"Tell me about Zack."

Putting his hands behind his head, he lounged back in his chair. "Unlike me, Zack desperately needs the money."

She chewed her lip in frustration. Would she have to pry every bit of information from his mouth? Which tidbit should she pursue, his remark about himself or Zack's plight?

"Wendy said Zack was upset about her taking maternity leave. I gather they need her income to make ends meet. Or at least they did until she became an heiress."

"You got it." Todd glanced around and lowered his voice. "Greenfield's investments soured last year when the stock market took a dive. He had to borrow money to pay off his clients who were demanding their funds. His creditors ain't too nice if you know what I mean. Zack owes his old gambling buddies, and you don't mess with them."

"So you're saying he's in debt."

"Right on. His job is in jeopardy, plus he needs to repay those hoods he owes. My mother's estate will give him what he needs to pull himself through."

"Do you think Wendy knows?"

"Not the whole deal. I think she's spooked, though. She knows how much Zack hated the old lady. Mokie— that's what I called my mother—dictated their lives and was always putting Zack down. He resented her interference."

"You said she cut you out of her will. What was the nature of your disagreement?"

He grinned. "She didn't like how I earn a living."

"And how is that?"

A lecherous look came over his face as he regarded her. "You should know, babe."

His pointed glance made her feel sordid. "Where were you the night before your mother drank the poisoned coffee?"

"I was right here at Scudders until I went home with a hot babe named Teena. Ask the bartender: Rocko will vouch for me." He leaned forward, his breath fanning her face. "I suppose I could ask you the same thing."

She bristled at his tone. "I didn't kill her."

"No? How come that detective was so interested in your relationship to my mother?"

Her face paled. "Detective Vail spoke to you about me?"

He nodded, smirking. "I didn't tell him what I know."

"And what is that?" she demanded, not sure she wanted to hear his answer.

He reached across the table and squeezed her hand. "Come back to my place, and I'll let you in on a little secret." Rubbing her skin, he added, "We can get to know each other better."

God, no. Whatever he had to say wasn't worth that price. "You have something to tell me, go ahead. I'm not going anywhere with you."

Laughing, he poked her arm. "You'll come. I'll just wait until you knock on my door, babe. Until then, good luck fending off the cops."

Saluting, he rose and lurched away.

It took Marla a few minutes of stunned silence to realize he'd stuck her with the bill.

7

The Strip was crowded with walkers when Marla left Scudders. Ten o'clock was relatively early by beach standards, but many of the throng were out for an after-dinner stroll. Party animals would cruise into the area later, drinking until their bleary vision forced them home.

Marla, needing time to think, crossed the street to parade along the sidewalk beside the undulating wall leading to the sand and ocean. Her ears picked up the foaming sizzle of the waves as they crashed onto shore and ebbed back to sea. A grim smile curved her lips as she compared her jumbled thoughts to the tumultuous water. Todd had given her much to think about, but for a moment she allowed her senses to absorb the salty night air and caressing breeze. Like most residents, she didn't come here often enough. Being near the sea relaxed her, but usually she was caught up in a busy routine that precluded leisure time. *Life is too short not to stop and look around,* she reminded herself. Against her will, an image of Tammy invaded her mind. The little girl would never know such beauty, and it was all her fault. She had to live for both of them in order to honor Tammy's memory.

Abruptly she halted and executed an about-face. Those were matters she didn't care to dwell on right now. Lifting her chin, she caught a startling glimpse of Detective Vail a few paces ahead.

She crossed the distance in several short steps. "Were you following me?" she demanded, thrusting her face in front of his. Her fists clenched as rage boiled to the surface. Despite what he believed, she would not be treated like a common criminal.

His insolent gaze met hers. "Why would I want to tail *you*, Ms. Shore? Is there something you have to hide?"

Planting her hands on her hips, she scowled at him. "You think I murdered Bertha Kravitz, but since you don't have proof, back off or I'll scream harassment."

His lip curled in amusement. "I'm just out for an evening stroll, like you are. Or did I just see you leave Scudders across the street?"

She wondered if he'd seen Todd Kravitz or made any connection between the two of them. "I don't have to answer your questions," she retorted. "If you'll excuse me, I'm returning to my car before the meter runs out." She had plenty of time left, which he'd already know if he'd followed her there.

"Wait," he said, holding up a hand. "How about that cup of coffee you promised me? Pirate's Cove is just rolling into action."

Hesitating, Marla considered her options. Going home was the most sensible course, but whoever said she had nothing but practical bones in her body?

"All right," she conceded. "But if this turns out to be another interrogation session, I'm outta here."

Tossing his head back, he laughed. The pleasant, masculine sound aroused her senses. A closer look revealed he wasn't attired for work unless the undercover mode counted. He wore a gunmetal gray knit shirt that brought out the silvery highlights in his hair. She liked the casual windswept style better than his usual slicked-back look, and it engendered an unwanted feminine response. Avoiding his perceptive gaze, she dropped her eyes to his broad shoulders which stretched the shirt fabric taut across his chest. Her glance trailed downward to his trim waistband. He kept himself fit, she realized, wondering what sports he engaged in. *Don't even think about it,* she warned herself. *So what if he's attractive? He suspects you of being a murderess. The man is off-limits, at least for now.*

Entering the restaurant, they were seated at a table facing the ocean. There wasn't much of a view as the blackness of night obliterated any hint of a horizon. Vail didn't seem to mind. He ordered two coffees and focused his attention exclusively on her.

"So are you going to tell me what you're doing on the Strip?" he asked, a steely glint in his eyes.

"I thought you weren't going to question me." His company made her nervous, which she tried to hide by twisting her fingers under the table.

He shrugged. "Call it curiosity. I doubt a pretty lady like you needs to frequent bars to get a date."

Inwardly she preened at his calling her pretty before reason took hold. Maybe he hadn't spotted Todd Kravitz after all. Deciding to test him, she confessed her assignation. "I met Todd Kravitz for a chat. He'd indicated at his mother's funeral that he had something important to tell me." Waiting for Vail's reaction, she was mildly disappointed when he merely raised an eyebrow.

Their coffees came, and she took her time adding cream and sugar. Vail drank his brew black, which she might have expected. It seemed strange to be sitting in a restaurant with a police detective who considered her the prime suspect in a murder case. Vail appeared remarkably at ease, as though he had asked her out for social reasons, but she knew that wasn't likely. Hoping to persuade him of her innocence, she continued.

"Todd said Zack Greenfield might have had a motive for killing Bertha." She repeated what he'd said about Zack's financial status.

"Did Todd mention the names of these creditors?" Vail asked, his heavy brows drawn together.

Shaking her head, she gave a negative response. She neglected to inform him about Lance's efforts, figuring Vail's department was already looking into the backgrounds of Bertha's relations. Would he share his information with her?

"What have you learned about the Greenfields?" she queried.

He took a sip of hot coffee. "Not much more than you at this point. Zack works for a large investment firm. He steered his investors down the wrong path and is now paying the price." Leaning forward, he captured her eyes with his piercing gaze. "What puzzles me is what game you're playing."

The intensity of his glare made her breath come short. "What do you mean?"

"Sounds to me like you're snooping in places you don't belong. Why?"

She clenched her jaw. "I want to expose Bertha's murderer as much as you do. She expired in my salon. That makes me partially responsible, but I didn't put the poison in her drink. I intend to find out who did."

Vail didn't respond immediately, as though weighing the truthfulness of her remark. "You should leave this investigation to professionals," he finally commented, his expression hooded.

"I'm not going to do anything foolish, and I'll tell you what I learn." Did he believe her, or did he already know about the envelope? Briefly she considered admitting its existence and what it signified, but she decided it would not be in her best interest at this time. Better to learn all she could about Bertha's connections first so he'd have other paths to follow. Maybe she'd made a mistake in the past that Bertha cashed in on, but that didn't make her a murderess. And if Bertha was blackmailing her, who else might she have victimized as well? When she went to meet Wendy on Friday, she'd search for other evidence along with her envelope.

"I got a threatening phone call last night," she blurted, hoping to engage his sympathy.

His hand tightened around his coffee mug. "What do you mean?"

Shrugging, she said, "I couldn't tell if it was a man or woman. Whoever it was advised me to mind my own business or I would be the next poisoning victim."

A scowl warped his features. "Why didn't you report this right away? Damn stubborn woman. You could be putting yourself in danger."

Bless my bones, is he really concerned for my safety? Maybe he had been tailing Todd tonight, and not her. How reassuring. "I attended Bertha's funeral," she said. "Her business partner, Roy Collins, threatened to bring a lawsuit against me. That's where I met Todd and the Greenfields. When I visited Wendy, she hinted that Todd and his mother didn't get along."

"You visited Wendy? When was this?"

She gave him a brief smile. "I paid her a *shivah* call the day after the funeral. I gathered she doesn't like Todd because she tried to raise my doubts about his motives. She said he manages to earn a living, but he doesn't have a regular job. Maybe Bertha found out he's doing something illegal and he decided to dispose of her."

"That's a pretty drastic way to silence your mother."

"Todd wouldn't tell me what he does in the way of money-making activities." A shudder racked her spine. He'd made her distinctly uneasy during their conversation. By alluding to events she should be aware of but couldn't remember, he'd just raised more questions in her mind.

"We're not sure, either, but it bears checking into along with everything else." Folding his hands on the table, he fastened his eyes on her face. "You said Bertha Kravitz gave you a loan to pay for beauty school. Your parents wouldn't help you out?"

He's raising the heat, she thought, contemplating her response. She'd needed money, all right, but cosmetology school wasn't the only reason. And Bertha wasn't the source for either need.

"My mother didn't approve of my career switch. I'd gone to college for two years as an education major, and she'd set her heart on my becoming a teacher. When I changed my mind, she got angry and told me I was on my own."

"So you met Bertha, and she agreed to give you a loan?"

"Right." After finishing her coffee, she patted her lips dry with a napkin. "Look, you aren't supposed to question me. I've offered you information, and I expect you to accept it in the spirit in which it's given."

"Touché." His face broke into a wry grin. "This isn't really what I intended when I asked you out for a drink. I just have trouble shutting off my inquisitive mind."

A loud commotion at the next table diverted her attention. A bunch of tank-topped males were clamoring for more beer. Glancing around, she noted the place had gotten crowded and raucous with laughter. Smells of charbroiled meats mingled with browned onions. Although it was well past ten, people were still ordering full meals.

Reverting her gaze to the man seated across from her, Marla smiled. "And just what did you intend, Detective Vail?"

He gave her a quizzical glance. "Please, call me Dalton. I'm not sure what I wanted ... Marla. I don't know whether to arrest you or date you. You're a woman of many layers, and I feel compelled to peel them away, see what makes you tick." He paused. "I haven't felt this way since my wife died two years ago."

Oh, joy. Should she be pleased by his interest, or was it another ploy to throw her off guard? She wasn't particularly thrilled by his desire to analyze her. It made her feel like a subject for his personality studies. Or maybe she was being too paranoid. Twisting her napkin, she wondered why he'd even admit to harboring a personal agenda unless he meant it. And if he was sincere, how did she feel about him?

"I'm sorry about your wife," she murmured.

"Yes, well, we're managing." At her inquiring look, he added: "I have a twelve-year-old daughter."

"It must be tough for her."

"Brianna doesn't say much, but I know she hurts." A pained expression crossed his face before he hid it behind a mask of impassivity. "She's coming to an age where she needs a woman to guide her."

Oh no, not him, too. Just like Arnie, he wants a mother for his child. "You might as well know I'm not the motherly type." Afraid he'd probe into her background, she held up a hand. "Look, this is getting too heavy for me. I'd rather not get involved while Bertha's murder is unsolved."

"And if that weren't an issue?"

She glanced away. "Let's deal with it when the time comes."

He compressed his mouth, and she got the feeling he wasn't used to being rebuffed. She hoped it wouldn't influence his opinion of her regarding the murder case.

"If you get any more of those anonymous calls, beep me," he said on their way out of the restaurant. After rummaging in his wallet, he handed her a business card.

She stuck it in her purse and stopped when he halted by the front entrance. He touched her elbow, his smoky eyes peering down into hers.

"I hope you're going to leave the rest of this investigation to me."

"Maybe I would if I trusted you, but I still think you suspect me. I need to preserve my reputation."

He glared at her in blatant disapproval. "You're absolutely right. You are my number one suspect. Being alone with the deceased, you had the perfect opportunity to do away with her without any witnesses. I'm still working on the motive, and you'd better hope I don't come across one. In the meantime, I've got a good excuse to keep my eye on you."

"Just make sure you give the others the same consideration," she said, her tone sarcastic. Their encounter had told her nothing new except to watch her back from all directions.

He escorted her to the parking lot, each of them lost in private contemplation. As she started the engine, she determined to act carefully over the next few days. The visit to Bertha's house became more imperative than any other avenue of pursuit. She had to get that envelope before Vail discovered it. Otherwise, she'd have a lot of uncomfortable explaining to do, and if she thought the murder case might impair her reputation, the contents of that envelope would do worse. While she was there, she'd sound Wendy out about the other principals in the case. The girl had to know more than she was letting on.

A sweet scent perfumed the air as Marla left work on Friday aftern. . She'd hurried through her morning appointments, her tension growing with each passing hour. She felt uncertain of Wendy's reception and anxious to recover the envelope whose contents could condemn her. Partially cloudy, the weather reflected her sense of dread as she drove east on Las Olas Boulevard.

"Is that you, Marla?" Wendy called. Her voice came from inside Bertha Kravitz's house. Marla had just pressed the front doorbell and stood outside waiting impatiently.

"Yes, it's me." Shifting her feet, she glanced at her rust-colored jumpsuit. The outfit was too constricting in this heat. Her throat tightening, she swiped a hand around the inner circle of her collar.

"Hi, come on in," Wendy said, swinging the door open.

She looked comfortable in a peach shorts set, her polished toenails sticking out from a pair of white sandals. From the dust on her knees, Marla surmised she'd been hard at work.

"How are you getting along?" Marla asked, stepping inside.

Gesturing for Marla to follow her into the adjacent living room, Wendy gave a sad smile. "I'm doing okay. It hurts to go through Aunty Bertha's things, though."

They seated themselves opposite each other, Marla claiming a gold-silk-upholstered loveseat. She spared a brief glance around the area, not surprised to see much hadn't changed since her last visit. With no pets or kids in the house, Bertha could afford to maintain a stiffly formal atmosphere.

Twisting her hands in her lap, she considered how to approach the matter of the envelope. *Delicately*, she advised herself.

"This must be a difficult time for your family," she commented, deciding to play the sympathetic listener.

Wendy glanced at the beige carpet. "I feel the loss more than Zack, and I can't speak for Todd except that he's not even interested enough to help me here."

"You're Bertha's personal representative?"

"That's right." Wendy gave her a curious look as though wondering why Marla was so concerned about her private affairs.

"I remember you said Bertha resented your husband," Marla persisted in a kindly tone, "but surely he can offer you his support. You shouldn't have to do this work all by yourself."

Wendy shrugged, her relaxed demeanor telling Marla she wasn't eager to return to her task. "You know Aunty

Bertha tried to tell us what to do. The only way she could exert control over Zack was to offer us money. If nothing else, that could sway him, but he always resented her interference."

"Did Zack know Bertha was getting her hair done that morning?"

"I-I may have mentioned it. We were both supposed to attend the luncheon with her."

"Were you and Zack home all that night before?"

Wendy shot to her feet. "I've answered enough questions for the police. What else was it you came here for, Marla?"

She released a long breath. "A manila envelope addressed to me. Have you located it?"

Wendy's dark eyes probed hers. "I've just begun to search through her study. That police detective took her appointment book, financial records, and the key to her safe, among other things. Do you want to look on her desk?"

"Sure." Marla sprang up, trying not to appear too eager as she followed Wendy into the old woman's home office. Inside, she approached a massive oak desk. Electronic gadgets were noticeably absent except for a Smith-Corona typewriter and a portable phone unit, the only concessions to technology. A couple of Mont Blanc pens sat in a marble holder on the desk top beside pencils with erasers in a matching container. The impression was one of quiet elegance. Three clocks ticked away in various corners, indicating that Mrs. Kravitz either believed in punctuality or collected timepieces as a hobby.

A pile of papers lay scattered about various surfaces, including the desk. She shuffled through them, her panic growing as she searched for the envelope and couldn't find it.

Was she too late? Had Detective Vail already recovered it? But then he would have said something when she'd met him the other day. Unless he was toying with her, trying to entrap her with her own contradictions.

Sweat broke out on her brow. She pushed a stack of papers aside to search again. Her fingers fell upon a sharp object, forcing an exclamation from her lips. Peering at it, she frowned. A screw-back earring? If she recalled correctly, both Bertha and Wendy had pierced ears.

Glancing to see if Wendy was still busy rummaging through a collection of unpaid bills, she turned it over in her hand. The pearl-and-marcasite setting was attractive albeit old-fashioned.

"Wendy, did this belong to your aunt?" she called, holding up the item.

Wendy squinted. "I've never seen that piece of jewelry before. Aunty Bertha wore gold mostly and never screwbacks."

"Nobody else has been in here for the past few days, right? Except for you and the cops?"

"As far as I know. I did accidentally leave a door unlocked the last time I was here, but the police were watching the place then." She held a hand to her stomach and grimaced.

"Are you all right?"

"Yeah, just feeling a little sick. It happens unexpectedly, not always in the morning like you'd expect. Zack says I should get over it soon."

"Maybe you need to rest for a while. You can't work yourself too hard when you're pregnant."

"I'm just glad I was able to get this week off from work, although I wish the circumstances had been different." A trace of sadness infected her words.

Feeling a surge of sympathy, Marla patted her arm. "Bertha will live on in your loving memories."

"She'd planned to write her memoirs, you know. She told us at Passover. Todd wasn't very happy, but he usually argued with her about everything."

Absently, Marla pocketed the earring. "Yes, I remember Bertha mentioned that she'd started her autobiography."

"Well, I don't know why it would make Todd so upset. He was practically shouting. Did you ever, uh, talk to him?"

You mean, did I tell Vail about your suspicions regarding Todd? "Yes, I did." She watched Wendy carefully. "Todd said Zack's business investments haven't been doing well. He needs the money your inheritance will bring."

A muscle twitched on the side of Wendy's jaw. "Todd is trying to deflect your interest in him," she said smoothly. "It's obvious he has something to hide."

Speaking of things to hide. "By the way, I can't find my envelope. Do you think Bertha put it in her safe?"

"If so, you'll have to wait until the police examine the contents. In the meantime, I'll let you know if I find it elsewhere in the house." She moved toward the front door. Not wishing to appear too desperate, Marla followed.

"I wish I could do more to help you get through this," Marla blurted, feeling sorry for the girl who had a heavy task to bear alone.

"Thanks. It just helps to talk, and you've been a good listener." Wendy hesitated, mixed emotions reflected on her face. "I-I'd like to count on you as a friend."

"Of course. Please . . . call me anytime."

"I will. Likewise, if you learn anything new."

8

Marla got into her car, pondering Wendy's last words. She was glad the girl considered her a friend, but wondered why Wendy wouldn't turn to her husband for support. Then again, why did Wendy always change the subject when Marla mentioned Zack? She'd never gotten an answer to her question about where they'd spent the night before the murder. Did that mean they hadn't been home? Surely Detective Vail had gotten their alibis. Maybe she could coax him to share information, but she needed something to offer in return.

It was time she paid a visit to Zack Greenfield, she decided, checking her watch. Damn, ten minutes until her next appointment arrived! She hated to keep customers waiting and pressed harder on the accelerator when her car veered onto Las Olas Boulevard. Even if she exceeded the speed limit, it would take her fifteen minutes just to get to her salon. Her heart pumping faster with nervous energy, she kept an eye out for police cars in the rearview mirror.

Zack would have to be a target for another time. This weekend? He'd probably spend it with Wendy, and she wanted to get him alone. How about Monday? Okay, go for it. She'd make an appointment for next week, pretending she needed help planning her financial future. During the rest of the drive, she constructed how she'd present her ruse and mentally devised a list of questions to be covered.

Starving since she'd eaten so little for lunch, she breezed into Bagel Busters when she had a break around four and ordered a corn beef sandwich on rye with a cream soda. Not much caffeine there, but enough of a boost to last her until bedtime. She had nothing special planned for tonight, not being in the mood to go out even though Ralph had asked twice.

"Hey, Arnie, got a free minute?" she called, waving.

Signaling to an assistant to take over his post, he approached her table. "*Shalom,* pretty lady. What's up?" Plopping himself into a chair, he leaned back with casual ease.

Her glance flickered to his hair, not slicked-back as usual but parted to the side. With his cocky grin, it gave him an attractively rakish look. "New hairstyle? I like it, pal."

"I aim to please. Any word on the murder investigation? We haven't had a chance to talk this week. Either I'm tied up when you come in for bagels, or you've been sending Lucille. I was beginning to think you were avoiding me." He slapped a hand on his broad chest, covered by another T-shirt from his brand-name collection. "I was deeply wounded by your callous insensitivity."

"Go stuff it. I've just been busy."

"So what's the score?"

Marla waited as the waitress served her meal. Chewing on a piece of sandwich, she responded. "Well, I've talked to Mrs. Kravitz's niece and her son. Wendy is suspicious of Todd and Todd is suspicious of Zack. They're each trying to place blame on the other." Between bites, she explained her findings.

"All right," Arnie drawled. "So you feel you've met Todd before but can't remember when. He wouldn't tell you what he does for a living but isn't hurting for money."

She nodded, taking a sip of cream soda. "The guy gives me the creeps. As for Zack, Detective Vail confirmed that he's in debt. I made an appointment with him for a consultation on Monday. According to Wendy, he resented Bertha's attempt to control their lives, but she doesn't believe he'd resort to violence."

"Of course not, she's his wife. And pregnant, besides. That gives him even more of a motive, especially if those gambling friends he owes are getting nasty."

"I hope Lance comes up with something useful. I'll give him a call later, although I'm sure he would have contacted me by now if he had news." Finishing off her sandwich, she frowned. "I remembered that the creamer jar was fuller when I used it last. Someone must have emptied it so only a spoonful remained and then added the poison. That person must have known Bertha was coming in that morning. Wendy and Zack knew about her appointment. I forgot to ask Todd."

"Didn't your staff know you were coming in early to do Mrs. Kravitz's hair?"

Playing with her spoon, she didn't answer immediately. "Yes," she finally replied, "and that about eliminates a customer from doing the deed unless Bertha confided in a friend. With the back door left unlocked, anyone could have entered during the night once the cleaning crew finished."

"Carlos never came back to work, did he?"

Marla slapped a hand over her mouth. "I forgot to follow up on that one, although Vail might have told me if he'd talked to the man." She eyed Arnie. "Any good gossip come through here?"

"Nope. Say, do you really think Vail is leveling with you?"

A small smile played about her lips. She dropped her hand, cupping her glass. "I believe he's attracted to me, but he can't trust me. I'm sure he's learned things he isn't revealing. If I could get a trump card, I'd offer to trade information with him. We ran into each other after I met Todd, so I told him about that conversation and seeing Wendy. You see, I'm willing to share."

"But he suspects you of poisoning Mrs. Kravitz."

"I was alone with her. So says Roy Collins, who sent me a letter from his lawyer. He's going to sue me for negligence."

"Oh Lord." He gave her a worried glance. "What are you planning to do?"

She grinned. "I've hired Lance to check into Sunshine Publishing. Lucille hinted that Roy had been involved in some activity detrimental to the company, but she wouldn't elaborate. Either it turned out to be insignificant or she's afraid of repercussions if she rats on him. After all, that's what got her fired in the first place. She told Bertha, and the old lady didn't believe her. Lucille said she doesn't harbor any resentment, but who knows?"

A puzzled expression crossed his face. "What's the difference if Lucille exposes Roy now? That is, if her hints are substantiated."

"I don't think Lucille would betray him. Don't ask me why." She thought a moment. "Maybe the old lady just found out Collins was siphoning off company funds. Bertha wouldn't accept the truth from Lucille, but seeing it for herself would be different."

Arnie followed her train of thought. "And if she threatened to bring charges against Roy, maybe he retaliated. You think Lucille suspects him of doing Bertha in?"

Marla pressed a palm to her forehead where a dull ache throbbed. "You can suspect anybody if you try. I wish Vail would be so smart."

"He wouldn't be in the detective department if he didn't consider all the angles."

"Tell me about it." Stretching, she rose. "Time to get back to work. Thanks for being such a good friend, Arnie." Flipping a couple of dollar bills on the table, she grabbed the check and headed for the cashier.

"Hey, you got plans for tonight?" Arnie said, resuming his post at the cash register.

"Yeah, I'm retiring early. It's been a long day."

His face brightened. "Any chance we could—"

"Sorry." She paid her tab, flashed him a brilliant smile, and strode out before he coaxed her into accepting.

Still smiling, she entered her salon. Arnie always had the ability to lighten her mood. Maybe one day she'd take him up on his offer, purely for a friendship outing, of course.

"Marla, you got a call from Mr. Thomson," Lucille stated. The receptionist looked harried, the phone receiver clamped to her ear while she scribbled in the appointment book with a pencil. Although Marla liked her to keep their schedule on the computer, Lucille insisted on doing some things the old-fashioned way as well.

At her news, Marla frowned. Thomson's call was probably about their lease, which came up for renewal next month. What was their landlord planning to do? Noting her next appointment waiting in the reception area, she signaled for her to go on to the shampoo station. Scurrying past, Marla charged into the storeroom where she picked up the telephone reserved for private calls.

"Mr. Thomson?" she said after his secretary transferred the line. "This is Marla Shore. I got a message that you'd called."

"That's right," his gruff voice responded. "I see your lease expires in June. I'm sure you're aware of how high insurance premiums have gone since that last hurricane hit so close to home. Costs have escalated with inflation, meaning my expenses have risen. What this means is that I have to raise your monthly rent and ask for a supplement to your security deposit."

Naming a figure that made her jaw drop, he continued before she could protest. "I realize this might prove to be a difficulty under your current circumstances, so I've opened to other offers. I have to say I'm tempted to take the one who says she'll pay me double your rent."

Marla sputtered for a reply, at first so outraged she couldn't speak. Doubtless he was referring to Carolyn Sutton, who'd been scheming to take over her salon. But where would Carolyn, whose business was declining, get the funding?

"I'm sure we can reach an agreement," she said in a smooth tongue, "as long as I have your assurance you'll honor my option to renew."

"You match those figures and the lease is yours. Get

back to me in two weeks. I'd like to wrap this up by June fifteenth.''

Two weeks! Frantically, Marla wondered where she'd get the money for the new security deposit without even considering the hike in rent. Was Thomson deliberately trying to ruin her? He knew her income wasn't sufficient for those requirements. But then neither was Carolyn's. Someone had to be backing her, Marla realized as she headed back into the salon. Her eyes narrowing with suspicion, she contemplated a likely source. Damn Stan, he could be so Machiavellian. She could just conceive of him setting up a plan like this. Force her to come up with a large sum of cash and she'd have to sell her share of their jointly owned property. Well, she'd find another way.

Gritting her teeth, she breezed through her last appointment. In a morose mood, she waved good-bye to her employees as they filed out at the end of the workday. *Just make it through tomorrow and you'll be done for the weekend,* she told herself, gathering her purse.

"Want to grab a bite to eat?" Nicole asked, lingering behind. Her expressive brown eyes reflected concern.

"I'm not hungry. I just ate a sandwich at four."

"Then how about a cup of coffee? You look done in."

Marla stiffened. "Am I that obvious?"

"Yeah, you are. What's wrong?" Nicole paced forward until she stood facing Marla. Planting her hands on her hips, the slender dark-skinned woman looked as though she wouldn't budge.

Heaving a sigh, Marla leaned against the reception counter. "Thomson won't renew our lease unless we come up with a lot more money. He's received a better offer, and you can guess who from."

"Carolyn Sutton? Oh, no. But how can she afford anything more than we can?"

"A loan, perhaps?" Marla sneered, knowing the true answer. "Maybe we should ask her ourselves."

"That might not be such a bad idea." Nicole shifted her feet. "Does our lease allow for such an increase? I thought there were limits."

"So did I, but if someone makes a better offer, Thomson has the right to accept it. At least I think he does."

Nicole frowned. "Shouldn't you consult your attorney?"

"The guy who originally handled my affairs moved to Connecticut, remember? And I don't have another good lawyer I can trust. If I did, I'd have already consulted him about this other business."

"Stan—"

"Is probably backing Carolyn Sutton. He wants me to sell a piece of rental property we jointly own, but I refuse. He's warned me he'll get his way."

"That's pretty despicable."

"So is he." Her neck snapped around at a commotion from the rear. Darlene was clattering out of the storeroom. Marla's eyes widened in surprise. "I thought you'd left," she said to the girl, who boldly stalked toward the front door.

"I, er, had to check my supplies for tomorrow. And there was a load of towels to fold. Dunno why you're not grateful." Sashaying by, hips swinging in a miniskirt, she tilted her chin defiantly.

"Sure, Darlene," Nicole spit while Marla stood to the side silently chewing her lip. Once they were alone, Nicole leaned forward. "She was listening to us," Nicole hissed.

"No kidding." Marla sighed. "I'll deal with her

another time. Right now, I need to figure out how to beat this latest problem." Giving a weak smile, she regarded her friend. "We'll have dinner together next week, okay?"

Nicole gave her a thumbs-up. "If you say so. Hang in there, Marla. Things will turn out all right."

Always an optimist. As she walked to her car, Marla wished she possessed such confidence. It seemed as though the burdens of the world were falling onto her shoulders. But then she thought of Tammy and everything focused into a new perspective. *You'll survive, just like before. Life consists of challenges but at least you're able to face them. Not like Tammy, who will never have the chance.*

Realizing she couldn't make any business calls until next week, she tried to relax at home. Anita phoned, and they agreed to a lunch date on Monday. Marla figured she'd be finished at Zack's by then, and she didn't relish spending the afternoon alone. After taking Spooks for a walk, she fixed herself a light supper: a bowl of red beet borscht that she'd mixed with sour cream and chunks of boiled potatoes. Along with buttered rye bread, it made a tasty meal. She surfed the Net for a while, checking the news sites, then retired early.

Saturday arrived with the sultry promise of rain. She'd just finished her second blow-dry when a walk-in called her name. Glancing up from the counter where she was straightening hairbrushes, she groaned. Detective Dalton Vail marched in her direction, a determined gleam in his steely eyes.

"What now?" she snapped, not in the mood for word games.

He grinned, and the transforming effect on his demeanor made her breath come short. *Bless my bones,*

Marla thought, *but doesn't he look smashing today*. Her quick perusal absorbed his camel sport coat enlivened by a geometric-patterned cocoa-and-crimson tie. His beige dress shirt tucked into dark brown pants. As he neared, she caught a whiff of spice cologne.

"I need a haircut. You busy?"

Marla muttered an expletive under her breath. *Just what I need. I'll probably snip too much, and he'll arrest me.*

"Not at the moment," she crooned, recovering her composure. "Have a seat." Waving to Lucille to put him down in her appointment book, she focused her attention on his hair. They discussed his style and she sent him to get shampooed.

This would be a good opportunity to question him about what he'd learned regarding Bertha's murder. Maybe she could disarm him enough so he'd talk readily. Naturally, it crossed her mind that he'd come in for the same purpose, and she resolved to reveal as little as possible.

Marla didn't count on the feelings engendered by sifting her fingers through his wet strands of hair. His silver highlights were more pronounced when she had him under the microscope, so to speak. Pleased to note the thickness of his layers, she didn't realize he'd closed his eyes until she glanced in the mirror. Pursing her lips, she withdrew her hand as though touched by fire. Handling his hair seemed too intimate a gesture, as though the distance between them had suddenly closed. She wasn't comfortable with that notion and showed her agitation by dropping the first comb she picked up. Snatching another, she jumped nervously when his eyes snapped open and met hers straight on through the mirror.

"You have a gentle touch," he said softly.

His voice lacked its usual arrogance, and she found the change to be disconcerting. Parting his hair, she proceeded to use the shears in quick, automatic movements.

"I was meaning to ask—have you been able to reach Carlos? From what I gather, he hasn't returned to the cleaning crew."

"His boat isn't in its berth, and we've been unable to track him," Vail responded, his tone grim. "I spoke to some of his friends at Seaside Marina. He'd bragged about a sum of easy money he had coming, so they assume he got it and took off."

"Interesting," Marla murmured, thinking he might have accepted a bribe to leave the back door unlocked so the killer could enter her salon and poison the creamer. Or maybe he'd been paid to do the deed himself. She said as much to Vail.

"We have a set of prints from the doorknob that may belong to him. Until we can check them out, this is all supposition. They don't match anyone who works in the salon."

"And if the prints belong to Carlos?"

He shrugged. "The killer may have worn gloves, or perhaps Carlos added the poison. Or maybe someone wants us to believe those options." His casual tone belied the clever look in his eyes. *He's trying to bait me,* Marla figured. *Sorry, pal. I won't bite.*

At the next station, she noticed Nicole had stopped talking to her customer. Their eyes met, a knowing smile curving the stylist's mouth. Marla wondered what amused Nicole the most, her clumsy attempt to interrogate the detective, or his smooth delivery that provoked her defensive response. Glancing at her other employees, she noted

Lucille staring at them in blatant curiosity. Darlene pretended an air of disinterest but she'd sidled halfway across the room to straighten magazines in the reception area, clearly within listening distance. The others were enclosed in their own private domains.

"Don't you feel it's significant that Carlos has vanished?" she said, annoyed that Vail continued to suspect her. "He wouldn't disappear if leaving the door unlocked was an honest mistake. Have you been checking into the movements of Bertha's relatives for that night? Todd was with a woman he met at Scudders, but how about Wendy and Zack?"

"Why don't you tell me," Vail said wryly. "You seem so well informed about this case."

In the middle of spritzing his hair with water, she paused. "That's only because I know I didn't kill Mrs. Kravitz. I'm trying to expose the real murderer. You, on the other hand, are blinded by your suspicions of me."

"Is that right? I'm glad you're such a mind reader." A sardonic grin curved his mouth. "What am I thinking about you now?"

"Who knows," she murmured, spraying more water on his head than necessary. He blinked his eyes, thick lashes glistening with moisture. Marla wanted to get this over with as fast as possible. Compressing her lips, she finished the cut, applied mousse, and blow-dried his hair into an attractive style that curved at his brow.

"Thanks," he said, rising from the chair after she'd removed his cape. "Anything else you figure I should know?"

Like I'd tell you when you're not leveling with me, pal? "Not really."

He gave a jaunty nod as though undaunted by her refusal. "Be seeing you around, then."

It wasn't until he'd paid his bill and gone that Marla realized she'd been outwitted again.

Detective Vail had neatly deflected her question about alibis for Wendy and Zack.

9

Marla arrived home just as the phone was ringing. Cursing, she dropped her purse on the kitchen counter and grabbed the receiver. Too late. Remembering the code for call return, she touched the keypad, then pressed number 1. To her pleased surprise, Lance's voice replied.

"Hi, it's Marla. You were trying to reach me?"

"How did you know?"

"I used call return. What's up?"

"I've got news. Wanna meet for dinner?"

"Sorry, I ate earlier."

"A movie, then."

Get on with it, Lance. Her hand tightened on the receiver. "Please tell me you've found something on Sunshine Publishing."

"Sure, but it's nothing earth-shattering. My report can wait. Come on, taking a break will make you feel better. I can tell from your voice that you're wired. I promise I won't hound you to see my web sites."

"No, tell me now." Annoyance rippled through her. Didn't he realize how desperate she was for information?

"If I spill the beans, will you still go out with me?"

"Blackmail, eh?" Marla's bones melted with fatigue, but she conceded his offer was tempting. Since Bertha died, she hadn't experienced a moment of enjoyment except for the show attended with Tally. Mental fatigue could dull your senses and impede logic. If she wanted to think clearly, she needed to allow time for recreation.

"All right," she accepted reluctantly. "Now talk."

He cleared his throat. "Sunshine Publishing's financial records don't jibe. I'm finding inconsistencies. I need to delve deeper but thought I'd let you know you might be on the right track regarding Collins."

Relief bubbled to the surface. "Way to go, Lance! You've earned yourself a date."

Male laughter cascaded through the phone line. "I'll pick you up at seven-thirty. We'll make the eight o'clock movie. See ya."

"So what did he say?" Tally asked, hands folded in her lap.

Marla glanced at her friend, seated in the passenger side of her Toyota. Tally appeared cool and comfortable in a red-linen shorts set, wavy blond hair brushed off her face. With her stature alone, she'd stand out in a crowd, but that glaring bright red drew eyes like a flag. Marla touched her cotton blouse tucked into a pair of faded jeans—more appropriate attire when she didn't care to call attention to herself.

"Lance said Sunshine Publishing should have higher profits for the income recorded. He's trying to trace where the funds are distributed. If there is a deficit, Collins might be responsible because he oversees the allocations. It appears Lucille was telling the truth about that tax-evasion problem. It was unjustified and dropped from any further investigation. This other lead might prove to be more useful.''

"I hope so. What else is new since I talked to you Thursday night?"

Wrinkling her brow, Marla thought hard. She'd called Tally after getting home from her appointment with Todd and told her about the run-in with Dalton Vail. What happened after that?

"Oh, yes.'' Her face brightened. "On Friday, I visited Wendy at Bertha Kravitz's house. I needed to—"

Stopping abruptly, she bit her tongue. *I almost told her about the envelope.* "Er, I wanted to see how Wendy was doing and find out more about her husband. She changes the subject anytime I mention him. It's obvious she keeps trying to shift suspicion onto Todd.''

Tally smoothed back a lock of hair. "What did she say about him this time?''

Marla shrugged. "Todd got upset when Bertha announced she planned to write her memoirs. I think Wendy was more interested in asking if I'd talked to Vail about him.''

"That's all?" She sounded disappointed, as though she'd been expecting more.

Keeping her eyes on traffic, Marla considered what else she'd learned from her interview with Wendy. "Wendy didn't say where she and Zack were the night before Bertha's murder. Nor did Detective Vail when he came in for a haircut yesterday. I wonder what he knows that I don't. Oh, Vail said there's a set of prints from our back doorknob that he hasn't identified. He thinks they may belong to Carlos.''

"Is that why we're going to the boatyard?"

Marla nodded. "Carlos is still missing, and his boat is gone. Vail was kind enough to mention he'd spoken to the guy's neighbors, who said Carlos had been expecting some money. They figure he got it and took off for parts unknown."

"Money from where?"

"You mean from *whom*. That's what I hope to learn. Anyway, I made an appointment with Zack for tomorrow morning. Maybe he'll reveal if he and Wendy were home that night. Todd had an alibi, and I don't know about Roy Collins."

Tally gave her a sly look. "What was it like, doing Vail's hair?"

For a moment, she didn't respond, her attention diverted by erratic traffic. *Damned slow drivers.* Zooming through an intersection, she got in front of a lady cruising at twenty miles per hour in a zone with a speed limit posted at forty. The woman was so short you could barely see her head above the steering wheel. The punk in the pickup truck changing lanes every couple of cars wasn't much better. She steered clear of that one, too.

"It felt weird," she admitted to Tally, shifting her mind back to their conversation. With a shameful shiver of pleasure, she recalled the silky feel of Vail's wet strands of hair sifting through her fingers. "Intimate, almost. It made me uncomfortable."

"Why? Because he suspects you of murdering your client, or because you like him . . . as a man?"

"Tally, quit it. The guy is off-limits."

"Yeah, for now. What happens when he solves the case?"

"Then I'll never hear from him again. His interest in me is purely professional." *Don't be so sure. He's another one of those fellows looking for a mother for his child. What gives? Do I come across as a maternal type, or what? Maybe it's my conservative clothes,* she thought, sparing a glance at her New Balance sneakers and then peeking at Tally's stylish sandals.

I'd better pay a visit to Tally's boutique and update my wardrobe before I get a bunch more widowers knocking on my door. The notion wasn't terribly flattering. Didn't anyone admire her intelligence and wit? Mentally, she ran down the short list of men she dated. Ralph called often, but he had more carnal interests in mind. As a friend, he was supportive and fun. Lance made her laugh, but he was married to his computer. And Arnie was a man with kids seeking female guidance. No one rated as a serious prospect, not that she was looking.

Tally had fallen into a glum silence, staring out the window. Instinctively, Marla knew she was thinking about her own problems with the male gender.

"Look, Tally, I called the golf club and they said Ken was out on the greens. He wasn't lying to you."

"Oh no?" Tally heaved a deep sigh. "Maybe he asked them to cover for him. He didn't invite me to come along this morning."

"Did you mention you wanted to join him?"

"Not exactly." Tally's blue eyes darkened with anxiety. "He just announced he was going to play golf. Didn't even care what I had planned for the day. Maybe he's meeting his girlfriend there."

Marla scoffed. "I doubt it. You'd hear gossip, and so far

nothing has surfaced to make you believe he's screwing around. Talk to him! There's got to be something else going on that's bothering him."

"How astute," she mumbled. "Well, I'm not waiting around for the lout to confess. I'm taking matters into my own hands to force the issue."

"What do you mean? Shit!" A brown Honda cut in front of them, causing her to hit the brakes. Thrust forward, she felt the seat belt dig into her lap.

"Crazy driver," Tally hollered, clutching the armrests. "Why don't you look where you're going next time?"

Marla slowed the car to achieve a short following distance. "I swear, some of these people shouldn't be allowed on the road."

"No kidding." Glancing out the side window to make sure no one else was about to cut them off, Tally asked, "Where are we going anyway? I've never heard of a boat-yard in this direction."

Heading east, they passed Tropical Acres, a landmark restaurant on Griffin Road.

"The place is called Seaside Marina. The directions aren't so great." Marla handed Tally a piece of paper scribbled with her hopefully legible scrawl. "When I talked to Vail, he mentioned the name of the marina where Carlos kept his boat. I called up and got these instructions. From what I understand, we need to cross Federal Highway. Somewhere east of here, Griffin Road turns into Taylor."

"What makes you think you can learn more than Vail by questioning Carlos's friends?"

She spotted her chance to change lanes. "Use your turn signal, pal," she yelled at the Honda driver as she veered into the left lane. "I'm hoping people will be more talkative since we're women. Less threatening, you know. Nor are we cops, so they might be inclined to confide in us."

Ahead she caught sight of flashing red lights. Train tracks. She pressed on the brake pedal, halting for a freight train. Coming up was the intersection to Federal Highway. Facing them were two lanes for left turns only. The right lane headed toward a narrow road that appeared to curve northeast.

"Now what?" she asked Tally, pointing ahead.

"The directions say to cross Federal Highway and go straight."

"Okay, here goes." She took the road lined on either side by thick tropical foliage. Nothing indicated a boat-yard ahead. Could she have made a wrong turn?

After they'd passed a Value Rent A Car lot on the right, Tally pointed excitedly. "Look at that sign. We're about to enter Port Everglades."

Frowning, Marla muttered, "Maybe the marina is part of the port. It doesn't make sense. Wait, there's the three-way stop sign, so we must be on the correct route. We make a right turn, don't we?"

Tally nodded, her face animated. "There's the truck-storage place. We've got to be close."

Cruising by, Marla read a sign for Caribbean American Shipping. "Hey, is that it—Broward Marine?" she cried, noting the wide entrance past a gatehouse ahead. The man she'd queried had mentioned passing through a gate.

"No, you're supposed to follow the curve in the road," Tally instructed her, frowning as she examined the writ-ten directions.

Marla continued along the narrow road, squinting at

the sign announcing ASSOCIATED MARINE ELECTRONICS.
Nope, that wasn't it either. "Wait, look up ahead!" She
spotted SEASIDE MARINA emblazoned in white against a
blue backboard, and her heartbeat quickened excitedly.

"We're here!" The gate turned out to be an opening
in a metal fence. She followed the paved road to its
end fronting the dockmaster's office, beyond which boats
bobbed in the water at numerous slips. With a surge of
excitement, she pulled the car into a parking space next
to a rusting white Jeep Wagoneer. Damned if her Toyota
wouldn't need a car wash after this adventure, she
thought, switching off the ignition.

Inside the office, a bearded man sat at a desk, his bare
feet propped up on a metal garbage can. He wore a
T-shirt advertising Budweiser, King of Beers. On a
counter behind him rested a modern communication
system with blinking red lights. Foodstuffs and bottled
drinks were for sale on rows of shelves opposite. News
blared from a radio in a back room, the noise adding to
the din of a parrot squawking in a cage by the window.

At their entrance, the man dropped the newspaper in
his hand and swung his legs down. His gaze scanned
them with obvious interest. "Yo, ladies, what can Ah do
for y'all?" he drawled in a classic Southern accent.

Ignoring Tally's broad grin, Marla stepped forward.
"We're looking for the slip where Carlos kept his boat,"
she said. "I'd like to talk to his neighbors. He's a friend
of mine, and I'm concerned about his absence."

The dockmaster squinted. "You don't look like no
friend of his, miss, if you'll forgive me for sayin' so."

She raised an eyebrow. "Oh no? We, er, met at the
bowling alley. I don't know a whole lot about him except

he said he lived here on his boat named . . ." She purposefully let her voice trail off.

"*Angelica.*" He nodded. "Nice sloop, a one-masted
vessel, kept it real clean. You'd see him paintin' and
sandin' every weekend. You could tell the man was proud
of his boat. Must have had strange work hours 'cause
he'd leave every evenin' and come back after the sun was
up. Don't know where he went. Just took off more than
a week ago and no word since. The cops been here lookin'
for him."

"Does he have a radio onboard?"

"Just an old handheld VHS. Y'all need to call Channel
9 to get past the bridges, you know. The tenders might
have records of when he passed through."

And Vail has probably checked them out.

"Which slip did you say was his?"

"Ah didn't, lady, but check out Number 33." He stood,
wafting stale cigarette fumes in her direction. "In case
Carlos shows up, who should Ah say was callin' on him?"

"Marla Shore." She whipped out her business card.
"Do me a favor and phone me if he pulls into dock, or
you hear anything more about him."

"For a pretty lady such as yourself, Ah'll do that. Your
tall friend got any requests?" he asked hopefully, eyeing
Tally.

"Not me!" Tally said, chuckling. "I just came along
for the company."

"Right, then." He winked. "Happy huntin', ladies."

Outside, the sun beat down, promising a sweltering
day. Sweat prickled the back of Marla's neck as she and
Tally strode out to the dock. Seagulls screeched overhead,
and a frigate bird soared high over the sparkling blue

water. A fresh sea breeze ruffled her skin and tossed strands of hair into her eyes.

"How do we find Number 33?" Tally asked, shading her face with a rigid hand as though saluting.

"We'll just walk around until we see it."

Marla, donning a pair of dark tinted sunglasses with ultraviolet protection, marched ahead to where several rows of boats faced them like silent sentinels. No, not so silent. Various creaks and groans met her ears, sounds of masts moving and rigging slapping and American flags whipping in the wind. Water trickled from through-holes and waves splashed against fiberglass hulls. Not being the seafaring type, she'd had little experience with boats, but she appreciated the serene atmosphere even though glancing at the rippling water made her uneasy. It reminded her of—*No, I won't think about Tammy now.*

The harsh whine of a power tool erupted, colliding with the pleasant sounds of nature. It brought home the reason they were here—mainly, because nature had been interrupted when Bertha Kravitz's life ended prematurely. Focusing her thoughts on their objectives, Marla advanced.

"Watch your step," she warned Tally, her sneakers padding on the damp wooden boards underfoot. They passed by a man stowing a coil of rope on a power boat and another guy rolling out some sort of blue-plastic sheeting.

"Here's the thirties," Tally cried, veering down an aisle to the left. "Gosh, this is fun. We don't get to the water very often, even though Ken loves the beach, because we've always got somewhere else to go." Her shoulders slumped. "At least we used to go places together before he decided he hates me."

Marla gave her a sympathetic glance. "He doesn't hate you, Tally. I'm sure he's got a reasonable explanation for his behavior. Look, do you want me to talk to him?"

"Certainly not!" Tally looked horrified. "I've got my own plans for setting him straight."

"Which are?"

A secretive smirk lit Tally's face. "I'm not telling even you. Not that I don't trust you," she hastened to add, noting Marla's expression, "but all the arrangements aren't finished yet. I'll just reveal that it coincides with our tenth anniversary next month."

Ah, some sort of surprise, Marla surmised. She hoped Tally wouldn't be disappointed by Ken's reaction.

A male mating whistle caught her ears. Glancing around, she spied a blond-haired fellow peering at them from a ketch. Unlike some of the other slips with expensive power boats, this section held modest sailing vessels. Waving to the guy, she kept on walking until they reached slip Number 33.

"Yep, it's vacant," Tally confirmed, facing the empty berth.

"Let's find someone we can ask about Carlos," Marla suggested.

"How about that guy hosing down his deck?"

Marla followed the direction of her gaze to a man on a single-masted sailing boat. He wore a T-shirt with a palm-tree design, a pair of tattered jeans, and reflective sunglasses on a face as tough as elephant hide and as brown as toast. His upper arm bore a tattoo that she couldn't quite decipher.

Cupping her hands to her mouth, Marla yelled: "Excuse me, can we have a word with you?"

The man's head snapped up, and he switched off his hose. "You talking to me?"

She strode forward until positioned beside a rail at the bow of his sloop. "We're friends of Carlos and wondering what happened to him." Gesturing at the empty slip, she frowned. "He's been gone over a week, and no one has heard from him."

Scratching his head, the man gave her and Tally an appraising stare. "You gals don't look like no friends of his that I can remember."

Tally broke in. "Actually, Carlos worked part-time for Marla. She doesn't take kindly to employees who fail to show up for work without offering an explanation."

"So what is it you want to know? The cops already been here. Carlos in some kind of trouble?"

"They just want to ask him some questions. We want to make sure he's safe," Marla said. "When was the last time you saw him?"

The man rambled toward her. "A week ago Wednesday. I thought something funny was going on. His boat needed a lot of repairs, and he said he'd be getting some money soon to fix it up. Lived on that tub of his for eight years now."

"Where is he from?"

"New York. Has a sister there. Had no one in Florida but an aunt who died last year, but he couldn't stand the cold weather up north. Bought his boat at a steal and worked on it himself. But these things can get right costly to maintain."

Marla wondered if Vail had checked with the sister to see if Carlos was there. She supposed he'd have said something if the janitor were located.

"I'm not sure I understand," Tally put in sweetly beside

her. "You're saying he came into some money and maybe took off to a drydock to make his repairs?"

The man laughed, a wheezing rumble. "He didn't go to no drydock, sugar."

"So where is he?" Marla snapped, impatient for answers.

"Well now, that's the thing. This lady came by on that Wednesday morning and gave him something. Wasn't no envelope looking like it held a wad of money."

Both Marla and Tally leaned forward eagerly.

"Yes?" Marla asked breathlessly, barely conscious of the sun's blazing heat on her back. She'd gladly wait in a desert if she could learn what happened to Carlos.

"Damned if I can figure it out. She must have been a friend of his, but I can't recall no light-haired dame like her visiting him before."

"Light-haired," Marla repeated. "Old, young, body stature?"

The man shrugged. "Slim-figured woman. I couldn't get a glimpse of her face, but I did spot what she handed over. Beats the hell out of me why she'd give Carlos a home-baked cake."

10

"A cake?" Marla felt like the parrot in the dockmaster's office. "How could you be so sure that's what she gave him?"

The man's face crinkled into a smile. "Well now, I saw Carlos take the plastic container and open it. Wasn't no store-bought dessert with that lumpy pink frosting. Carlos grinned, licked his chops, and closed the round holder."

Marla grimaced. "You don't suppose the woman hid the payoff inside a cake?"

Tally frowned at Marla as though she were losing her marbles. "That's a bit far-fetched."

"This whole thing is far-fetched." She turned her attention to the sailor. "Is there anything else you can tell us?"

"Nope." He lifted his hose. "Watch out, or you'll get wet. I gotta finish my work. Good luck to y'all."

"Okay, who do we know with connections to Bertha who's a light-haired female?" Marla said as they trudged back to her car.

Tally brushed a hand through her wavy hair. Sweat glistened on her brow, and her face was flushed from the heat. She looked as hot as Marla felt. "You tell me," Tally said.

"It's not Wendy. She's a brunette," Marla replied, unlocking the driver's side. "Someone from Roy Collins's office, perhaps, like a secretary sent on an errand?"

"But why would Roy send a cake to Carlos? That makes no sense."

"I could ask Zack when I see him tomorrow. I'm hoping he'll be more talkative than Wendy once I steer the conversation toward Bertha Kravitz. He can probably tell me more about Roy."

Tally cast a meaningful glance at Marla. "You're over-looking another alternative. The woman could be someone you know more intimately."

Marla's throat constricted. She'd been denying the other possibilities. "Darlene has blond hair, and she's been nosy lately. But I don't think she's capable of murdering anyone. She has no motive against Bertha." *Unlike me. I wonder what you'd think if you knew the truth.*

"Get real, Marla. You can't trust anyone until this is solved."

Starting the engine, Marla fell into a glum silence until after she'd steered onto the main road heading west. At least driving gave her a clear view of things. Bertha's murder directed her down less obvious paths. Not trusting her staff was the worst. She'd prided herself on her ability to judge people accurately. Turnover at the salon was at an all-time low, thanks to her careful selection of personnel. But now her confidence had been undermined, and the only person she could truly rely on was herself.

"How about a woman wearing a wig?" she offered, still unwilling to believe a staff member would betray her.

Tally raised a skeptical eyebrow. "Sure, Marla. If Vail learns about this, he might believe it was you."

How right you are. She said nothing more on the subject, lost in her own musings. They stopped for a bite to eat, but Tally was impatient to get home so they didn't linger. Marla could tell her friend's thoughts were deviating because she kept glancing at her watch. Tally was probably wondering if her errant husband had returned yet. She felt a swell of sympathy, wondering what to do to offer comfort.

Tally still had room in her mind for Marla's troubles. "Keep me informed," she said, wagging a finger at Marla. "I want to help you solve this mess. We're here for each other, remember?"

"That goes for me, too." As they approached Tally's house, her friend's shoulders tensed. Marla spotted Ken's gold Acura sitting in the driveway. "You see, he's home waiting for you," she said reassuringly. "Maybe the two of you can do something together this afternoon."

"If I have anything to say about it, we will. This has got to end, Marla."

"What about that little surprise you're planning?"

"It's my last resort."

"I can't believe you're not going to tell me what you have in mind," Marla said, tapping her chest. "You wound me deeply."

Tally laughed. "You're such a good friend, but this is one secret I won't reveal. You'll learn about it afterward." Her expression sobered. "I'm hoping such tactics won't be necessary, but I am prepared to carry them through.

In the meantime, I'll keep working on him. He's never been this close-mouthed before."

Thank goodness Tally's spirits had rallied. It was better to confront one's problems straight on. *No pain, no gain.* The truism applied to relationships as well as sports. Had Marla followed that advice with Stan, she'd have relieved herself of much suffering. But sometimes you learned things the hard way, and they were the lessons that really stuck.

"Maybe I can entice him to go to the Strip," Tally commented, her hand on the door latch as Marla pulled alongside the curb. "We haven't seen the new shopping plaza yet, and Ken is one of those rare men who enjoys browsing." She waved her hand. "Call me tomorrow after your appointment with Zack, and we'll exchange news."

"Good luck," Marla cried, as Tally swung from her seat.

She could use some of that luck herself, Marla realized during the drive home. She seemed no closer to learning who Bertha Kravitz's killer was than Detective Vail, although most likely he wasn't telling her everything. Why should he? She was still a suspect. For some reason, Marla felt it was important to win him as an ally. Only when the case was solved could she preserve her reputation and move on. Only then could she absolve herself from the guilt she felt over Bertha's demise. But there was still the matter of that damned envelope. Until she had it safely in her possession, Vail might use it to pound the nail into her coffin. For all she knew, he'd already seen it and was waiting to gather more evidence against her.

Frowning, she pulled into her driveway when, out of the corner of her eye, she noticed a package tilted against the front door. Her foot faltered on the accelerator but she continued into the garage. Today was Sunday. How could she have gotten a mail delivery?

Her curiosity mounting, she retrieved the package which was wrapped nondescriptly in brown paper. *Odd, there's no return address.* Turning it over in her hands, she noticed the lack of a postmark as well.

A few moments later, she entered the town house. Spooks yipped wildly, wagging his tail and running circles around her. Smiling, she placed the bundle on the kitchen counter and bent to scratch his ear before letting him outside.

Her skin felt sticky from the humidity. Better to get comfortable before opening that package, she thought, heading into the lavatory. After freshening up, she allowed herself to approach the mysterious box.

Her examination yielded little information. Shiny sealing tape secured the edges. A white mailing label listed her typed name and address. Otherwise, there was no indication of the sender's identity.

How peculiar. Throwing caution aside, she withdrew a pair of scissors from a kitchen drawer and sliced through the tape. Nothing momentous happened—like an unexpected explosion—as her fingers separated the edges of the wrapping. Slowly, she released the breath she hadn't realized she'd been holding. When the last vestiges of package wrapping fell away, her eyes widened.

Marzipans. My favorite!

Thrusting the brown paper aside, she slid the box open. The fruit-shaped candies looked like the typical confections she bought for herself at Christmastime. But which friend knew how much she loved these treats?

A slip of paper fell onto the counter when she lifted the

box. She snatched it up, hastily scanning the typewritten message: *From Your Secret Admirer.* That's all. No signature or any other indication of who'd sent her a gift.

Detective Vail? She'd mentioned marzipan to him the first day they'd met, but she hadn't told him her own preference for the sweet. Nor would Tally send her a gift in this manner. It could be someone from the salon, she realized. Her staff knew she turned into a marzipan freak during the holiday season.

Selecting a rosy apple shape, she sniffed its almond fragrance. Her mouth salivated with anticipation.

Arnie, of course. The dear man had sent her this gift to cheer her. It couldn't be any of the other guys she dated. Lance brought her electronic gizmos that usually ended up in a drawer. Ralph gave corny gifts but rarely food, and basically, he just remembered her birthday. Nah, it had to be Arnie.

Her lips poised to take a bite, but then she paused. Now that she thought about it, Arnie wasn't so subtle. He presented his gifts personally, like that bottle of Beaujolais he'd given her after the wine festival. He'd insisted they share it at an outdoor concert over the weekend. But if not him, then who else?

The faint aroma of almonds prodded a memory from her mind. *No,* she thought. It wasn't possible.

Her blood chilled as she replaced the firm candy in its box. Grabbing her purse, she rummaged inside until her fingers touched the business card belonging to Detective Vail. Within reaching distance of the telephone, she dialed his beeper number with a trembling hand. Probably she was being totally paranoid, but better safe than sorry.

A thumping noise at the door made her scurry forward

to let Spooks inside. She stepped back as he dashed into the kitchen. Standing by her side, he shook his body, flinging moisture onto her clothes. The odors of fresh air and rich humus clung to him.

"Good move, Spooks," she said, brushing off her blouse. The phone rang, and she grabbed the receiver off its hook.

"Hello?" She hardly recognized the breathless voice as her own.

"Vail here."

Her stiffened spine relaxed; his gruff voice was oddly comforting. "It's Marla Shore. This may be foolish, but I found a package at my front door. I-I'm not sure who sent it."

"Have you opened it yet?"

She could imagine his wolf's eyes narrowing in thought. "Yes, it's a box of candy. My favorite kind, actually. Marzipan."

A leaden silence followed. "I'll be right over."

Marla used the intervening time to change clothes. By the time Vail arrived, she was neatly attired in a navy pantsuit with a red shell and dark pumps. Her hair freshly brushed, she'd applied a dab of powder to her tanned complexion. At least she hadn't lost her coloring, she thought, a fresh attack of nerves assaulting her. What if those treats were really poisoned? Her gaze swept to the countertop. No way would she taste one to find out. One thing she knew for a certainty: Vail hadn't sent them.

Her fears diminished when he arrived. Hearing his sedan pull into the driveway, she dashed to the foyer. Her hand fumbled with the doorknob in her haste. A moment later, she stood in the open doorway, watching him stride toward her.

Dressed in a plaid shirt tucked into a pair of form-fitting jeans, he looked more like a lumberjack than a clever detective. Her defenses wavered as she surveyed his thick hair, craggy features, and wide shoulders. He looked damn good, and she had a hard time remembering to maintain her cool.

Clearing her throat, she extended a greeting. "Hello, Dalton." She used his first name purposefully, more to put herself at ease than him. His piercing gaze affected her more profoundly than she liked to admit. "I'm glad you could come. I wasn't sure if you were working today or not."

His mouth quirked in an easy smile. "It gave me a reason to leave the office. I'm supposed to be off today, but I was getting caught up on paperwork. I can't say I'm sorry you interrupted. Sometimes I get too carried away."

So he's a workaholic. What does he do in his spare time? "Please come inside," she said, her tone formal. She didn't mean for them to get too personal.

"Where's the package?" he demanded, stalking past her.

"In the kitchen. Want some coffee?"

"Okay, thanks."

He's just here for business, she repeated to herself, recalling the last time he'd been in her kitchen. He had been searching for clues that she was a murderess. What did he believe about her now?

She showed him the box of candy, then put on a pot of coffee. The hot brewed aroma filtered into the air, making her mouth water. Time for her early afternoon caffeine fix.

"Where did you find this?" he demanded, his expression serious as he regarded the package.

"On my front stoop. You saw the note?"

"Uh-huh. Any idea who might have sent it?"

"Obviously not you," she said in a teasing tone.

"Marla," he began, a warning gleam in his eye.

She sobered immediately. "I just want to make sure those candies aren't tainted with . . . you know." Shuddering, she turned away to retrieve a couple of mugs.

Ceramic mugs. Like the one Bertha Kravitz had been holding when—

"You're trembling," Vail observed, coming up behind her. His big hands rested on her shoulders—warm, strong hands that caused a sudden awareness to swamp her senses, especially when a whiff of spice cologne drifted her way.

She shrugged him off. "I'm fine."

"No, you're not, but you won't admit it. We'll talk about that later. Got a couple of plastic bags handy?"

"Right here." She scrambled in the pantry, moving aside the salad shredder Anita had given her that she'd never used, and the jar of matchbooks collected at various restaurants. She found the Ziploc carton buried behind a pile of aprons.

Vail gave a low chuckle as he surveyed the chaos. "Your pantry reminds me of my daughter. Her bedroom looks neat but that's because she jumbles everything inside her closet."

Handing him the plastic bags, Marla sniffed indignantly. "I'm a very organized person. I know exactly where everything is in this kitchen."

"Naturally." He bundled up the package wrapping, typed note, and box of marzipans while Marla poured them each mugs of coffee. She noted he was careful not to finger the items himself. A pang of regret forced its way into her mind. Maybe the candy was legit. She could be giving away a perfectly good box of marzipans.

Then again, maybe not.

"Care to sit for a few minutes?" she asked, gesturing at the kitchen table.

"I'd like that, thanks." Taking his mug, he claimed a seat. Marla averted her eyes from his capable hands wrapped around the coffee cup.

"As far as I see it, we have two possibilities here," he said, taking a sip of his beverage. "One is that an admirer really did send you a box of candy. The other is that these are contaminated. If so, whose pile of dirt have you stirred up?"

When he took her seriously, Marla couldn't help offering her insights. Clutching her mug, she mentioned her visit to the boatyard.

Vail's brow furrowed in anger. "What the hell did you go there for? Don't you think I'm doing my job?"

"I'm sure you are, but I felt a woman might get more information. I'm not as intimidating as you."

"Intimidating?" he growled.

"You do come across as rather authoritarian. People are more apt to confide in a woman. Less threatening, you know."

He appeared thoughtful. "Even so, your visit there wouldn't have given anyone enough time to get a package over here by this afternoon. So if these candies are tainted, someone you'd met previously would be responsible."

"Right." His logic made sense. "I did find out that a

light-haired woman saw Carlos the day before he vanished. She gave him a pink-frosted cake.''

"A cake. How odd.''

"Don't you see? She might have been giving him a payoff. Maybe she baked his money into the cake so no one would see the exchange.''

"And presumably, she's the one who entered the unlocked back door at your salon to put poison in the creamer jar?" He leaned forward. "Just who do you think she is, Marla?''

"I haven't a clue." Her fingers tightened on the mug. He was regarding her closely, as though suspecting any moment she'd confess to having contaminated the candy box herself. It would be a clever ruse to throw off his suspicion.

"That woman who works at your salon—Darlene?— she's got blond hair," he continued, making her feel a rush of relief that he wasn't targeting her. "I checked out her address. You might be interested in knowing where she lives . . . or rather, with whom.''

"Darlene has her own apartment.''

"That's what she told you?''

"Sure. She dates different guys she picks up on the beach. That's how she gets her kicks on the weekends. She's always bragging about her conquests.''

He shook his head. "She's painted a false picture for you. That tells me she's got something to hide.''

"What do you mean?" Marla shifted uncomfortably in her chair. She wasn't certain she wanted to hear his report.

Vail watched her carefully. "Darlene is shacked up with Roy Collins.''

"*What?*" she cried, bolting from her chair. "Darlene . . . and Collins? But she just met him at Bertha's funeral."

"Apparently not. They've been together for a while."

"Well, bless my bones." Obviously, Darlene didn't want anyone at the salon to know about her connection with Roy, but why not? Did it have something to do with Bertha Kravitz? "Do you think Darlene paid Carlos to leave the back door unlocked so Roy could enter the salon?" she asked, resuming her seat.

Vail ruffled a hand through his hair. "We didn't match any prints to Collins, but that doesn't mean he wasn't there. As Bertha's business partner, he stands to gain her half of their publishing company by right of survivorship."

"That doesn't prove anything. Wendy inherits her aunt's fortune." She paused. "Actually, why wouldn't Bertha leave everything to Wendy?"

"Bertha's husband helped to fund the business when he was alive. He brought Roy in as a partner. He may not have regarded Wendy with as much favor as his wife."

"Well, I'll talk to Darlene. She might know more."

"Marla, this isn't your case," he reminded her gently. "I'll handle things from now on, okay? You've already received two warnings, assuming this package isn't what it seems. We won't know until the lab report comes in, but I have a bad feeling about it. You were smart to call me."

She studied him for a long moment. "I'm not used to depending on anyone else, Dalton. I like to do my own footwork."

"So I've noticed. But you could end up like the proverbial cat who was too curious."

She smiled. "How did you become interested in being

a police detective? Was it because you like to be the one in charge? Or do you just like to tell helpful citizens like me to buzz off?"

"I guess you could say I like puzzles." He lounged back in his chair, seemingly content to linger. "It's the challenge, you see. The intellectual part is what stimulates me."

"Really?" He'd surprised her. "Don't tell me you're the type of guy who works the *New York Times* crossword each Sunday?"

"You got it. Now tell me why you became a stylist."

"That's easy. I love doing people's hair. Besides, I get to schmooze and make women look attractive and experiment with different styles. It satisfies a need within me, you know? I have to do it, like an artist who's driven to paint."

"So you consider yourself to be a creative person."

She nodded. "A lot of stylists have an artistic side."

"But you also must like being around people. You work with women all day who treat you as their personal confidante."

"It's boring sitting in a chair for an hour. Sure, customers talk to me. And usually I don't divulge what they say."

"Hear anything relevant about Bertha Kravitz?"

Now she knew where he was going. "Nothing important."

His jaw flexed. "Obviously, you find your work satisfying. Did you always want to go to cosmetology school, or was this something you realized later?"

"At first I wanted to be a teacher. But after the accident—" Marla cut herself off, cursing inwardly. *Oh, he's good,* she thought.

"Go on."

His shrewd gaze made her wonder how much he already knew. "I changed my career direction," she blurted.

"Why?"

"Because . . . because . . ." *Lord save me.* She didn't want to talk about Tammy.

A series of blips sounded and he withdrew a cellular phone from where it was clipped to his belt. "Excuse me," he said to her before answering. "Vail here." A pause. "I see. Where and when?" He listened with a grim expression on his face. "Okay, I'm on my way."

Standing, he regarded Marla with cool detachment. "I've got to go. They've found Carlos." He put the phone back on its clip. Taking the plastic bagged box of marzipans, he strode toward the front door.

She hurried to catch up. "Where was his boat? Did he say anything about the murder?"

Vail halted, turning to face her. His eyes were flat as pewter.

"Carlos won't be telling us anything. He's dead."

Marla's mind shifted into overdrive. Carlos was dead. Did he die of natural causes? Where had his body been found? Were there any clues to Bertha's murder aboard his boat?

En route to Zack Greenfield's office on Monday morning, she barely focused on the road ahead. Her brain filtered through the information from yesterday. Dalton Vail had dashed off, leaving her with dozens of unanswered questions. She'd spent a restless night pondering their conversation and the new possibilities that Carlos's death presented. Damn, why hadn't Dalton called her? Didn't he believe she had a right to know what was going on?

Of course not, you idiot. He still considers you a suspect. Under the circumstances, she shouldn't expect him to share information with her. Having hoped to gain his trust, she felt a stab of disappointment slash through her. Maybe he liked her, but he wasn't the type of man to let his emotions outweigh his sense of logic. Trusting her was not something a person in his position could afford.

An alternative explanation arose that chilled her blood. Since she hadn't heard from Wendy regarding the envelope, it was possible Vail possessed the photographs contained therein. That might explain the mixed signals he generated in her presence. On the other hand, she'd have sensed it if he'd discovered her secrets. Usually she was a pretty good reader of nonverbal cues, and his behavior didn't suggest any inner certainty on his part that he'd caught her. But even if he realized that motive and opportunity were hers, he still needed to prove she had the means to conjure up an exotic mixture of poison.

What was monkshood, anyway? Some obscure herb? And who would know about such a thing, much less how to turn it into a powdered form not easily discernible? Cyanide was the main ingredient, she recalled. Maybe you could buy it as rat poison, or was that arsenic? Perhaps she should look them both up later, either at the library or on the Internet if such references existed. Any knowledge would be helpful, although she shuddered as an image of Bertha's death grimace returned to haunt her.

Letting her optimism surface, she thought maybe Wendy had found the envelope but just didn't have time to phone her. She'd ask Zack about it this morning.

At least traffic heading downtown on Broward Boulevard was light by ten o'clock. She'd figured it would be better to avoid the rush hour. The rest of the ride went smoothly, and soon she was turning into a parking garage.

As she ascended the elevator to the fourteenth floor of a tall office building, Marla reviewed her plan. She'd pretend ignorance about financial matters, which shouldn't be too hard, considering how she'd learned about the subject in the first place. She'd gleaned her knowledge from whatever pearls of wisdom Stan had condescendingly dropped her way, then continued her education by reading financial magazines until she got too depressed by all of the self-made millionaires interviewed in their articles. Her main investments consisted of mutual funds, bank CDs, and a few individual stocks. She didn't trust insurance companies or most brokers, so she probably was a good candidate for financial analysis. But that was not her prime purpose in coming. After flattering Zack, she'd tackle him with more personal questions. If she infused just the right amount of innocence into her voice, he might talk freely.

Giving a nervous tug to her navy blazer, she faced forward with a resolute clench of her jaw. The elevator halted, and the door slid open, revealing a reception area dominated by a blonde seated behind a mahogany desk. The woman glanced up at her arrival.

"Hi, I'm Marla Shore. I have an appointment with Mr. Greenfield." Stepping onto the carpet, Marla eyed the secretary appreciatively. Groomed impeccably, she exuded competence. From her emerald green suit to her button earrings, she was the picture-perfect image of an administrative assistant. Even her polite expression showed dignity mixed with discipline.

Holy highlights! Could this be the mysterious light-haired woman who'd visited Carlos at the docks? Marla's eyes narrowed as she considered the possibility.

"Ms. Shore, please have a seat." The woman indicated a standard sofa arrangement. "I'll notify Mr. Greenfield that you've arrived. He should be just finishing with his last appointment. May I offer you a cup of coffee?"

"No, thanks." Much as she'd have liked to hike her

caffeine intake, she declined. Already her heart was racing with anticipation, and she didn't need to be overly wired. "By any chance, were you at Seaside Marina recently?"

Sharp green eyes met hers. "Sorry, what was that?"

"Did you run an errand to Seaside Marina near Port Everglades in the past couple of weeks?"

"Not me, I get seasick looking at the water." Smiling, she turned back to her computer, effectively closing down any further conversation.

Marla took a seat and picked up a copy of *People* lying on a table. She flipped it open to an article about a young actress and her latest paramour. Way to go, girl, she thought, reviewing her own love life. None of her male friends exuded an aura of power like Dalton Vail. If not for the murder case, how would he feel about her? Warmth stole upon her senses as she thought about him. Why did the man keep invading her mind? Better to focus her attention on that envelope. It was more important she retrieve the photographs before he learned of their existence.

Reaffirming her purpose, she glanced at her watch, a square-faced Rado with a scratch-proof crystal that Stan had given her on their first anniversary. The dial read ten minutes past the hour. Compressing her lips, she dropped the magazine on the table and tapped a foot to allay tension.

A buzzer sounded, and the secretary lifted her receiver. "Yes, sir," she said. Signaling to Marla, she pointed to a closed door that presumably led to the inner sanctum. "You can go in now. Go straight down the corridor. Mr. Greenfield will be in the last cubicle to your left."

Her blood surging with excitement, Marla rose from

her seat and headed for the door. She swung it open and stared. Facing her was a wide aisle with executive offices to the right and small cubicles opposite lined like boxes. She'd walked halfway down when a familiar figure emerged from around a corner. Stopping short, she gasped in surprise.

"Ken! What are you doing here?"

Tally's husband approached, his slate gray suit fitting attire for an insurance claims representative. His wheat brown hair swept across a wide forehead creased with worry lines. Anxious blue eyes gazed at her from a clean-shaven face. Wondering why he was here, she watched as his mouth curved in a guilty grin. Disaster claims were his specialty, unless Zack's predicament counted. Not likely!

"Marla, good to see you."

"Who did you come to visit?" she asked bluntly.

"I had an appointment with Zack Greenfield," he said, a look of puzzlement crossing his expression.

"What a coincidence. I'm here to talk to Zack, too. I didn't know you consulted him for financial advice."

He shuffled his feet. "We went to grad school together in Boston. That's where we got our MBA degrees."

Marla raised an eyebrow. "Exchanging stories about old times, were you?"

"Not exactly." He gave a furtive glance over his shoulder. "Look, don't tell Tally I've been here, okay?"

"Why is that, Ken?" She didn't like the notion of keeping secrets from Tally. In view of Ken's nervous manner-isms, she could tell more was going on here than friendly reminiscences.

"I just don't want her to know. You're not going to

say anything, are you?'' he asked, his casual words belying a mildly threatening tone.

"Not if you insist, but I should tell you that Tally is pretty upset with the way you've been treating her lately."

"I've got things on my mind. Zack is helping me out, so you don't need to concern yourself."

Marla felt hurt by his attitude. Here she was trying to help them, and Ken wouldn't confide in her. Now she understood Tally's feelings. How did you deal with a man so stubborn?

"I think Tally would feel better if you shared your worries," Marla advised. "She's your wife, and she feels you're excluding her. It makes her wonder if you're seeing someone else as in, you know, another woman." She gulped, hoping she hadn't overstepped the bounds of friendship.

Ken's eyes widened in astonishment. "You're kidding!"

Leaning against the wall, she regarded him calmly. "No, I'm not. Yesterday when you left to play golf, she was sure you were going to meet a lady friend. You've been tuning her out lately, and she feels neglected."

"Well, it's not that at all. This is something I have to deal with on my own. Besides, why should she care? She's so busy at her boutique shop that I rarely see her anymore."

Marla couldn't believe his bitter tone. "Maybe the two of you need to sit down and talk. It sounds as though you both have some misguided ideas about each other." Reaching out, she touched his arm. "Please, Ken."

He shook her off. "I'll get things straightened out first, then we'll talk. I promise," he added, noting the doubtful look on her face. "You've always been a good friend. Don't let me down now."

"Ms. Shore?" Zack peeked around the corner of his cubicle.

"I'm coming." She waved in his direction, thinking Zack could tell her what was bothering Ken if she played her cards right. Returning her attention to her friend's husband, she offered a reassurance that pained her.

"I won't say anything for now," she told him. "But talk to Tally, will you? And let's go out together again soon." They'd double-dated before. Maybe she'd ask Dalton to be her escort. A delicious shiver shimmied up her spine at the thought. *Play with fire, and you might get burned, girl.*

"I'll keep in touch," Ken said. "And don't worry. Things will turn out okay."

"I hope you're right," Marla muttered on her way to Zack's cubicle. With Zack being a prominent financial advisor, she'd have expected him to inhabit an office like the vacant one across the aisle with an expansive window view of downtown Fort Lauderdale. Either he'd fallen on hard times, or he rented a smaller space because of frugality. This tiny space didn't inspire confidence. In order to attract prosperous clients, he should make an effort to appear more successful.

Zack, sitting at his desk, which was curiously devoid of papers, leapt up at her arrival. He must have seen her talking to Ken and figured he could wait a few more minutes for their appointment to begin. A gratified smile curved her mouth. She'd always felt her time was as valuable as the next guy's. Why not return the favor and let him wait for her? Doctors' offices were the worst. You might wait two hours to see the specialist who'd spend three minutes with you and then send a bill for hundreds of dollars. Someday she'd mail an invoice for the hours she lost while in the waiting room.

Zack's limp handshake and artificial smile put her on alert. "Please take a seat," he said, gesturing toward a chair with torn vinyl upholstery. The man didn't even rate decent office furnishings. What kind of advice could he give to people when he needed some himself? "How can I help you?" he asked, lowering his slim frame into a chair in worse condition than hers.

Marla managed a smile. "I'm sure Wendy told you I visited her after the funeral. She'd mentioned you were a certified financial advisor, and I need help with my investments." Her tone had a singsong quality on purpose. If she came across as the ditsy type, Zack might lower his defenses. She'd play into the common male misconception that women were financially inept.

He straightened his spine, letting her know the strategy worked, and gave her a supercilious look over his long nose. "I'll need a list of your current assets," he informed her.

Marla handed him a paper she'd prepared listing her allocations. A discussion ensued in which she was pleasantly surprised by his sound advice. Giving him a disarming smile, she crooned: "You know, I can't understand why someone with your expertise isn't inhabiting one of those larger offices with a picture window." She swept her hand in a vague gesture.

Zack's expression darkened. "You're absolutely right."

"The one directly across from this cubicle is empty."

He regarded her with cold, dark eyes. They were small and round in his narrow face, almost overwhelmed by bushy eyebrows and a wide mouth. "You take a wrong turn around here, and your efforts aren't appreciated. That's what happened to me.''

"Yes, I recall Wendy mentioning some concerns about your situation, but I don't understand.''

"She'll have nothing to worry about soon.'' He leaned forward, lowering his voice. "My personal fortune took a downturn recently, but I've a big comeback planned.''

"Oh dear, then what I heard is true?'' she asked in her most childlike tone.

"What's that?''

"Well, I don't believe it, of course. You're obviously a competent advisor, so you'd know better.''

"What did you hear?'' he snapped.

"In addition to your own loss, you've had to borrow money to repay clients whose investments soured last year. And the loan is being called in.''

Hunching forward, he scowled. "Who told you that?''

"Todd Kravitz. He suggested you might need his mother's money to dig yourself out of a hole.''

"That scumbag. Ask him how he makes a living! Why, he was spooked when Aunty Bertha said she was going to write her memoirs. I'll bet he was afraid she'd reveal his dirty deals.''

Marla's heart thumped wildly at this new information. "How does he manage to get by?''

Zack grimaced. "I've been in his apartment. He's got stuff lying around that doesn't belong to him. Fancy electronics, jewelry. You get my drift?''

"I'm not sure that I do.'' She fluttered her eyelashes, attempting to appeal to his masculine ego.

Zack snatched up a ballpoint pen and clicked it on and off. "Those goods are just passing through his place. He finds a buyer. Get it?''

Marla slapped a hand over her mouth in pretended shock. "Oh, my goodness!"

"You can't rely on anything he tells you."

"Well, you may be right. So this business about you taking out a loan isn't true?"

"Oh, it's true all right." He puffed out his chest. "But I'll be repaying it pretty soon. Wendy shouldn't worry about things so much. Ken trusts me, and we're in this together. You'll see, we'll surprise everyone."

Marla felt a rush of alarm. What if Zack was talking about Wendy's inheritance? In what way was Ken involved? Did the threads of this reach farther then she'd imagined? Her mind flitted to the possibility that whoever paid Carlos might have poisoned the creamer. Where had Zack been that night? For that matter, how about Ken? He could just as easily have sent one of his female colleagues to take a cake to Carlos. What was the significance of the cake?

"The night before Bertha—" Her throat squeezed, but she forced herself to continue. "The night before she passed away, were you home with Wendy?"

Zack threw her a startled glance. "Why are you asking?"

"I'm just curious," she said, smiling sweetly. "Detective Vail questioned me about my activities. Remember, I was alone with Bertha in the salon. I gave her the cup of coffee, and although I wasn't the one who poisoned her, Roy Collins has threatened to sue me. I've no doubt Vail considers me a suspect. In case he asks me about you, what should I say?"

His eyes narrowed. "I was home that night. Vail has no reason to blame me."

"So who do you think did it?"

He scratched his head. "How should I know? Collins gets the business, and Todd gets off the hook if his mother was going to expose his illegal schemes."

Inwardly, she sighed. It appeared this track was leading in circles. "Bertha kept an envelope addressed to me that I need returned. Did Wendy mention finding it yet?"

Zack shook his head. "Not that I've heard."

"I like Wendy," she said softly. "This must be a difficult time for her, especially when she's pregnant."

"It's been tough," he agreed. "Wendy always felt close to her aunt, even after we were married. She could use a friend like you, Marla."

"Is Todd her only living relative?"

"Yeah. Wendy had just turned twenty-two when her father died. That was ten years ago. Her mother, Maureen, passed on four years later. Maureen was Bertha's younger sister. Bertha took over as a surrogate mother, treating Wendy as the daughter she'd never had."

"She must have been excited to learn Wendy was pregnant."

"Naturally." His mouth curved downward. "It gave her a better opportunity to offer unwanted advice."

"Wendy said you and Bertha had problems getting along."

His scorching look spoke volumes. "She was always giving us orders, believing her money entitled her to rule our lives. At first, we needed her help, so I swallowed my pride. But I hated her for meddling, especially when Wendy supported her views instead of mine."

Jumping to his feet, he paced the tiny space. "*Do this, Wendy, come with me. Zack doesn't need you today, dear,*" he mimicked. "She even offered us a mortgage if we'd buy a house in the same neighborhood. No way I'd live near the old lady. We were too close even where we settled. I financed the place on my own, thank you."

Was this proud man capable of murdering his wife's aunt to obtain her money? Doubts plagued her. Since he didn't deny his disagreements with Bertha, Marla leaned toward believing him innocent. But even if he weren't guilty of killing Bertha, what nefarious scheme had he and Ken cooked up together?

"How did Bertha's husband fit into your relationship?" she queried, curious to know more about Bertha's family.

"Walter was very generous," Zack said, sinking back into his chair with the air of a man relieving himself of a burden. Maybe he'd kept these feelings bottled inside himself after Wendy's aunt was killed. It wasn't in good taste to malign the dead, plus he might alienate his wife by bad-mouthing her loved one.

"Walter never really knew Bertha's secret pleasures," Zack continued, leveling her with an assessing glare as though daring her to refute him. "A rich banker, he gave her the funds to establish her publishing company. He didn't realize she had the ruthlessness to build it from the ground up. When Sunshine Publishing needed to expand, he brought in Roy Collins. It was his idea that they become partners. That was a big mistake. Bertha made Roy into much more than a partner."

Marla leaned forward. "What do you mean?"

Zack gave her a knowing smirk. "Bertha and Roy were a number. Bertha was forty years old when she started the company. Todd was just entering school full-time. She was restless by the time Roy entered the scene. With her husband occupied at the bank, she involved herself with the business and her new lover. Wendy knew about it because Bertha would share her feelings of admiration for Roy."

He noticed her disapproving glance. "Oh, she didn't come right out and say they were having an affair," he reassured Marla, "but Wendy figured it out. You could see how they acted together. It's amazing Walter didn't notice, but he was the type who focused so totally on his job that he forgot birthdays and other social events."

"What was Roy's relation to Bertha at the time of her death?" Marla asked. "Were they still together?"

"Hell, no. Roy always did have a wandering eye for the ladies. That's why he never married. Bertha said she was going to include him in her memoirs, just like Todd. She never approved of Todd's disreputable lifestyle, you know. She wished he'd get married and give her grandchildren. But Todd likes women, too. He's got a different gal in his place each week. You'd think he'd be worried about catching AIDS."

Marla remembered the sleazy looks he'd given her in the nightclub. If she never encountered him again, she'd be happy. "If Bertha was no longer hooked up to Roy, who's his latest interest?" Wondering if Zack knew about Darlene, she held her breath for his answer.

"None of my business." Raking her, his gaze darkened. "I think our appointment is finished. I've said enough."

"I'm just trying to help." Standing, she spread her hands.

"You know what I think?" he replied, rising. "This interview was just a fishing expedition. You have no intention of following through on my recommendations."

"You gave good advice, Zack. I promise I'll consider your suggestions." She paused, leveling him a direct gaze.

"If you have anything to add to our discussion, you know where to find me."

"Good-bye, Marla. I'll tell Wendy we saw each other. She'll be pleased."

12

Marla left Zack's office with more questions than answers. While driving to the restaurant where she was supposed to meet Anita for lunch, she reflected upon their exchange. Zack had claimed he and Wendy were home the night before Bertha died, but was he telling the truth? His motive seemed stronger than ever for gaining the inheritance. With a child on the way, a large debt owed to creditors, and a workplace that needed serious redecorating, he could use a hefty infusion of cash. Otherwise, what else was this big windfall he expected in the near future? And how was Ken involved?

She felt dismayed at the notion that Ken was keeping secrets from Tally. At least he wasn't involved with another woman. That had been Tally's main concern, although she didn't believe her friend would be too happy about his association with Zack, whatever it meant.

Roy Collins had had no scruples about shacking up with Bertha while she was still married. Even if Bertha had made the first move, his deceit indicated he lacked principles. Now he'd turned to Darlene, and Bertha's death left him in control of Sunshine Publishing. Did the drive for power motivate him, or was he fired by greed? Or perhaps he sought a more powerful position believing he'd be more appealing to women. Marla wondered how Bertha might have reacted if she'd found out about Darlene. Was the older woman finished with him, or would she have been furious at his betrayal?

She'd have to talk to Lance to see how his inquiries were proceeding. If he gave her a solid rock to stand on, she'd approach Roy. Or maybe Darlene would be a better road to follow. They both might have had reasons to get the old lady out of the way.

"So what are your conclusions?" Anita asked, facing her across the table at Brasserie Max in the Fashion Mall. Marla was digging into angel hair pasta with sun-dried tomatoes and minced garlic while Anita enjoyed tomato basil soup and Caesar salad. Her mother looked perky in a bright daffodil-and-black outfit, her red nail polish vibrant as she waved her hands to animate her speech.

Marla swallowed a gulp of iced tea. "I don't know. I wish Dalton . . . Detective Vail would get back to me about those marzipans. I'd like to find out if they were legitimate. If not, maybe he was able to get some prints off the box."

Anita put down her fork. "You're not doing anything dangerous by talking to these people, are you? Because if you're being threatened, stop being a *yenta*. You'd be better off minding your own business."

"This is my business." Warmth gripped her heart. From the look of anxiety in Anita's eyes, Marla realized her mother was worried about her, but she felt compelled to learn the truth. She couldn't explain the guilt she experienced over Bertha's demise without reviving painful events. Nor could she explain her fear that Vail would find the envelope and expose her disgraceful past.

"I'm not a *schnook*, Ma," she said. "I can watch my back. I called Detective Vail when I got those candies, didn't I?"

Anita nodded sagely. "So when am I going to meet this paragon of authority?"

Shoveling a forkful of pasta into her mouth, Marla regarded her obliquely. "Who said anything about meeting you?"

"Come on, I can tell he attracts you. You sort of roll your shoulders in a suggestive manner when you mention him."

"I do not!"

"Is he Jewish?"

"No, he isn't. Anyway, he has no interest in me except as a murder suspect."

Anita looked her in the eye. "You'd be smarter to choose Arnie. He's a nice Jewish man who makes a good living. You could do worse. Besides, he's handsome as the devil, wouldn't you say?"

"If you like him so much, you ask him out." She drew in an exasperated breath. "Ma, I didn't come here to discuss my love life."

Anita raised a penciled eyebrow. "You'd rather talk about killers? Charming topic. Your brother was asking about you. He's back from his trip. It would be nice if you called him to say hello."

"He could call me, too." A flush of shame crawled up her neck. She should have phoned him last week but had been too caught up in her own problems. "I'll get in touch with him tonight," she promised, feeling an upsurge of resentment at the way Bertha's death had taken over her life. Whoever had poisoned the old lady had done Marla a grave disservice. More than ever, she vowed to bring the perpetrator to justice.

Errands occupied the greater part of the afternoon, but she made time to stop off at the library. Unfortunately, they had a dearth of books on poisons, so she gave up and went home. Maybe the Internet had a forensic site she could explore.

After letting Spooks out and refreshing his water dish, she headed across the foyer toward her bedroom. A folded white paper by the front door caught her attention. Staring at it, she felt her throat tighten. Now what? Someone had slipped a message under her door. Was it the same person who'd sent her the box of candy?

Swallowing with a dry tongue, she picked up the note by its corners, by now aware she should keep her fingers off the evidence. Carefully unfolding the paper, she quickly scanned the scrawled handwriting. "Thank God," she burst out in a tremulous voice; it was from Moss.

Marla, here's my latest effort. See what you think.

Beyond my front door an anthill stood
I covered it with a pesticide hood
The creatures scurried about
Having lost their clout
Now nothing remains of their brood

Marla laughed until she doubled over and the tears ran down her face. What a sweet old man. She sincerely hoped he published his poems someday so he could bring good cheer to others like he did to her.

Sparing a moment from her chores, she dashed next door to compliment him. Emma, his wife of forty-some years, opened the door. Dressed in a housecoat which outlined her thin body, she looked frail. Marla felt a twinge of concern. Emma's complexion seemed awfully pale.

"I was looking for Moss to tell him how much I liked his latest limerick," she said, smiling.

"He went to the drugstore, but I'll be sure to let him know you approve. He's just crazy about writing these things. He guards his papers as though they were the crown jewels."

"It's wonderful that he has such a fun hobby."

Emma's rheumy eyes filled with pride. "I've been urging him to join a local poet's society, but he's too embarrassed to show his work to other writers yet. I think it would be helpful to him."

"Undoubtedly." Marla peered at her more closely. "Are you not feeling well, Emma? You look a tad off color."

Emma swiped a hand across her brow. "I might be coming down with the flu. Moss went to get some Tylenol."

"Oh, dear." She glanced toward their open garage door. "He forgot to put out the trash, but the truck hasn't come yet. Let me do that for you." Hastening over before Emma could protest, she hauled the heavy bag to the curb. "Is there anything else I can help with? Make you a cup of tea, perhaps?"

Her neighbor flashed a weak smile. "You're so kind,

but I'll be fine. If you don't mind, I'm going inside to rest.''

"Shall I stay with you until Moss returns?" She knew how distraught Moss would be if Emma got into trouble in his absence.

"That isn't necessary. Run along, child. You've got enough problems on your mind."

So Moss had told his wife about Marla's difficulties. She supposed most of the neighborhood knew about the murder at her salon by now, either from word of mouth or by hearing it on the news. Notoriety had never been her goal.

Hoping Emma would be all right, she trudged back to her town house and let Spooks inside. He danced in front of her, an entreating look on his pedigreed face.

"Okay, pooch, here's a treat." She threw him a rawhide bone from a package in the pantry. After changing into shorts and a cotton blouse, she returned phone calls and did some chores. Finally, she headed into her office and turned on the computer. Using the search function, she entered poison as a key word. Over twelve thousand finds resulted. Scrolling down the list of links, she passed by Poison Prevention, Poison Ivy, and Poison Arrow Frogs, and clicked on Poison On-line Entrance, thinking it might be some sort of index. This led her to the site for Poison Songs, a Billboard Live Show, and Sound Waves from a Bret Michaels solo CD.

"This isn't about poisons," she muttered, backtracking until she found a Poison home page. This, too, was a site referring to the music group. She backed up again, bypassing the comic book Poison Elves. Achieving no progress there, she switched to Yahoo.

"Ah, ha!" she exclaimed, her gaze falling upon Health:

Medicine: Toxicology. At last, a forensic link! More links took her to other sites about toxicologists, government laboratories, forensic expert witnesses, but nothing on poisons per se. Frustrated, she raised her hands and gave up. A visit to the bookstore might prove an easier method to gain information, but that would have to wait.

Actually, why not just call Vail and ask him if he'd gotten a report on the candy? Then she could question him at length about the poison used to kill Bertha. Dialing his number, she was pleased when his gruff voice answered.

Bravely, she forged ahead. "Hi, it's Marla. Have you gotten any feedback about the marzipan? I'm anxious for the results."

"I imagine you would be," he replied dryly. "Nothing is back yet. It takes a few days."

"Find out anything relevant about Carlos?"

A pause. "We're checking into a few things."

"Such as?"

He chuckled. "You're damned persistent, aren't you?"

"A lot is at stake." Something soft and moist tickled her ankle. Glancing down, she smiled at Spooks, who was laving her with his tongue. Idly, she scratched his head.

"You haven't gotten any more threats, have you?"

"No, thank goodness." She hesitated then told him about her interview with Zack. "Where was Roy that night? Did you question him?"

"Roy Collins went to the west coast on business. He'd booked a room at the Ritz-Carlton in Naples on the Gulf. I called the hotel. He checked out the next morning."

Her eyebrows lifted. "His budget must be generous. So he remained conveniently out of town."

"His girlfriend didn't. She stayed in Fort Lauderdale."

"I should talk to Darlene."

"No, you shouldn't. Look, Marla, you could screw up my investigation. I appreciate your input so far, but let me do my job. Stay out of this."

"You still consider me a suspect?"

"Until I expose the perp, I do. Everyone involved with Bertha Kravitz is a suspect." His voice lowered. "But I don't really want to believe you're guilty."

She swallowed hard. "I'm trying to understand all this so I can help. Those toxins that were in Bertha's drink . . . cyanide and monkshood. How do you obtain them? I'm wondering who would have such knowledge."

"So am I."

"I've been open about sharing news with you."

An exasperated growl met her ears. "Marla, cut it out. In my official capacity, I'm not able to be more specific."

Okay, she got it. Unofficially, he'd relate relevant data when possible. "I see. Well, happy hunting." Ringing off, she rubbed Spooks's belly while considering her next move.

Questioning Darlene was definitely a priority regardless of what Vail said. She'd approach the girl tomorrow. What else could she accomplish today? Frowning, she considered who might provide her with the information she sought. Wasn't Tally's brother-in-law some kind of chemist?

"You're in luck," Tally said when Marla phoned her. "Give Phil a quick call. He'll be able to help you. Let me know what you learn, okay?"

"Right. Talk to you later."

Fortunately, Phil was like most men when asked to share his expertise, especially when Marla offered the rationale she was assisting Detective Vail. Flattered by her attention, Phil was more than eager to cooperate.

"Hydrocyanic acid acts rapidly and occurs naturally in various seeds and pits, such as peaches, apricots, and plums," he informed her in a didactic tone. "Cyanide also has industrial uses, so there are different ways to obtain it. Monkshood is less common. It's a plant often mistaken for wild garlic. The entire plant is poisonous. Ingested as a drug, monkshood has a rapid effect. Death can occur from ten minutes to a few hours."

"How would you get the plant into a powdered form?"

"Hold on a minute while I check my references."

Marla patted Spooks during the interval, wondering who'd have access to exotic plants besides a landscape worker. Maybe monkshood grew wild and a knowledge-able person could cultivate it.

"The roots can be dug up and dried in the sun," Phil explained. "You have to protect your nose and mouth or the fumes from the roots can cause dizziness because they contain aconine. Drying them out takes three or four days."

"Do you pound the roots into a powder?"

"I suppose. Here's another method. Take a handful of leaves and steep them in hot water. After letting the brew cool, pour the water into a small pot. Add five ounces of alcohol to the herbs. Blend the ingredients together and let sit for a few hours. Decant the alcohol solution into the leftover water and discard the leaves. Cover the pot and simmer on low heat until a dry powder results. Scrape out the residue and you have your poison."

Marla didn't respond immediately. Who would go to such trouble, or even know what to do? "Why a mixture

of two toxins?'' she asked, confounded by the options.
"Wouldn't cyanide have worked by itself?"

"Sure. My guess is the monkshood was insurance, or
vice versa. If one didn't have any effect, the other would
kill the victim."

His matter-of-fact tone chilled her bones. Someone so
diabolically clever had planned Bertha's demise. Hadn't
she read that women preferred poison as a lethal method
of choice? It was a clean way to dispose of an unwanted
victim. No violence; no blood. But not all men were bent
on bludgeoning or stabbing, either.

Darlene certainly had the opportunity. Working in the
salon, she could have added poison to Bertha's creamer
many times over when no one was looking. The open
back door could have been a red herring, or maybe Roy
had come in that night to assist her. But he'd been in
Naples, right? Or at least he'd checked out from his hotel
on the west coast early the next morning. Unless he'd
used express checkout, in which case he could have left
anytime during the night. His alibi required further
examination, she decided. Another factor against Darlene was knowing Marla's schedule. The stylist knew Bertha was coming in early the next day, and that Marla and
her customer would be alone. Had Darlene planned to
make her a scapegoat?

After expressing her gratitude to Phil and getting his
pledge of confidentiality, she hung up and took Spooks
out for a walk. She needed the fresh air to clear her
brain. As she strolled along, her taut nerves unwound and
her muscles relaxed. Moisture suspended in the humidity
filled her lungs, and an earthy scent pervaded her nostrils.
Slate gray clouds scudded overhead as though in a race,
charging forth with fury. Lost in her thoughts, she barely

noticed the impending weather or the clatter of fleeing birds.

Returning through the garage-door entrance, she unfastened Spooks's leash in the kitchen and grimaced when he shook his body. Dirt particles splattered in a circle.

"You like getting me messed, don't you?" she muttered, while he gazed at her with a smug expression. After washing her hands, she checked the answering machine in the study. Three calls registered. Pressing the play button, she retrieved two hangups and one call from her landlord demanding her response to his terms for the new lease.

"Damn, this is the last thing I need. I'll bet he isn't allowed to raise my rent much. If only I had a good lawyer." No way she'd call Stan. *Maybe Lance knows someone,* she thought, after wracking her brain for ideas. He'd bought a condo recently. He might have used an attorney.

Lance was happy to give her his lawyer's name. "I'm still checking on that Collins character. The deeper I get into public records, the more things don't jibe. I've got some friends who owe me favors. Hopefully they'll get something solid for you."

"I'll be forever grateful." She'd interview Roy now except for his lawsuit threat. Otherwise, he'd probably add harassment to her offenses.

Lance's voice deepened. "How grateful, luv?"

"I promised I'd come to view your favorite web sites, didn't I?"

"Oh, yeah. So are you busy tonight?"

"Get me a handle on Roy, and I'll free my schedule."

He laughed. "Check your e-mail. I sent you a couple of jokes."

"Thanks, pal." She replaced the receiver, a smile tilting

her lips. Leave it to her friends to cheer her when things were rough. And speaking of friends, she needed to call Tally back.

A loud crack of thunder rattled the windowpanes. Glancing outside, she was startled to note the churning clouds presenting an ominous edge on the horizon.

The phone clamored along with the next peal of thunder. She sprang to answer it, her nerves agitated by the darkening gloom. In her haste, her fingers brushed a small item on the desk. Oh, yes, it was the earring she'd found at Bertha's house. She'd taken the pearl-and-marcasite piece from her pocket and forgotten about it.

"Hello," she mouthed.

A sharp intake of breath came from the other end.

"Hello," she repeated, the hairs rising on her nape. She put the earring in a drawer, her attention diverted. "Is anyone there?" Lightning streaked across the sky, forcing trees and pitched roofs into sharp relief. Through the receiver clamped to her ear, she heard a muttered expletive. Then there ensued a *click* followed by the dial tone.

Frozen in place, Marla stared out the window. A fierce wind had blown up, whipping branches against the house along with a driving rain. Splattering sounds pelted the roof. Another blast of thunder brought Spooks yelping at her feet. Replacing the receiver in its cradle, she bent to scoop him into her arms. His small quivering body gave her comfort, but it wasn't the storm that made her fearful.

Someone hadn't been too pleased she was home, safe and dry. Someone who didn't wish her well.

13

Marla sniffed the freshly brewed coffee as soon as she stepped inside the salon. Apparently, Lucille had beat her to work that morning. The receptionist sat at her desk peering at the computer screen, a frown of concentration between her eyes. Upon Marla's entrance, she glanced up with a startled look.

"Marla! I didn't expect you . . . s-so early."

"It's nine-thirty," Marla answered, stashing her purse in a drawer. Actually, she was later than normal. Being the owner, she tried to arrive by nine to prepare for the day and sometimes to grab a bite to eat at Arnie's place. But some of her staff, including Lucille, had keys in case they needed to come in for an early customer.

Straightening, she gazed approvingly at Lucille's groomed appearance and attractive hairstyle. The older woman's golden highlights glinted in the bright overhead glare. She'd need a touch-up to her coloring in a few weeks, Marla realized as her trained eye observed the gray roots. She'd drop a hint to Giorgio later. Usually he did Lucille's hair, utilizing a reddish gold tint to complement her skin.

"Why did you come in so early today? You must have been here for a while." Marla nodded at the coffeepot and neatly stacked magazines on a low table.

"I thought I'd update our customer profiles," Lucille said in a flat tone. "It's been a while, and I know you have too much on your mind to bother." Her expression softened. "I hope you didn't take work home with you this weekend. You really looked done in last week. Did you have a chance to relax?"

Marla grinned as she reflected upon her busy two days off. "Not really. I had some interesting events happen."

"Oh? Like what?" Lucille gulped down a sip of coffee from a mug resting by the mouse pad, activating Marla's salivary glands. She'd love to indulge herself in a third cup.

"Nothing worth reporting." Standing by the refreshment table, Marla poured herself a drink. Bringing the mug to her nose, she inhaled deeply to sniff for any unusual odors. *Stop being so paranoid!* she chastised herself as her nostrils hovered over the steaming brew. Satisfied it was worth the risk to get another shot of caffeine, she allowed herself a long drink. Someday she'd be sorry she consumed so much coffee, but she hoped that wouldn't be soon.

Putting the mug down at her hair station, she counted supplies. "How's my schedule look for today?" she queried Lucille. Tuesdays usually brought a steady workload, while Wednesdays were the slowest day of the week.

"You're pretty heavily booked." Lucille shut down whatever program she'd been revising.

"Nice blouse," Marla remarked, nodding at her beige-silk top. Reconsidering her decision not to talk about the past few days, she realized Lucille might have the answers to some of her questions. Sauntering over to the reception desk, she leaned casually against the counter. "Can I ask you something?"

"Sure, go ahead." Lucille's pale blue eyes regarded her warily.

"I heard a rumor that Bertha's partnership with Roy Collins involved more than just business. What do you know about them?"

"Who've you been talking to?" Lucille demanded, pursing her lips.

"I consulted Zack Greenfield for some financial advice yesterday, and we got to discussing mutual acquaintances."

A play of emotions crossed the receptionist's face. "Roy always was a womanizer. Instead of appreciating how willing *I* was to listen to his problems, he chose to consort with Bertha. I knew why, of course. He hoped to dazzle her so she wouldn't find out about his—" Lucille bit her lip, her face reddening.

"His what?"

"I'm not at liberty to say."

Marla leaned forward, her probing gaze making Lucille glance away. "Was he fixing the books, Lucille? Is that what you discovered, and when you tried to tell Bertha, she didn't believe you?"

The receptionist clenched her hands together, her knuckles white. "I can't talk about Roy."

"Why not?" Marla persisted. "Has he threatened you?"

"Ha! As though he'd dare!"

Marla still couldn't figure Lucille's relationship to Roy. To provoke her into further revelations, she offered a tidbit of information. "Did you know he's seeing Darlene?"

Lucille stared at her, openmouthed. "What did you say?"

"She's been lying to us about all those guys she picks up on the beach. She and Roy live together."

Lucille's face suffused with a purplish hue. "He wouldn't . . . no, that can't be true."

"Remember when Detective Vail accused Darlene of giving us the wrong address? She scribbled something down and handed it to him. The paper had her current residence, which I'll bet you won't find in your computer files."

"So what does that prove?"

"Vail checked it out and told me she's shacked up with Roy."

Lucille shot to her feet, eyes blazing. "If what you're saying is true, it's her fault. That hussy! No wonder he didn't seek . . . his true friends when he lost interest in Bertha. She stole him away."

Marla stepped back. She'd never seen Lucille so emotional. "Was Bertha aware that he was seeing Darlene, do you think?"

"No, she would have said something when she came here to get her hair done. As far as I knew, he still gave Bertha the impression they were together. It wouldn't have been smart for someone in his position to turn his back on her. But she was aware he was losing interest, and it made her vengeful. She cursed him and called him a cheating liar."

Sinking back into her chair, Lucille ran a shaky hand across her face. "She'd discovered what he was doing with the company funds. She wouldn't believe me, you understand, but she confided to me that she'd caught him at it herself. My guess is that she was irked because he wasn't paying her enough attention, so she planned to publish her memoirs to expose him."

Well, Marla thought, *so Bertha's impending memoirs affected others besides Todd.* Maybe Roy wanted to stop Bertha from revealing his deceit, and Darlene had gotten involved. What was the girl's role anyway? Was she planted here as a spy, to warn Roy if Bertha got wise to him? And when Bertha did turn against him, had he and Darlene decided to eliminate her as a threat to their security?

Marla bit back her next question when the phone rang. While Lucille was occupied, she headed toward the deli to buy bagels before their first customers arrived.

"Hey, sweets," Arnie greeted her with his usual enthusiasm. She marveled at how he managed to look like a hunk wearing an apron over jeans and a T-shirt.

"My usual order for the salon, please."

He shouted to an assistant. "Two dozen assorted." There being no one else waiting at the cash register, he leaned forward and grinned. "I've got something for you." Reaching behind the counter, he withdrew a large-size brown paper bag and thrust it at her.

"What is this?" Marla liked surprise gifts when she knew the giver's identity. Inside the bag was a square box labeled: JACK DANIEL'S TENNESSEE WHISKEY-FILLED GOURMET CHOCOLATES. "Oh, Arnie, you're a doll!" Selecting a confection, she popped it into her mouth. The liquor drained down her throat, leaving a burning trail mingled with the taste of semisweet chocolate.

Arnie's dark eyes twinkled playfully. "I figured you'd need a boost. How'd your weekend go?"

"Delightfully," she muttered, unwilling to elaborate. "Would you like one?"

"No thanks, I know you'll enjoy them." He waggled his eyebrows. "I want you to think of me each time your luscious lips close on one of those sweets."

"Come off it, pal. I've got a better idea. Isn't your daughter's dance recital next month?"

"Yeah, that's right. She's got her dress rehearsal soon."

"Well, if you haven't already asked another hot date, you can buy me a ticket. I'd like to go." It was the least she could do when he was so kind to her.

His expression brightened. "You're on! Want to do dinner first? Lisa and Josh will be with us," he warned with an apologetic shrug.

Great, a romantic dinner with the kids along. "That'll be all right."

Their conversation reminded her of some other calls she needed to make. Rushing back to the salon, she quickly put the bagels on a platter, retrieved the cream cheese and spreading knife, and laid them beside the coffeemaker. Then she closed herself in the storeroom and dialed the number of Lance's lawyer. Briefly she outlined her situation with the landlord and promised to drop off a copy of her lease during her lunch break. Thus relieved, she called the child-drowning-prevention coalition to find out the date for their next meeting. Last week's had been canceled, and she'd forgotten to get in touch with them. She didn't want to neglect her duties in the wake of recent problems.

Tally was on her mind, too. They'd touched base last night, but Tally had been on her way to a meeting. She'd invited Marla to come along to a metaphysical study group, but Marla had no desire to connect with her spiritual side. Enough matters confronted her on the earthly plane. "I'll go shopping with you but I won't join analysis groups," she'd replied in a bantering tone. In her heart, she knew Tally was seeking answers to her own difficulties, but that wasn't the route Marla chose to follow. Making her last call, she caught Tally just as her friend was starting work.

"I can't talk now," Tally gushed. "Can we meet later?"

Marla hesitated. Face-to-face, she might inadvertently let slip that she'd seen Ken. "Er, I'm not sure. Why don't I contact you this afternoon?" Then she thought maybe Tally had news. "Has anything different happened since we spoke?"

"Not unless you count Ken saying a few civilized words to me at breakfast, not to mention eating at home."

"That sounds like progress." Pleased that Ken might be making an effort to ease Tally's anxiety, she hung up just as Nicole burst into the storeroom.

"Marla, why are you hiding in here? Your first customer has arrived."

"Already?" She was losing track of time these days, and that didn't translate well for her mental state. Exchanging pleasantries, she left Nicole reaching for a pile of towels and entered the salon.

The day whipped past in a flurry of activity. Having meant to question Darlene, she didn't get the chance. People were always nearby, and she dared not invite eavesdroppers. Another alternative presented itself as six o'clock neared. She could confront the girl on her own turf, and besides, Marla was curious to see where Darlene headed when she left work.

Crouching behind the wheel of her Toyota, she waited in the parking lot for Darlene to leave the salon. She'd gone as soon as her last customer finished, using the excuse she was meeting a friend for an early dinner. Hopefully Darlene wouldn't notice the white car following behind.

The trail led to a condo high-rise near the ocean. It was a swanky development with a guardhouse at the entrance and a gate surrounding the community. Initially, Marla cruised past at a slow pace. No way Darlene could afford a place like this on her salary as a stylist. She'd need a sugar daddy like Roy to afford such an expensive lifestyle. When she was certain Darlene had cleared the guard's vicinity, she drove through the entry.

"I was supposed to be following my friend," she explained to the uniformed security man with a dazzling smile. "She went too fast and got ahead of me. This is my first visit here, and I'm not sure of her apartment number. Darlene Peters is her name." Anxiously, she scanned the road leading to an underground garage. Darlene must have pulled in there because her Corvette wasn't visible outside.

"You'll find Ms. Peters at B-507 in the second tower," the guard said after consulting a clipboard. "I'll ring her that you're on your way."

"Oh, that won't be necessary since she's expecting me. Is her roommate in, do you know?"

"Mr. Collins usually gets back around seven, miss." He gave her a curious stare that warned her she'd best move on. She'd already gotten information which confirmed Vail's report. Darlene and Roy were definitely sharing the same living quarters.

Going inside to talk to Darlene probably wouldn't be a good idea right then, she decided after glancing at her watch. Roy might arrive soon, and it wouldn't be safe to confront them together if they'd conspired against Bertha. Tomorrow presented another opportunity to question Darlene. Somehow Marla would find a way to be alone with her.

She went directly home, exhausted more from mental fatigue than physical exertion. Her answering machine was flashing, but she didn't feel like retrieving messages right away. Probably some customers who wanted special accommodation. Running a weary hand through her hair, she headed to the bedroom to change. Peace and quiet were not on her list, however, because the phone rang just as she stepped onto the cool tile floor in her bare feet.

"Marla, it's Wendy. Zack told me he saw you yesterday. It was kind of you to choose him as your financial counselor."

Marla settled onto the edge of her bed, legs dangling. Apparently Zack hadn't confided in his wife the full gist of their conversation. "He gave me good advice."

Wendy cleared her throat. "I guess he showed you the beautiful view out the picture window from his office."

Didn't she know his work space consisted of a tiny cubicle with no view except walls? "Yes, it was lovely. You sound as though you haven't been there in a while."

"Right. Zack . . . doesn't like to be bothered at work. Did he, er, mention anything to you about my aunt?"

Marla's brow folded into a frown. "Sure, we talked about her. Zack resented her interference in your lives, but I believe he understands how much she meant to you."

"Oh, dear."

"Wendy, what worries you?" Did she know something

about Zack's activities that would implicate him in Bertha's death?

"Nothing . . . nothing at all. Actually the reason I called was because I found that envelope you wanted."

"What!" Marla rolled off the bed, rocketing upright. Her fingers gripped the receiver with an iron fist.

"There was a secret compartment in her desk. I found the Manila envelope addressed with your name like you said. There was another item in there, too. I-I'm not sure where Bertha got it or what I should do, so I'll give them both to you. Can you meet me tomorrow at lunchtime?"

"Of course. Want to join me for a meal?" Her heartbeat skipped erratically. The envelope . . . at last it would be hers!

"I can't spare the time. I only have a half hour for lunch, but if you come to the hospital where I work, I'll give these to you." She rattled off her location, then disconnected.

Marla hung up, then realized she was shaking from head to toe. *Dear Lord, let this be an end to my problems in this arena,* she pleaded. *I can't afford for Vail to get hold of those photographs.* Speaking of Detective Vail, maybe he'd left her a message. Forty-eight hours had passed since she'd given him the marzipans. That should be enough time for a lab report, right?

Indeed he had left a voice message, but when she returned the call, no one answered. Frustrated, Marla fixed herself a prepackaged Caesar salad and microwaved chicken drumsticks for dinner. Afterward, she responded to messages from friends and called her mother before picking up a mystery novel and relaxing on the couch. She'd promised herself not to work on salon business since clearing her mind was more important.

Reading a book was a luxury she usually denied herself. In her spare time, she scanned through fashion and hair magazines for the latest styles. Nicole devoured mysteries as though they were candy and often tried to enlist Marla in her hobby. She'd loaned Marla a medical thriller but there just hadn't been time to pick it up. Maybe reading it now would help her solve Bertha's murder, Marla thought hopefully, snuggling into the cushions.

Bleary-eyed the next morning from staying up too late reading a story she couldn't put down, Marla consumed three cups of coffee before deeming herself ready for work. No wonder she didn't normally absorb herself in a good book. A sleepless night and a throbbing head were the result. Better to stick to lighter fare, at least until she could decrease her work hours.

Her morning passed with lightning quickness for which she was grateful. Eager to meet Wendy, she left without explaining her departure to anyone. Her next two customers had canceled, so she had several hours free before her four o'clock appointment arrived for a routine haircut.

Marla knew where the hospital was located but not the physical therapy department. She asked directions at the front lobby and proceeded through a series of twisting corridors. Ignoring the antiseptic smell, she passed by a hematology lab and a respiratory unit. *Hospitals are not my thing,* she told herself, feeling a surge of pity for the patients being transported by wheelchair. *If I worked here, I could never go home without taking a part of these people with me.*

The physical therapy department was a bustling center of activity. Patients with assorted degrees of mobility, some dressed in street clothes as outpatients, others in flapping hospital gowns, were exercising using various mechanical devices. Now there was a procedure she could happily endure, she thought, observing a stout woman getting her shoulders massaged.

She connected with Wendy, who'd been watching for her, and they slipped inside an empty office. Marla was too anxious to get hold of the envelope to exchange pleasantries.

"Do you have it?" she asked, giving Wendy the once-over. The young woman's pregnancy was barely showing, her peach smock taut over white trousers. She'd tied her hair neatly back with two barrettes, and looked harried, with a sheen of sweat on her pretty face. Marla felt guilty for interrupting her work schedule, but she rationalized that obtaining the envelope was of greater importance.

Wendy strode to the desk and opened a drawer. Beneath a pile of papers nestled a manila envelope which she withdrew. "Here you go. The document with your name on it is inside along with that other item I'd mentioned."

Marla gingerly took the folder and peeked inside. Hmm, the original Manila envelope with her name on it had been larger. The negatives hadn't taken much space, but the photos did. This one looked too small to hold everything. She didn't bother to glance at the other item, some sort of magazine.

"I really appreciate this," she said to Wendy, facing her. "You didn't, uh, mention finding it to anyone else?"

"No, I didn't, not even when Detective Vail inspected the contents of Bertha's safety-deposit box."

"Oh?"

Wendy pointed at the envelope. "I didn't want him to

see that . . . trash Bertha kept hidden. I can't conceive of what she'd been doing with it unless Todd was somehow involved. You'll see what I mean."

Marla's curiosity threatened to ignite. Clutching the envelope to her chest, she grinned weakly. "If that's all," she said, letting her voice trail off and hoping Wendy got the hint.

"For now. I've got to get back to work."

"Me too. Thanks for your help, Wendy. If I can ever do anything for you, please give me a call." Waving, she left.

Inside her Toyota, she turned on the air-conditioning before opening the Manila envelope. Her eyes widened in shock as she drew out the contents. A magazine showed full color scenes of naked couples entwined in erotic positions. How did this get into Bertha's possession? Experiencing a sinking feeling, Marla squeezed her eyes shut momentarily to block out the vivid images. Thank God her pictures had never made it into this format. Gathering her fortitude, she tore open the smaller envelope with her name on it.

A cry of disbelief escaped her lips.

The negatives were there, but where were the photographs? Desperate, she searched through the magazine pages in case the photos had fallen inside, but no luck. Could Bertha have stashed them separately for extra insurance against her blackmail scheme?

Damnation. Now she still had to get those pictures. She only hoped they hadn't been placed in Bertha's safety-deposit box.

14

Taking a closer look at the magazine, Marla gnawed on her lower lip. The lurid poses blurred with her shame until she imagined herself in each of them. Thankfully, her supple young body had never been displayed in such a public fashion. It was bad enough copies of her pictures had been sold under the counter to perverts who wanted to view them in private. At least that's what the photographer told her was being done with them. Now she wondered how many had been circulating before Bertha got hold of the negatives and original prints. Her stomach churned as she mentally revisited her sordid past. You couldn't abolish regrets; you could only learn to live with them.

Too distraught to return to work, she changed gears and drove around aimlessly while her mind wandered back to the day Bertha Kravitz had confronted her with the evidence of her shame.

"I wanted to surprise my husband with an album of boudoir pictures," Bertha had explained after calling

Marla to her home ostensibly to get a haircut. Marla had come eagerly, hoping to acquire the wealthy client as a regular customer. She'd had no idea the old lady planned to drop a bombshell.

"The photographer asked if I wanted normal poses or something more erotic." Bertha had grinned, a toothy smile that showed off her capped teeth. It wasn't so much a smile as a predatory snarl, like a hungry tigress preparing to pounce on a helpless victim. "Imagine my surprise when the examples he showed me were pictures of you, Marla. I'd only been to your salon once, but you made quite a favorable impression. I can't tell you how shocked I was to discover your secret."

Marla wished the floor would dissolve so she could sink through to a bottom level, which in south Florida probably meant the Biscayne Aquifer. Sweat dampened her palms as she faced Bertha in her office. "I only took that one job," she croaked, her tongue so dry it scraped her palate like sandpaper. "I needed the money."

Bertha didn't care about her explanations. In return for keeping silent, she'd demanded free hair appointments and other salon services in perpetuity. Forced to comply, Marla had tried to put the interview behind her. She'd survived worse things, and she could get past this, too, except for the days Bertha came in and gave her a disgustingly smug smile.

Oh yes, she did have a motive for wanting Bertha out of the way. Gripping the steering wheel, Marla drove slowly through a winding residential complex in an unfamiliar neighborhood. She didn't want to be seen or recognized. Pulling alongside the curb by an empty lot, she idled the engine.

Fifteen years ago, she'd been a naive young woman

whose moment of neglect had let a beautiful child drown. Unintentional though it might have been, Marla had to pay the price. Modeling jobs had provided her with pocket cash before, so this time she accepted one that offered to pay a great deal more. Posing for lingerie ads wasn't shameful, after all. Store models did it all the time for catalogs and newspaper advertisements. So how could one stint hurt her reputation?

Unfortunately, the photographer wasn't someone she'd worked with previously. Noticing the vulnerability in her eyes, he'd approached her with a better offer. Sweet young things like herself were highly in demand for more risque poses. If she were interested, the money rewards would be fabulous.

Needing funds desperately to pay the lawyer defending her against Tammy's parents and not wanting to burden her own family, she'd agreed. *Stupid girl,* Marla railed now. Little had she realized what would be required from her until a muscular male model sauntered into the private back room at the photographer's studio. Only then had Marla become suspicious, but she still figured that a few photographs, even nude pictures, might not hurt if they were destined for sale to closet voyeurs. At least the photos hadn't been designed for a magazine like the one in her hand.

Flipping through the pages, she looked for a date. It had been issued fairly recently. Could there be a connection between this photographer and the one Bertha had sought out for her boudoir pictures? As far as she'd known, the man who took Marla's photos had left town. Maybe he'd just changed his place of business, and Bertha had still been connected to him. And if so, perhaps she'd been blackmailing other former models like herself. That notion chilled her because then there might be a whole slew of people who'd wanted Bertha dead.

Perhaps she could coax the printer into revealing the photographer's whereabouts. Even if it had nothing to do with her own sordid pictures, the lead was worth investigating. She noted a post office box address for Fort Lauderdale.

Shifting into drive, Marla shot forward and headed onto a main road.

An hour later, she had her answer. After standing in line at the main post office, she got the name and address of the person renting the box by claiming she was answering an ad in a promotional brochure. This led to another downtown location. Gritting her teeth, Marla debated whether she should return to work or risk being late by following the trail. It wasn't worth it to make her customers angry, she finally decided. She could always return after working hours.

Her afternoon appointments passed quickly, but she'd nearly forgotten her dinner date with Ralph. She met him at the Italian Bistro in Davie. Marla was still dressed in her work clothes, a floral-patterned skirt and a cranberry short-sleeved sweater. In contrast, Ralph had spiffed himself for the occasion. Dressing up for him meant putting on a clean T-shirt that displayed his muscular physique and a pair of snug jeans. His spiky black hair looked as though he'd stuck his finger in an electrical outlet. Marla resisted the urge to advise him against using so much gel as she greeted him outside the restaurant.

They were seated at an alcove by the window. After giving her order, she dropped her gaze to his grease-stained hands. He might be less refined than some of her other friends, but Ralph was sincere, and that's what appealed to her the most in a man. She'd met him when her car needed some work, and she had realized he was one of the few honest mechanics in the area. That they were physically attracted to each other became evident right from the start. *He's the brawn and Lance is the brains,* Marla thought, suppressing a smile. So what if she divided her attentions? Ralph, at least, had his feet firmly planted on the ground instead of in cyberspace.

"Wanna go for a ride?" Marla asked after she'd paid her half of the tab. "There's a place downtown I need to check out. A printer's shop."

Ralph gave her a crooked grin. "Sure, babe. Is there a parking space?" The way he emphasized *parking* told Marla what he had in mind. No problem. She knew how to fend him off.

The locale was across from the railroad tracks near Old Dixie Highway. A small, nameless store was wedged between a row of warehouses and a bicycle-repair shop. The number on the facade corresponded with the address she'd been given at the post office. Hovering near the closed front door was a fellow with a blond ponytail, a bandanna around his head, and a torn T-shirt proclaiming Life's A Beach.

When he gave Marla the once-over, she sidled closer to Ralph. Flexing his muscles, her companion glared at the stranger. *Brawn can come in handy,* Marla thought gratefully.

"The place is closed. I'll come back another time," she told Ralph, swallowing her disappointment. "Let's go." With darkness descending, she didn't care to linger in that part of town.

Ralph took her elbow and guided her to his battered Chevy. She'd already observed that he spent his time fixing other people's cars but didn't bother with his own. Somehow the trait tickled her fancy. Unlike many other men, Ralph didn't derive a sense of power from his set of wheels. His value system emphasized more important goals such as going to night school. She admired his ambition to earn a college degree and wished him well.

Settling onto the cracked leather seat, she heaved a sigh. Although her nerves screamed with frustration, she'd have to be patient about contacting the printer. Tomorrow, she could try to run down here during business hours.

"What's the problem, babe? Why did you want to come here anyway? It's not the sort of joint you normally visit." Ralph patted her arm.

"It's related to Bertha's murder. She's the woman who expired in my salon," she explained at his puzzled look.

"Aren't the police working the case?"

"I'm trying to learn things from a different viewpoint."

"You're prying, you mean," he said perceptibly. "That could land you in a heap of trouble."

"I'm already in trouble. The detective suspects I did the dirty deed." She noticed they weren't driving back to the restaurant where she'd left her car. "Where are we going?"

"You're too uptight. I figured we'd take a walk along the river and then have coffee on Las Olas. You game?" His dark eyes sparkled mischievously, and Marla understood. He felt she needed comforting, which he was all too happy to provide. Of course, the offer of coffee was a temptation she couldn't deny.

"Sure, I'd like that."

He parked on a side street near Las Olas Boulevard and they skirted the dinner crowds to head toward the

New River. Strolling along the waterfront, Marla averted her gaze from the rippling current. It reminded her of things she'd rather not think about right then.

Without being consciously aware of her purpose, she leaned closer to Ralph. He'd been walking beside her, holding her hand and keeping silent as though realizing she needed space to calm herself. When she felt his solid chest wall, her composure broke and she turned into him, seeking his strength. Responding, Ralph tightened his arms around her.

Despising herself for her weakness, Marla gave in to the need for protection, burying her head against his shirt and closing her eyes. Her past mistakes kept returning to haunt her. Would she never be free of this anguish?

To her distressed surprise, Dalton Vail's angular features floated into mental view, and an imagined whiff of his spiced scent invaded her mind. Where'd he spring from? A guilty conscience?

Marla disentangled herself, her breathing rapid. "S-sorry, I . . . I guess things are just taking their toll."

Ralph smiled gently. "That's all right. Let's go for coffee. Caffeine always gives you a boost."

It gave her a boost okay, but not the kind she wanted. She spent a restless night, tossing in her bed and dreaming about the gruff police detective. Whether a good dream or a nightmare remained to be decided. *I should tell him about the photographs,* she thought, but she was hesitant to sully his impression of her. Not to mention revealing she had a motive for doing away with Bertha Kravitz. The fear of being arrested held her tongue more than anything. Even if Vail believed her story, he might be forced to act against her.

"You look like something your dog might drag inside,"

she grumbled to herself in the morning while peering into the bathroom mirror. Dark circles marred her complexion and even a heavy concealer couldn't erase them. After fluffing powder on her face, she applied a light touch of blush before doing her eyes with a putty-colored shadow.

Spooks stood by, watching her with baleful eyes. They'd already gone for their morning walk, but he still craved attention. Marla stooped to scratch behind his ears. "You behave while I'm gone. No digging on the sofa today, you hear?"

Having her own business preserved her sanity. When she'd been married to Stan, she used to spend hours in the kitchen concocting tropical delights in order to please him. Nothing she did seemed to earn his appreciation. Now she worked for herself. She didn't have to answer to anyone for her time and got her rewards from her customers. She'd earned her reputation and intended to keep it from being demolished.

She'd just gathered her purse and was about to leave for the salon when the phone rang.

"Marla? Dalton Vail here. I have a new lead regarding Carlos. Want to take a ride with me this morning?"

"Where to?" she rasped, warmth flooding her at the sound of his deep voice.

"You'll see. Can you get out of your appointments today? I'm not sure when we'll return."

Mentally, she reviewed her schedule. "I can ask Miloki and Nicole to take over for me. We have a light load today. Where do you want to meet?" Part of her wondered why he wanted her along. Was it to keep her in sight because she was a suspect? Or did he genuinely desire her company? Probably the former, she told herself cynically.

"I'll pick you up in fifteen minutes."

"Wait a minute, what do I wear? I mean, do I need to dress up or anything?" Her glance swept over her belted bronze jumpsuit. No way her clunky work shoes could be appropriate.

A low, masculine chuckle erupted through the line, sending a delicious thrill along her internal circuitry. "Just be comfortable," he advised.

Yeah, right. Be comfortable when she was about to spend the day with the sexiest detective this side of the Mississippi. As soon as he hung up, she dialed the salon. Drat, no one answered. But then, it was just after nine. Even Lucille usually didn't come in this early. Marla left a message on the machine notifying her staff she'd been called away and wouldn't be in. They'd have to juggle their schedules to accommodate her appointments.

That task done, she dashed into her bedroom to spritz herself with Obsession. Spooks, excited by her bustle of activity, charged into the room. He zipped around madly, barking as he darted in and out. Marla didn't have time to coddle him. Checking that her hair was properly styled, she threw on a pair of gold-button earrings. Ouch, that right ear pinched. Her lobes were small and couldn't support big dangling earrings like the ones she'd worn yesterday. Tally looked better in that kind. Thinking of her friend reminded Marla she needed to visit her shop. Tally had put away an outfit for her to try on, and she'd never gone over. It wasn't fair to hold it that long. Just chalk up another omission to Bertha's death!

Slipping into a pair of low-heeled pumps, she finished primping in time for her ears to pick up the sound of a honking horn. Swinging her purse strap over one shoulder, she scrambled to the front hallway.

Marla couldn't get used to seeing Dalton in casual clothes. When he got out to open the car door for her, she caught a glimpse of his broad chest encased in a hunter green knit shirt. Forcing her gaze away from his massive shoulders, she let her eyes trail downward past his trim waistband to a pair of black trousers. *Very preppy,* she decided approvingly, and nondescript for a man who preferred to blend in with the crowd.

They made small talk until Marla noticed they were heading west into Everglades territory. On either side of the road, sawgrass extended as far as her eyes could see. A snowy white egret soared over the soggy plain, its long neck a graceful arch.

"What's our destination?" she queried, ready to get down to business. He seemed reluctant to steer the conversation toward personal matters, and that suited her just fine.

"We're going to see a *santero* priest," Vail admitted with a sheepish grin. "I contacted Carlos's sister, who lives in Elizabeth, New Jersey. She didn't have anything relevant to add to the case but said her brother used to visit this man. He lives in Hialeah, but they'd meet out in the Everglades to go fishing together. I'm hoping he can shed some light on Carlos's activities."

"What's a *santero* priest?"

"Someone who interprets the rituals of *santeria,* a religion that mixes African and Catholic beliefs. It's been popular among Cuban immigrants. Chants, drum ceremonies, charms, and animal sacrifices are part of the practice."

"Sounds like voodoo."

"Some people equate *santeria* to satanism, but most

folks go to a *santero* to cure an illness or ask for good-luck charms.''

"Oh, sort of like a medicine man?"

"Exactly."

"So you think Carlos may have talked to this priest about his plans?"

"Right, I'm counting on it."

Summoning her resolve, Marla asked the question burning in her mind. "What caused Carlos's death?"

Vail glanced her way, his face impassive. "Poisoned."

Marla gasped. "What?"

"The cake was contaminated. Whoever gave him his payoff also gave him a plateful of death."

"W-which, uh, poison was used?" Was it the same thing that killed Bertha?

"According to our forensic expert, the derivative came from a climbing pea plant commonly found in Florida," he said in a matter-of-fact tone as though they were discussing vegetable gardens. "Prayer beans, Seminole beads, Indian licorice—those are just some of the names it goes by. When the beans are crushed, the seeds provide abric acid, a highly toxic substance. Symptoms can take up to several days to occur."

A shiver wormed up her spine. "So Carlos wouldn't have felt the effects right away. That latent period would have worked to the killer's advantage. Give Carlos the cake as a parting gift. That night, he leaves the salon door unlocked. He's gone in the morning and dead a few days later. Good-bye witness." She swallowed a lump in her throat at the heartlessness of it all. How easy to dispatch someone who was considered expendable.

"Seems like we have a bad guy who knows his plants."

"Or bad woman," Marla added, thinking of a certain

light-haired female working in her salon. She didn't believe Darlene knew much about botany, but then, how well did she know the girl?

"So who's this *santero* we're going to see? And why did you bring me along?"

Again he spared her a glance, but this time his brows were furrowed. "I have some other news to share. We also got the lab report back on the candy."

"Don't tell me . . . I missed eating some perfectly safe marzipans." She spoke lightly but a tremulous voice betrayed her anxiety.

"Actually, they contained cyanide—the same form that was found in Mrs. Kravitz's powdered creamer."

Marla's face lost its color. "Oh, joy. Just what I needed to hear. What's next?" Thinking about her close call, she felt a surge of anger stir her blood. *No one has the right to threaten me!* Bad enough Bertha had been murdered in her salon. It was almost as though someone had a grudge against Marla to set the scene where it hurt her the most.

Pressing her lips together, she guarded her silence as they sped toward an area of higher ground thick with pines and cypress trees. A charred section lay to her right, blackened stumps reaching from the muck like frozen hands. Wildlife thrived in the river of grass which was dotted by hammocks, but although she strained her eyes, she couldn't spot a single alligator by the banks.

Carolyn and Stan came to mind, both predators in their own ways. Carolyn must be the one who'd offered to pay Mr. Thomson a large sum to take over Marla's lease. If Stan were subsidizing her effort to force Marla out, he must be figuring Marla would sell their jointly owned property to stay afloat. But would they go so far as to murder her customer?

Glancing at Vail's set jaw and distant expression, she refrained from confiding her thoughts. She could be totally wrong, leaving herself open to a defamation-of-character lawsuit if word got out. No, better to keep her mouth shut until she learned more.

Staring out the window, she let her mind wander. Freed from restraint, a certain thread surfaced among her memories, and then her mental record kept playing the same tune.

Carolyn was a bleached strawberry blond. In her high-school days, she used to work in a Publix bakery.

She could have been the woman who baked the cake.

15

Vail turned his car off the main road about an hour west of Miami. They sped past a souvenir shack selling seashell trinkets. A sausage tree shaded the gravel lane, its oblong shaped fruit hanging down from vinelike branches. Sabal palms dotted the landscape, higher ground in the endless wetlands. Peace descended upon Marla as she sank against the seat cushion and allowed her cares to drift away. Here among the tall grasses with an expanse of azure sky stretching in a 360-degree panorama, it was easy to lose your sense of reality in a communion with nature. Living in a semitropical climate, she should take advantage of her surroundings more often.

Yeah, right. Like I have so much extra time.

Several miles ahead, they came upon a sign advertising an Indian village and airboat rides. Straightening her spine, she gave Vail an inquisitive glance.

He responded with a quick grin. "We're almost there. I hope you don't mind loud noises."

Marla gave him a teasing smile. "That depends. If it's a strange animal growling, that might alarm me."

"I thought you were a dog lover."

"Oh, I am. But some animals can be more ferocious." She thought of Stan, nearly frothing at the mouth when he got angry. "What about you? Do you have any pets?"

He nodded, his eyes the color of flint. "I bought Brianna a golden retriever when her mother died. I thought having a pet might help . . . but it didn't, not really. She still has a hard time handling her feelings. She loves the dog, though."

Marla resisted the urge to touch him. "And you?" she added softly.

He shrugged. "I manage."

A wealth of pain hid behind his words, but Marla didn't get the chance to pursue it. A squat concrete building loomed ahead, identified by a sign, INDIAN SOUVENIRS. Besides the usual gift shop and a storage shed, this compound also had a gasoline pump. *Who'd stop here for gas?* Marla wondered, glancing at the deserted road. Vail veered into an unpaved lot. Shifting the sedan into park, he shut off the ignition and turned to her.

"Let's go check out this place."

Marla wished she'd chosen a shorts outfit when she emerged from the car. Laden with humidity, the warm air filled her lungs. Creeping toward its zenith, the sun blazed a trail overhead. Insects droned in the background like a hungry chorus. Curving around the rear of the shop ran a slough on which were docked several airboats. Thick tropical vegetation lined its banks. Yellow water lilies sprouted from the shallow water, whose stillness was broken by an occasional ripple as a fish leapt into the air. A gentle breeze ruffled the hairs on her skin as she followed Vail inside the shop.

The sweet smell of orange-blossom perfume drifted her way on waves of air-conditioning. Marla stepped past painted heads made from coconuts, a selection of colorfully dressed Indian dolls, and stuffed miniature crocodiles. Beads hung on a rack by the cash register, which was manned by a bronze-skinned woman who smiled as they approached. High cheekbones accented a face devoid of makeup. It was difficult to assess her age, Marla decided. Ebony hair, twisted on top of her head in a braid, was sprinkled with gray, although the woman's complexion remained wrinkle free.

"May I help you?" The Indian put aside her sewing and regarded them with undisguised curiosity.

"We'd like an airboat ride to Blue Heron Hammock," Vail announced. Even though his posture reflected casual ease, his commanding tone indicated a man used to giving orders.

The woman responded to his authority, rising immediately. "One minute, please," she said, vanishing through a door that presumably led to a back office.

While they waited, Vail placed a hand on Marla's shoulder. Her eyebrow lifted in surprise. He was seemingly unaware of his gesture, but she felt the warmth of his hand seep into every bone of her body.

A muscular man accompanied the Indian woman back into the shop. His hands were greasy, and he wiped them on a rag, which he then stuffed into his jeans pocket. Tattoos were etched onto his bulging forearms. Marla couldn't discern their design because her eyes were drawn to his face. A timeworn expression shone from his bottomless dark eyes, the crinkles beside them suggesting he possessed a sense of humor. He stood, thumbs hooked into his belt loops, like a warrior on the prowl.

"I'm Sammy. You wanna ride?"

"That's right," Vail said. "Have you got a boat available?"

"Sure, if you've got the dough. It'll be twenty dollars each for the round trip with a ten-minute stop at the village."

Detaching himself from her, Vail withdrew three twenty-dollar bills from his wallet and thrust them at the man. "I'll make it thirty dollars each for extra time."

"How much extra?"

"A half hour should be enough."

"Who you going to see?"

"A friend."

"This friend, he expecting you?"

"Not really. I was referred to him by someone else. Maybe you know him . . . *Santero* Manuel."

The Indian's eyes brightened. "Ah, now I understand." He glanced between Vail and Marla, his eyes sparkling. "This your woman? *Santero* Manuel can make you a blessing, no?"

Marla almost laughed aloud when Vail's face turned a bright shade of crimson. "We'll see," he muttered, striding toward the rear door.

As they climbed into the flat-bottomed boat with its aluminum hull rising out of the water, Marla considered asking the *santeria* priest for some blessings herself. *Help me find Bertha's killer, please. Then get Stan and Carolyn Sutton off my back.* There were lots of things she could pray for, but mostly Marla relied on herself rather than divine intervention. She wondered how Vail felt about religion. Off duty, he didn't display any religious symbols that she noticed. Marla's feelings about her own heritage were mixed, and she never wore a Star of David or other outward sign of her faith. Meeting a *santero* should be an enlightening experience, she decided.

Vail stood aside so she could precede him to one of the three rows of black-plastic benches situated behind a wide, curved windshield. She took a seat, reaching into her purse for sunglasses. Thus able to see despite the glare off the water, she examined the pilot's chair that towered over the flat deck behind them.

"I've never been on one of these," she confessed to Vail. He levered his large body down beside her, but she made no effort to scoot away when their hips touched. If this thing took off like she thought it might, she might need to grab something solid, like his beefy arm.

"That's a 240-horsepower airplane engine driving the propeller shaft," he told her, nodding at the apparatus.

A metal frame, forming a semicircle around the propeller, held the pilot's seat in place. Sammy, having reached his elevated perch, donned goggles and earphones. *Oh joy,* thought Marla, *we're really in for a thrill ride.* Clutching the bench when the powerful engine kicked into life, she risked a glance in Vail's direction. His face held a look of heightened anticipation, his full attention being centered on the waterway ahead. Sammy flipped some switches, stepped on the throttle, and eased out on the stick with his left hand. Just like airplane controls, she recognized. The twin air rudders shifted, and the boat slid forward.

"This is fun!" Marla said, as they cruised around the back of the gift shop and passed a cluster of banana plants. She spotted a baby alligator sunning on the bank and tapped Vail's shoulder to show him. He grinned but didn't speak because the roar of the engine drowned out all other sounds. Sammy stepped on the gas, sending the boat into a broad sideslip until they were heading south, away from the shop. Their speed increased so that Marla's eyes teared despite the sunglasses and her hair whipped about her face. Vibrations from the motor rumbled through her bones as they cleared the narrow river bordered by tall grasses and custard apple trees. Soon they were making a straight run down the wet grass prairie. The horizon was visible on all sides, its sheer immensity stealing her breath.

They bumped over a mound of black muck, and she felt the seat rise beneath her, then drop as the boat skimmed over the blanket of grass. Occasional hammocks dotted the landscape like islands in a swamp. She watched a flock of white ibis take flight as the noise of the engine neared them.

The boat hit another clump of mud and her attention redirected itself forward. Up ahead came an area of higher ground, and they were aiming directly for it. Blue Heron Hammock, she figured.

Reaching the oasis, Sammy cut the motor and side-slipped the airboat into a slough beside a wooden dock. Marla felt a rush of silence and an eerie calm as the boat's vibrations ceased.

Sammy put aside his earphones. "I wait here."

Vail stretched his tall limbs. "A half hour, remember?"

Grinning, Sammy gave a thumbs up-sign.

"Come on," Vail urged, taking her elbow and guiding her off the boat.

Stepping onto the wooden dock, its planks weathered and rife with splinters, Marla surveyed the scenery. "This is lovely," she murmured, indicating the flowering plants and fruit trees. Purple hyacinths lined the banks where a blue heron stood feeding in shallow water. A strong floral scent mixed with the smell of decaying vegetation.

"It's peaceful, isn't it?" Vail proclaimed, his keen gaze absorbing every detail. His body tensed as his eyes fell upon the only two visible inhabitants of the village. One was an old woman weaving a wad of material; the other was a man chopping wood. Neither was the priest figure they'd expected.

"Let's see what that woman has to say," Marla suggested, aware of Sammy's eyes on their backs. She strode forward, assuming a pleasant expression. The older female sat near a display of colorful Indian blankets strung on a clothesline. She didn't waver from her task as they approached but remained with her head bent, a frown of concentration on her face. The black hair knotted tightly on her head made her profile appear sharp and angular. Her fingers kept up their steady work without interruption.

"Excuse me," Marla said sweetly before Vail got in a word. The woman might react better to another female than to him. "We're looking for *Santero* Manuel."

The Indian tilted her head slightly and yelled to the man busy chopping wood across the clearing. Marla couldn't understand what she said and wondered where everyone else had gone. Obviously, this wasn't where the Indians resided, so it must be just another tourist attraction. Maybe at some point it had been a real Indian camp, but most of it was overgrown by now with only one chickee hut left intact, its palmetto-thatched roof sagging where a new cypress pole was needed. Sawgrass reached nearly to the roof, which lacked new fronds. Not much shelter from rainstorms there, she concluded. A smoldering fire, a half-rotten wooden table, and a small pile of logs completed the village decor. Surrounding the hammock rose fields of sawgrass, ready to overwhelm the island should it be abandoned.

"Greetings," Vail said to the wood chopper. Marla heard the wary note in his voice and couldn't blame him for his caution. As the muscled man approached, she shivered involuntarily. Dressed simply in a T-shirt and baggy pants, he nonetheless appeared menacing with an ax in his hand and a scowl on his swarthy face. Stringy hair fell to his shoulders, bluish highlights in the jet-black strands.

"Is the *santero* expecting you?" he gritted.

Marla kept silent, letting Vail take the lead. "We didn't call ahead," he said in a sardonic tone. "But we're here on an urgent errand. We need to see him today." A muscle worked in his jaw, and he glanced at her. Marla smiled back, reassuring him this trip would be worthwhile.

The Indian seemed to draw some conclusion by her reaction. "This way." He pointed to a trail leading into the bush. They followed him to a clearing beside a murky pond where the village site was hidden from view. Along the way, he dropped his ax. The gesture prompted Vail to relax his posture.

At the water's edge, a short man wearing a cotton guayabera shirt squatted beside a plastic bucket. A fishing pole lay on the ground along with various supplies. Having an aversion to live bait, Marla had never been drawn to fishing. Her lip curled at the sight of worms squiggling in the bucket.

"This is *Señor* Manuel," said the wood chopper. Giving them a curt nod, he strode back toward the village.

The *santero* rose and faced them. His shirt hung half-open at the bottom, showing a sprinkling of wiry gray hairs on a generous belly. An unlit cigar stuck from his mouth. His eyes, a piercing charcoal, considered them appraisingly. "So why have you come to see me?" he asked in accented English. "Let me guess. You would like a blessing for your union, no?"

"That's not it," Vail cut in quickly, avoiding her amused glance. Introducing himself and Marla, he stated their purpose: "We're here to talk to you about Carlos."

The *santero's* expression saddened. "Ayee, poor soul. I made a prayer to *Ochun* in his name." He eyed them curiously. "You are familiar with the origins of *santeria*?" When they indicated a negative response, he gestured to the riverbank. "Please, sit. I would like for you to understand." Removing the cigar from between his thin lips, he stuck it in a pants pocket.

With a grunt, Vail lowered himself to the hard ground, and Marla followed suit. Reeds rustled as a breeze blew up, gently swaying the sawgrass over the swamp. A raucous bird cry broke the otherwise peaceful stillness. Her hands splayed on the dirt as she settled into a comfortable position.

Assuming a perch on a nearby log, the *santero* directed his sharp gaze on them. "*Santeria* evolved from the religious beliefs of African slaves, many of whom came from the Yoruba people in what is now called Nigeria. They needed to hide their culture from white slave owners so they turned to Christianity. Through contact with Roman Catholics, the religion evolved into a fusion of elements from both belief systems. We worship African deities and Catholic saints together. *Ochun* is our beloved virgin."

"What is your role?" Marla asked curiously.

"I help my people to rid themselves of illness, to get

a better job, to keep a husband from wandering. Whatever is needed, I try to do, although sometimes faith is the best therapy."

Vail shifted his large body. "Did Carlos come to you for spiritual guidance, or were you just fishing companions?"

The *santero*, seated with his knees folded, fingered his glass-bead necklace. "Carlos was a good man," he said, his expression sobering. "He sent dollars home to his widowed mother still living in Cuba. I don't know what she'll do now that he's gone. Carlos has . . . had a sister, but she's struggling to raise two young ones on her own."

"Did he seem bothered by anything recently?"

A thoughtful gleam entered the Cuban's eyes. "Ayee. He was troubled at our last session. Fishing was our excuse to get together," he said, answering Vail's previous question, "but he'd always want to talk. I think he didn't want to appear superstitious, but he couldn't disregard *santeria* either. In this case, he was disturbed by a request made to him."

"How is that?"

"Someone wanted him to do a deed that made him feel uncomfortable. His conscience troubled him. It just meant leaving a door unlocked, but he was worried about the reasons why. He'd always been an ethical man, and this decision plagued him." He paused. "Carlos came over on the Mariel boatlift in 1980. He took this job as janitor soon after. He'd always sent dollars home, but the need increased after his papa died last February. I think that's why he agreed to the request despite his reservations."

Marla leaned forward to catch Vail's next words. "Who made the request?" Vail demanded.

"A woman."

"Description?"

The *santero* shrugged. "He said she looked good for her years."

"Did he mention her name? Or where she worked?"

"No, *señor*. Carlos didn't actually say the words, but I believe he was afraid she planned to burglarize the place. Your salon, eh?" he directed to Marla.

"That's right, but we have nothing valuable in our salon. What could anyone take . . . hair solutions and accessories? I suppose you could sell them at a flea market."

"Carlos wondered what to do. He wanted the extra dollars to send home, but his heart told him this deed was wrong. He asked me for an amulet against evil spirits."

"And in the end, he complied with the woman's wishes. Did he mention a final meeting between them?" Vail grated, idly scratching at an insect bite on his arm.

"He said he might go away for a few days just so he wouldn't be associated with whatever she'd planned." The *santero* bent his head. "I could only offer advice. I gave him an amulet and warned him to follow his instincts."

"If he had done so, he might still be alive." Vail compressed his lips.

Not a person to sit quietly for long, Marla piped in. "By any chance, did he say what color the woman's hair was?"

Señor Manuel withdrew his cigar and stuck it between his teeth. "Ayee, he'd said light-haired females always had their way with him."

A few questions later and it was clear they wouldn't gain any new information. Thanking the *santero*, they rose. Marla brushed dried grass needles off her butt and realigned her sunglasses. Her skin felt prickly with sweat. The breeze wasn't enough to cool them under the blazing sunlight. Throat parched, she yearned to return to the gift shop, where she could purchase a cold soft drink.

They were climbing into the airboat when the *santero* waved to them. "I just remembered something else," he called.

"What's that?" Marla and Vail chimed in unison.

"Carlos mentioned one more thing the woman said: " *'I'm doing it for him.'* "

16

"**W**hat do you think Carlos's words meant?" Marla asked during the drive home along the east–west corridor.

"It appears the woman wasn't working alone." Vail hadn't said much during their thrill ride back to the souvenir shop. Mouth clamped shut, he'd stared straight ahead, hair tossing into his face while Sammy pushed the throttle. The Indian seemed determined to unnerve them and rode his pilot's chair like an aeronautical acrobat.

"Darlene and Roy?" Marla said now, mentioning the first names that popped into her mind.

"I'm not so sure."

Marla gave him a suspicious glare. "Why do you say that?"

"We shouldn't overlook other possibilities."

She liked his use of the word *we*. "Darlene has light hair. She's hiding her relationship to Roy, and she has easy access to storeroom supplies. I'd say she's the most logical suspect."

Vail raised his eyebrows. "Aren't you forgetting someone?"

She couldn't tell by the gleam in his eyes if he were serious or not. "I have dark brown hair," she reminded him.

"If I'm not mistaken, you carry an array of wigs in your salon. You were alone with the victim, and you served her the contaminated drink. I'm just not sure how you'd know about poisonous plants when you seem to have a black thumb where greenery is concerned."

"No kidding. I'm not a *maven* in that department." Any plants left under her care died a hasty death. Marla noticed how he'd touched upon means and opportunity but failed to mention motives. Presumably he could have her damning photos, meaning the clever man was trying to trick her into a defensive blunder.

Groping for a response, she averted her gaze out the side window. Her glance carried beyond the wire fence blocking off the road from a canal and rested on the water's coating of brown slime. "Unlike Darlene I don't have a partner in crime," she pointed out. "Darlene could have paid Carlos to leave the back door unlocked as a red herring and put the poison into Bertha's creamer herself, or else Roy entered that night and did it. Oh wait, he was in Naples then." She frowned, thinking.

Vail patted her thigh. "We know he was in Naples up until dinner the night before the murder from tracing his charge accounts. But he used express checkout, meaning he could have left anytime in the night. When the maid knocked on his door in the morning, he was already gone."

Marla sucked in a breath. "So he could have been at the salon! He may have met Darlene there."

"Poison is still not the usual MO for a man."

"Well, if you don't think Roy did it, Darlene still might have been acting under his instructions. He inherits Bertha's business interests. Lucille led me to believe he's skimming funds from the company, and she thinks Bertha found out. Her memoirs might have exposed him. Faced with possible legal action, he may have taken matters into his own hands."

"What else did Lucille tell you?"

"She confirmed that Bertha and Roy were having an affair."

"Did that seem to bother her?"

"No, why should it? She left the company eight years ago." Something niggled at her consciousness, but Marla pushed it away.

"There's also Zack and Wendy," Vail commented casually.

Marla sat up straight. "Wendy was fond of her aunt. She wouldn't have harmed Bertha."

"Zack's resources are depleted. He owes people money, and his wife is pregnant. He's got a motive."

"I'm telling you, Wendy isn't involved in this case. Zack is expecting an investment to come through."

"Yeah, his wife's inheritance."

Realizing he was baiting her, she fell silent for the rest of the ride. Other possibilities entered her mind, unpleasant ideas she didn't want to consider but forced herself to confront.

Ken was involved in Zack's money-making scheme. His recent behavior indicated something was wrong, but he wouldn't confide in Tally. Or was one of them lying? Tally's blond mane of hair came to mind, but Marla quickly discarded the notion. The sailor would have recognized Tally if she'd been the one to visit Carlos at the dock. And what about the *santero's* remark that Carlos said the woman looked good for her age? Tally, Darlene, and even Wendy kept themselves youthfully in style.

Wishing she'd get home, Marla shifted her position. Who else looked good for her years and had light hair?

A lump rose in her throat. Carolyn Sutton. But her competitor wouldn't stoop this low to put her out of business. If anything, business had swelled after the murder. People were curious to visit the place and gossip about Bertha Kravitz. That didn't explain the rival bid to her landlord unless Stan truly belonged in the equation. Regardless of whether or not they'd been scheming behind her back, Marla determined to pay Carolyn a long-overdue visit.

"Want to stop for lunch?" Vail asked unexpectedly.

Marla glanced at her watch. It was nearly one o'clock. They'd made good time. In no hurry to return to the salon, she agreed. "Sure, what did you have in mind?"

"I know of a Cuban place not far from here."

"That sounds great."

Over a meal of sauteed chicken breast with fried plantains, black beans, and rice, Marla attempted to gauge his impression of her. He still wasn't sharing all he knew about the case, but that could just be his natural caution rather than a conviction on his part that she was guilty.

"You puzzle me," he admitted after bolting down a swallow of beer.

"How so?" Marla sipped her iced coffee, appreciating the restaurant's soft decor. White tablecloths and fresh flowers combined with muted lighting gave the place an intimate atmosphere. She felt strange being there with a police detective.

"Not too many other women would get involved in a

murder case like you've done. You've gotten some pretty useful information."

"Bertha died in my salon. That makes it my responsibility to find her murderer."

Reaching across the table, he took her hand. "You're wrong. It's *my* job to solve this case. You're putting yourself at risk by snooping."

Marla withdrew her hand. "You don't understand. If I find her killer, that absolves me." Folding her hands, she redirected her gaze to the tiled floor. "I should have detected something unusual in her creamer. It'll always be my fault that I fixed her that cup of coffee. It wasn't my intention to harm her." Her pleading glance rose to meet his bewildered expression.

"Why do you insist on accepting blame?"

A small smile played about her lips. "You mean you're not accusing me of doing the deed?"

"If you didn't, why do you persist in feeling guilty?"

Her shoulders slumped. "This isn't the first time," she murmured. She hadn't meant to say it. The words just slipped from her mouth. Clenching her hands together, she blurted out her disgraceful history. If he'd been digging into her past, he knew about most of it already anyway. Except for the photos, and she wouldn't mention those. In a faltering voice, she told him about Tammy.

"No wonder," he said, a hint of admiration in his tone.

"What does that mean?" She'd just bared her soul, describing her grief and guilt-ridden agony, and his response was an oblique remark. Her hackles rose in self-defense.

"I can tell you're a strong person from the way you handle yourself under fire. Now I know why. You were scorched by the flames of hell, and you came out unscathed."

Her eyes reflected her anguish. "No, not unscathed. The wounds may not be visible, but they're still here."

Leaning forward, he captured her gaze. "They'll always be with you, but you've learned how to go on. By your work with the coalition, you help others. That's really the best way to deal with pain."

"You've experienced bad times yourself. How do you manage?"

He lounged back, his face hooded. "We're not talking about me."

"Why not? If you ask me, you need to talk to someone."

"Well, I didn't ask you."

"Fine, suit yourself. But you'll never get close to another person with that attitude. Maybe that's the point. You're afraid of experiencing another loss."

"Aren't you?" he retorted. "You act like you're trying to prove something by finding Bertha's killer. And whenever I try to get more personal, you shy away. I've learned more about you today than from our previous talks."

"That's swell. Pat yourself on the back."

A bitter silence fell between them as they left the restaurant. Marla resented his remarks and how he was able to get under her skin so easily. Just as well she'd never see him again after this case was solved.

Neither one spoke during the drive back to her town house. Finally, Vail broke the ice. "Look, I'm sorry about what I said back there." Pulling into her driveway, he shifted into park and shut off the engine.

"No problem." Surreptitiously, she glanced at the time. Three o'clock. She could still make it to the printer's shop before business hours ended and have time left over to check on things at the salon. "I've got to go."

"But I'd like to talk about this."

"Not now."

"You don't have to go back to the salon. Isn't another hairdresser covering for you?"

"I've got things to do." Opening the door, she shoved herself out. "Thanks for the lunch. It's been a great day."

"You're welcome." The words bit out of his mouth. Eyes narrowing, he didn't say another word.

Feeling a twinge of guilt, she pushed it aside. Too many chasms lay between them to be bridged so readily. Bertha's murder was the biggest hurdle. Better to leave things between them on a business level.

After greeting Spooks, who leapt for joy at her arrival, she freshened up before heading out again. Three stops were on her agenda. First was the print shop, then her salon to make sure things were in order. Then if she still had time, she'd direct her attention to Carolyn Sutton.

Luck followed her to the store. When she pushed on the door, it swung open. She'd even been able to find a parking meter down the quiet street. Inside, a balding middle-aged man sat behind a counter reading the newspaper. At her entrance, he stood up, stuffing the paper into a drawer.

Marla caught a glimpse of machinery in a back workroom. Male voices raised in argument told her they weren't alone. Nervously, she wet her lips. From the magazines displayed on the walls, this appeared to be a legitimate business.

"Excuse me, I'm looking for the proprietor," she said, approaching the fellow behind the counter.

"That's me. Kurt Jarvis, ma'am." He regarded her with a wary expression.

"I'm, uh, doing an article on local entrepreneurs. You were recommended as someone who represents an unusual occupation." Leaning forward, she lowered her voice to a conspiratorial whisper. "My readers like to get the real juice, you know what I mean?"

"Who do you work for—one of the tabloids?"

"Of course."

He probably doesn't get too many classy women in this part of town, she realized. Figures he'd add her to his sleaze list thinking she could only work for a sensational news service. Then again, if he sold dirty magazines, his walk-ins could be well-heeled. Perverted tastes knew no social boundaries, or so she'd been led to believe. Maybe he sold the things through mail order, she thought suddenly, spotting a stack of brown-wrapped items at the far end.

"I notice you have these glossy publications." She waved at the displays on the walls. "But a friend gave me a sample of something else, which I was hoping to buy."

She smiled, noting the twitch in his double chin. It matched his belly when he moved. A half-filled box of doughnuts rested on the counter, a telltale smidgen of powdered sugar stuck to his mouth.

"Really? Who's your friend?"

"That's not important. I have a sample in my purse." Lifting out the magazine, she showed him.

His glance flickered toward the front door. "Put it away, ma'am. I don't carry that stuff here."

"Oh no?" She opened the first page and indicated the post office box address. "I asked at the post office where this originated, and they gave me this address. Since it's registered as a business PO Box, they can give out that information." She made her remark sound like a veiled threat.

"Just a minute, please." A sheen of sweat had broken out on Jarvis's face. Giving her a nervous glance, he turned away and scurried into the back workroom, where she heard him confer with his colleagues.

Marla used the time to saunter around the room. She noticed that the pile of brown-wrapped items bore a different post office box address than the one on the magazine and made a mental note of the box number. A colorful calendar on the wall drew her attention. Did they produce those, too? But when she took a closer look, her eyes widened. Another business was listed. Apparently this was a promotional gift from—guess who?—a photographer. Sure she had struck gold, Marla scribbled down his name on a pad of paper before the printer returned.

He didn't return alone. Backing him were two scroungy men who looked like bouncers. One had wiry hair and tattoos on both bulging biceps. The other one leering at her looked like he needed a good dentist. From the smell of him, a bath would have helped, also. Marla inadvertently took a step backward.

"You looking for dirty pictures, missy? This ain't the right place," growled the man with broken front teeth. "But if youse is interested, I'll take you somewhere else." His hot gaze raked her body. "I know where you can get a fix."

"No, thanks. I must have made a mistake." Clenching her purse to her side, she made for the door.

The two men were around the counter in an instant. Bad Teeth blocked her path. Spinning about, she faced Muscle Man square on. "I'm leaving now," she said, her tone firm. "Please ask your friend to get out of my way."

"Not so fast, sister." Muscle Man's voice grated like chalk on a board. "We'd like to know who sent you."

"I'm a reporter for the tabloids," she repeated, hoping

they wouldn't ask for identification. Her heart thumping wildly, she struggled to maintain her cool.

"Come into the back with us. We'll show youse what you want," coaxed Bad Teeth from behind.

Marla edged sideways, hoping he'd follow so she could aim for the door from a different direction. "First tell me if those magazines are printed here."

"You're not an undercover cop, are you?" sneered Muscle Man. He advanced until she was forced to stare into the bulging whites of his eyes. Sweat mingled with the smell of printer's ink. Resisting the urge to retreat, she lifted her chin.

"No, I'm not. I guess I was wrong about finding a story here. You've got to let me leave."

A harsh chuckle sounded from behind and then hands roughly cupped her buttocks. She jerked around, elbow swinging. Pain splintered her arm as she connected with Bad Teeth's cheekbone. Grunting in surprise, he lurched backward just as the front door crashed open.

"Need some assistance?" drawled Detective Vail. His steely gaze challenged her assailants. Never had she been more glad to see the tall, athletic police officer.

Sensing his authority, the two men backed off. "We was just having a little fun," whined Bad Teeth, quick to disengage himself under the threat of retribution.

Marla rushed toward Vail. "Let's get out of here," she pleaded, tugging on his arm. Scowling down at her, he gave a quick nod. Evidently he was more concerned about her safety than pursuing these miscreants.

"What the hell were you doing in there?" he snarled outside on the sidewalk.

"I was asking questions. Thanks for the rescue," Marla mumbled, too unnerved to explain further. As she

directed him to her car down the street, she stiffened
her spine to control her trembling. It wouldn't do to
show Vail how scared she'd been. Okay, so it was pretty
stupid to come here alone. Bad neighborhood, disreputable shop. Possible illegal activity if they were sending
those magazines out via the mail. Dumb move, Marla.
Her nose wrinkled; diesel fumes from a truck guzzled
down the road.

"Why were you here? Were you following me?" she
snapped, grateful he'd shown up at the right time but
wondering how he came to be there in the first place.

He kept pace with her fast stride. Fury darkened his
face, as turbulent as those storm clouds approaching on
the horizon. His thick brows were so close together they
reminded her of a cold front line marching south. Even
the corners of his mouth curved downward, expressing
disapproval. With his broad shoulders hunched forward,
he appeared ready for a fight.

"I didn't like the way you got rid of me," he said in
his gruff tone. "Thought I'd tail you to see where you
were going in such a hurry."

"What?" Whirling to face him, she tapped his arm.
"Is that a measure of your trust? I'd hoped you believed
in me." Hurt mixed with anger in her tone. She couldn't
help feeling betrayed. His actions merely served as evidence to the huge gap between them.

A distant rumble of thunder reached her ears. Dust
clogged her nostrils as a breeze blew in. The air smelled of
impending rain. It was a fitting end to a bad experience.

"You have the *chutzpah* to talk about trust?" he scoffed,
his gaze glittering with disappointment. "Why don't you
tell me why you were here. What questions were you
asking in that place?"

Marla wavered. She could just mention the magazine Wendy had found, but that might lead to the photographer and her own sordid past. Vail already knew about Tammy; maybe he'd understand why she'd been so desperate for money. Or maybe he'd consider Bertha's blackmailing her to be enough of a motive for Marla to murder the old lady. His menacing stance made her decision easy. He wasn't in a tolerant mood. Better to deflect his attention.

"Sorry, but I'm afraid that anything I say to you may be used against me."

"Ah ha, so you are hiding something. I figured as much." An exultant look crossed his face.

Fearful she'd say more than was wise, Marla resumed her walk to the car. Vail's long-legged gait quickly overtook hers. Taking her arm, he jerked her to a halt.

"I want to help, Marla. Honestly. You're putting yourself in danger, and I'd like to know why."

His earnest expression almost convinced her, but she knew cops sometimes took sympathetic tacks. It wouldn't work on her, much as she wished he could be an ally.

"No, thanks, this is a private matter." Loosening his grip, she fled to her Toyota and unlocked the door with shaking fingers.

"I'll be watching you," he warned without making an attempt to delay her.

Marla glanced at him standing by the curb. Peppery dark hair swept his forehead. Eyes glimmered with unfathomable lights. His body tensed, fists clenched by his side with restrained anger. He made a formidable opponent. She'd rather have him for a friend.

Feeling saddened, she crawled into her car. Until this case was solved, she couldn't call anyone *friend*.

17

Realizing Vail might still be following her, Marla headed for work. She doubted the police detective would hang around the parking lot until she finished for the day. After their latest encounter, she wasn't eager for a rematch.

"Hey, Marla!" Giorgio called, as she entered the salon. He was busy sweeping the floor to remove discarded hair cuttings. His handsome Italian features split into a broad grin as he regarded her. "What are you doing here? I thought you were out sick today."

Marla tucked her purse into an empty drawer at her hair station. "I had to go somewhere. Where's Lucille? The reception desk shouldn't be left untended."

"I'm keeping watch." He thumbed toward the rear. "Lucille's in the back arguing with Darlene. You should tell them to keep their voices down. We can hear them in the salon."

Picking up her clean coffee mug where she'd left it on the counter, she marched toward the storeroom. If those two had a case together, they should pursue it on their off time. A murmur of voices reached her ears as she approached. At first, she couldn't discern any words, but when she got nearer, their conversation became clear. Hesitating outside the partially ajar door, Marla focused on listening to the women.

"You're just taking advantage of him for his money," Lucille's voice hissed. "I can't believe Roy doesn't see it, but then again, he's always been easy prey to women like you."

"Roy cares for me," Darlene retorted. "You're just jealous because he never gave *you* a second glance."

"That's not the reason! You've blinded him to the truth."

"Face the facts, Lucille. He doesn't want you."

"Bitch!"

Lucille stormed from the room. The receptionist didn't even notice Marla's presence as she breezed past. Using the opportunity, Marla bounded into the storeroom to corner Darlene.

"What was that all about?" she demanded. Darlene had a stricken look on her face which was quickly replaced by an innocuous smile, but Marla was no longer fooled by her performance. Wise to her act, Marla wouldn't underestimate the girl's craftiness hereafter.

Tossing back a wave of blond hair, Darlene gazed at her defiantly. "Lucille found out about me and Roy. She said you know, too. So what?" She thrust her chin forward. "Like we weren't announcing it to the world."

Marla gave her a chastising glare. "You kept your liaison a secret. Why, Darlene? Were you afraid Bertha would find out? Or is that why you were working here, to spy on her?"

"That's none of your business."

Doggedly, Marla pressed on. "My guess is that Bertha discovered your little arrangement and was furious. You and Roy decided to get rid of her before she could make trouble."

"I don't know what you're talking about."

A dangerous gleam entered Darlene's eyes. Unabashed, Marla continued her interrogation. "When did Roy return from Naples? Was he here the night before Bertha died? Or did he actually get in that morning?"

"Don't ask so many questions or you'll be sorry."

"Did you send me a box of marzipans?"

Startlement crossed the girl's face. "Huh?"

"Never mind." Darlene's reaction indicated she wasn't privy to that incident. That didn't preclude Roy's involvement, however. Blocking the doorway so Darlene couldn't exit, Marla changed tactics to coax more information from her. "Why does Lucille get so riled over Roy? Did they have a thing once?"

Darlene smirked. "Not from Roy's viewpoint. Like she was always the one running after him. Just because he opened her eyes about Harvey doesn't mean he desired her."

Taking a chance that Darlene would talk about another staff member rather than herself, Marla poured herself a cup of coffee from the new machine in the storeroom and added cream and sugar.

"So tell me, who's Harvey?" she asked in a casually friendly tone. Bringing the mug to her lips, she took a careful sip of the steaming brew.

Darlene hooked her thumbs into her jeans pockets and leaned against a counter. "Lucille was dating Harvey Moore when she joined Sunshine Publishing. Like the man was using her but she couldn't see it. Being divorced, he had kids from his previous marriage and didn't want any kind of commitment. Lucille agreed to his terms. Stupid woman, she let him use her money for his own gain."

"So how did their relationship involve Roy?"

"Roy recognized what was going on and told her. I'm not sure what happened, but Harvey was a health nut. One day he made himself a pitcher of sun-brewed tea, except he used the wrong kind of leaves and poisoned himself. Lucille hoped she would gain Roy's attention then, but he'd already turned to Bertha."

"Sounds like Roy doesn't want commitments, either."

"That's not your concern, Marla."

"If he's involved in Bertha's murder, it is. You're not withholding vital information from the police, are you? Because you could be considered an accessory to the crime."

"Get lost." Eyes blazing, Darlene stalked past, heading into the salon.

Reeling from their conversation, Marla sagged against the counter. *Bless my bones, but Darlene is touchy about Roy.* Was one of them guilty, or both together? Or worse, neither one? Because then she'd have to look elsewhere for Bertha's killer.

Maybe Lucille could provide more information. Striding outside, she made a beeline for the receptionist's desk. Lucille sat staring at the computer with a distant expression. Lips pursed, she appeared to be miles away in thought.

"Nice plant," she commented, noting the new addition to the front counter. Deep purple blossoms and hairy green leaves sprouted from rich soil in a hand-decorated ceramic pot.

"Thanks," Lucille said, rousing herself. "African violets are my favorite indoor plants. Lately, I've been having fun with lemongrass, though. I managed to grow a patch in my garden. You'll have to try the tea I made with ginger." She smiled gaily, crinkles transforming her lined skin. "It's good for hot flashes. Makes you sweat more."

"Terrific." Marla leaned forward. "Have you ever heard Darlene mention an interest in gardening?"

"Hah! That girl wouldn't know basil from a bay leaf! Roy used to care more about those things. Sometimes we'd go to the Rare Fruit and Vegetable Council meetings together. He'd bring home batches of herbs."

"Oh, really? I didn't know he liked to grow plants."

"He likes to cook. He just uses the edible parts."

"He doesn't grow the more exotic varieties?"

Lucille's eyes narrowed. "What are you implying, honey?"

She shrugged. "It's not important." Pointing at the calendar, she added, "Who's next on my schedule? I can finish out the day." Feeling something was out of place, she scanned the salon. "Say, where's Nicole?" God, her brain cells must be deteriorating. She hadn't even noticed that her friend was absent. Items scattered across her station indicated Nicole had been there earlier, but where was she now?

Lucille patted her coiffed hairdo. "She had a break, so she ran over to Arnie's place. It's been a busy morning, and no one's had a chance for lunch. She's getting sandwiches for us now that things have slackened off."

"You should have asked Arnie to deliver." Marla's face flushed guiltily. It was her fault for dumping her appointments on them, but she'd figured today would be slow. They must have had a slew of walk-ins.

"My apologies, guys," she said to Miloki and Giorgio, who were listening in. Miloki, busy with a customer, smiled amiably. Giorgio, straightening his combs, waved one at her in response.

"Marla, any news on Bertha Kravitz's murder investigation?" called Miloki's customer. It was Raney Weston, a gossip *maven* who liked her hair teased into a cotton-candy puff of bleached gold.

"The police are still working on it."

"I heard someone else turned up dead."

All eyes turned in Marla's direction. "Yeah, Carlos the janitor. They found his body aboard his boat."

"What happened to him?" the woman persisted, blatant eagerness in her expression.

"Poisoned."

Lucille gasped. "How did you find out?"

Marla refocused her attention on the receptionist. "Detective Vail told me. We went to interview someone who'd known Carlos. That's why I wasn't here this morning."

"B-but why did Vail ask *you* to go? I thought you were a suspect."

"Gee, thanks, Lucille."

"Sorry, I didn't mean—"

"Forget it. So, who's coming in next?" she asked, pointedly directing her gaze at the appointment calendar.

Lucille smoothed her skirt. "Martha Rogan for her usual cut. After that, you've one more appointment, so you should be out of here by six."

"Great," she announced brightly. Inwardly, she frowned. It was great that she was busy, but not so wonderful in that she wouldn't have time to visit the photographer before business hours closed. That meant another delay in her investigation and one more day that Vail might find the original photos. Don't forget the new post office box number, either. That involved another trip to the post office to find out if it was registered to a business other than the printer. Oh, joy. Lots of leads to follow and no time.

"How's my schedule look for tomorrow?" she asked Lucille, drumming her fingers on the counter.

"Booked solid. Looks like a busy Friday."

Normally, she'd be ecstatic. But now every minute was crucial. She had the feeling things would become more urgent hour by hour.

Despite the time crunch, she stopped at Publix on the way home to buy groceries. She'd intended to make chicken soup for Emma, who was still feeling ill. Concerned about her neighbor's condition, she called Moss as soon as she put her purchases away.

"Hello, mate," his gravelly voice answered. "Nice of you to check on Emma. We're still waiting to hear from the doctor regarding test results. He said her blood count may be low."

"Well, I'm making her some chicken soup. If it's okay with you, I'll bring a container over later."

"You're an angel! We'll be here. Hey, maybe you'll take a look at my latest poetic effort."

"Sure, Moss." He could use some good cheer, after all.

After hanging up, she busied herself in the kitchen making cheese tortellinis for dinner. While waiting for a pot of water to come to a boil, she rinsed off the four chicken-breast halves she'd bought and put them in a soup pot. Covering the poultry with cold water, she set the stove burner on high. Next she peeled an onion, a couple of carrots, and cleaned off a handful of fresh dill.

Using a prepackaged salad, she poured out a single portion into a bowl and sprinkled on a tablespoon of raspberry vinegar. Low calorie and healthful, it was her favorite dressing. Then she made a few quick phone calls to her mother and Tally to catch up on their news, and to customers who'd left messages. No way she'd have time to do Marcia's hair at home before the Save the Manatee benefit luncheon on Sunday. Sorry, pal.

Sizzling noises popped and sputtered. Both pots had reached the boiling point. Working quickly, Marla tossed the tortellinis into the smaller pot. Setting her Mickey Mouse kitchen timer for seven minutes, she grabbed a serving spoon. The dirty scum rising to the water's surface in the soup pot needed to be skimmed. That done, she threw in the onion with an *X* cut through its flat end, the carrots, and the dill, and added a pinch of kosher salt. Sealing the top with a lid, she turned down the burner to low. She'd eat her supper while the soup simmered for an hour. The fragrant smell of dill mingled in the air with the stinging aroma of cut onion.

Marla thought about herbs as she poured tomato sauce onto the drained cooked pasta and added a sprinkle of dried basil leaves. So Roy dabbled in raising herbs, did he? Or at least he used them for cooking purposes. How familiar was he with the more lethal properties of plants?

The question repeated itself in her mind on Friday morning after she'd gone to the post office and inquired about the new box number. Interesting what company name was on the card: Sunshine Publishing. Bertha

Kravitz was listed as the contact person. So Bertha supported the publication of those dirty magazines, Marla thought. Was Roy a partner to this subsidiary venture, too? She supposed the only way to find out for sure was to ask him herself. At least she had protection from his proposed lawsuit now that Lance had found evidence against him. Her computer expert friend had called last night, his words tumbling over themselves in his excitement.

"We've got him! That crook has been embezzling money from the company for years." He'd rattled off his sources of information, and Marla crowed with triumph.

This morning Roy wasn't her target, however. She'd get to him later. First she'd interview the photographer, since he might provide more fuel for the fire.

Approaching the photographer's studio took more courage than she'd known she possessed. Not until late that afternoon when she had a cancellation did she run out of the salon on what she told everyone was an urgent errand. Later she'd agreed to meet Tally in her boutique to try on clothes, after which they'd go to dinner. Ken was out of town, presumably on business, and Tally needed mood lifting. So did Marla, and buying new outfits always made her feel better.

She'd need a major mood lift after this visit, she thought, pushing open the door to the photographer's studio. Her knees quaked and her stomach heaved. Not since her shameful episode had she set foot in a place like this. Huge framed photos decorated the walls: wedding couples, family portraits, graduation pictures, children with a look of purity in their eyes. Marla glanced away, her gaze seeking the receptionist's desk. No one was about, but when she *dinged* a bell, a strawberry blond woman wearing glasses emerged from the back office.

"Hi there, how may I help you?" she croaked in a raspy voice. Her chin disappeared into her neck, Marla noticed, making her seem weak-minded by virtue of appearance alone. Or maybe it was the jerky motions she used to accompany her words with gestures. This wasn't someone *she'd* choose to tend the front desk, Marla thought cynically. Possibly she could use the woman's insecurity to her own advantage.

Although she'd rehearsed her speech, when she went to say them, the words faltered on her lips. "I-I'm working with Bailey's print shop. He said you had a pickup for me?"

The photographs in the magazine had to come from somewhere, and it was her guess that this was the place. The calendar might have been given as an innocuous business gift, but the imprint had led her here. She realized the erotic photos would have to be delivered to the printer, or at least the negatives, whereupon he'd assemble the magazine. Or else the printer picked up the items here. Either way, she hoped to gain some useful information from her inquiries.

"What happened to the young man who usually comes for the package?" the lady asked, frowning.

Marla smiled knowingly. "He couldn't make it. I'm not sure about your schedule, but he told me to stop by."

"Well, I don't know. I'm only supposed to release it to him. If you'll wait a minute, I'll check in the back."

Boy, wouldn't she be lucky if the woman gave her the package, she thought after being left alone. Of course, what would she do with the evidence? Bring it to Vail? A bundle of erotic pictures by themselves meant nothing.

Glancing up when the door to the office opened, Marla felt her heart figuratively leap into her throat. That distinctive carrot-colored hair couldn't belong to anyone else, and she'd seen those leering cobalt eyes before. Maybe he'd gained weight in the past fifteen years and now walked with a waddle, but she recognized the man who'd shot her photos as though the humiliating event had happened yesterday.

A light of recognition dawned in his face as he regarded her closely. "Why, Marla, my dear. What an unexpected pleasure." She shuddered at his syrupy tone. "It's been such a long time since you were here last. I'm so pleased to see you. Come, let's go into a consultation room so we can have some privacy."

Rounding the desk so they were face-to-face, he slid his fingers along her upper arm. She got a strong whiff of garlic as his hot breath caressed her cheek.

Recoiling, she gasped, "Get your filthy hands off me." Just remembering how he'd fondled her during the photography episode made her skin crawl. Oh God, how could she face this man again? Yet he might have the answers to her questions. It was worth a bout of self-imposed trauma if she learned something valuable. Dex's presence confirmed her hunch that she'd come to the right place.

"My, you've certainly changed," he cooed. "No longer the lovely young girl desperate for money. Or is that why you're here today? I must say, you're looking swell." His glance raked her body in a slow, leisurely manner that made her feel ill. If she weren't so determined to garner new data, she'd leave now. But this man was too important to let go out of her own feelings of disgust and embarrassment.

Letting resolve firm her expression, she stared back. "I've just come to talk, not to work for you again, Dex."

"Is that right? We'll see. This way, please."

Her fists curled by her side, Marla followed him to a private alcove, insisting that the door remain partially open as she seated herself in a comfortable armchair. Dex levered himself into a leather swivel chair behind a desk strewn with wedding albums.

"So what's this visit about, Marla?"

Sensing an undercurrent of menace to his words, she thrust herself into the fray. "You're sending sexually explicit photos to Bailey's print shop, where they're scanned into porno magazines. The finished products are sold via mail order. Sunshine Publishing is financing the venture."

Dex's shrewd expression bored through her. "I don't know where you came up with these absurd allegations, but that's all they are, I assure you."

"Who else besides Bertha Kravitz is in on the deal? Does Roy Collins know about this little subsidiary business?"

"Huh? What are you talking about?"

She hesitated. Could she be mistaken? "Bertha told me how she'd come here for boudoir pictures and you showed her a racier set of photos. That's where she got the idea for the porno magazine from, I'll bet. Were you aware she was blackmailing me? She insisted on getting free hair services or else she'd publish my photos in her popular regional magazines. For years I've been demeaning myself to accommodate her. I've spent too much time and effort building up my reputation to have her ruin it with a single mistake from my past."

His look of puzzlement took her aback. "I don't know anything about blackmail. You're confusing me, Marla."

"Bertha came here to get her pictures taken, and that's when you showed her my photographs. At least that's what she told me. You've been working with her ever since."

"You've got it all wrong," he said, scratching his head. "It's that male model who bought your photos and came up with the scheme for an erotic magazine."

"What?"

"Bertha Kravitz never stepped foot in here. Wasn't she the dame who was murdered in your salon? Hey, I follow the news," he added at her astonished glance. "You didn't do her in because she was blackmailing you?" His frightened glance strayed to her handbag as though she might have a loaded weapon inside.

"Don't be ridiculous. I'm trying to uncover Bertha's killer."

He sagged in relief. "Well, you're not going to tell the cops anything about me, are you? Because I'm not doing anything illegal. People pay me to take pictures, that's all."

"Who pays you?" Marla demanded. "If Bertha wasn't the one, who then? Roy Collins?" She supposed he might be the courier who picked up the photos and delivered them to the print shop. Maybe he'd even given Bertha's name on the post office box card. But if she wasn't involved, how did Bertha get hold of Marla's negatives? Obviously, she'd lied about coming here for boudoir pictures. So how else could she have obtained the goods?

A link. She needed the link between them all.

"Don't sic the cops on me," pleaded Dex, wringing his hands. "I swear I don't know any Collins character, either. You want to pin the deal on someone, ask Todd."

Marla leaned forward. "Excuse me? Who did you say?"

"Todd Kravitz, the old lady's son. Don't you remember? He was the male model who posed with you for those sexy shots."

18

"So you think Todd killed his mother?" Tally asked.

Marla shrugged. Seated across from Tally at the Olive Garden restaurant, she debated how much to reveal. Her heart burst with the truth. After recognizing that Todd was the man who'd posed with her for those shameful pictures, she needed to unburden her anguish. Who else but her best friend might understand her motives? Certainly not Detective Vail. He'd accuse her of withholding vital information and construe her actions as corroborative evidence against her.

"Marla, spill it." Tally wagged her index finger. "You're not telling me everything."

Marla had a reprieve while the waitress delivered their entrees. Staring at her steaming dish of eggplant parmesan, she murmured, "You won't think badly of me if I confess, will you?"

"Don't be silly. I'm your friend. We can tell each other anything. Now what has you looking like you've just swallowed a blasted bullet?"

With difficulty, Marla raised her eyes to meet Tally's compassionate gaze. "I've never told anyone," she whispered.

"Go on, I'm listening." Shooting a longing look at her plate of spaghetti and mushroom sauce, Tally politely waited.

Twisting her hands, Marla bent her head. "After Tammy's accident, her parents decided to sue me. If you recall, my father had just recovered from his illness. I didn't dare inflict this further injury upon him. Daddy and Ma already shared my grief, but they didn't need an additional burden. I consulted an attorney—Stan's law firm—and resolved to pay the fees myself."

Squirming in her seat, she drew in a tremulous breath, grateful for Tally's encouraging silence. *I should have told her long before this,* Marla realized. *It wouldn't have been so hard to bear if I wasn't alone.*

"I'd done modeling jobs before to earn money," she went on, eyes still cast downward. "I thought I could work to pay off my debts, so I answered a call for a lingerie ad. I assumed the job would be for something like the Victoria's Secret catalog or weekend newspaper ads. But the photographer wasn't anyone familiar to me, and he offered me a lot more money if I posed . . . in an indiscreet manner."

"How indiscreet?" Tally's fascinated expression told Marla her friend was getting a kick out of this story. *Well, at least she's not horrified by my moral ineptitude . . . yet.*

"I, er, put on this black lace merry widow . . . with garters and a thong bikini, no less . . . and figured I'd have different outfits to try on. Well, the photographer, who couldn't manage to keep his hands to himself, had me recline on this couch. I should have been suspicious because we were in a back room, not his usual studio."

"And he wanted to pose with you himself?" Tally guessed, too engrossed to eat her meal.

Marla had completely lost her appetite. "Worse," she said. "He offered me an incredible amount of money if I'd pose with a male model. He'd sell the photos to a small audience who preferred to keep their voyeurism private. The pictures would never be made public, so no one else would ever see them. How could I refuse? I needed money desperately, not only to pay the lawyer, but also for beauty school. Ma was devastated I'd dropped out of college, and she didn't support my career change. I felt totally alone, so, naive *schnook* that I was, I agreed.

"Well, this man came out of another room wearing nothing more than a jock strap. Good-looking, blond hair, big chest. Okay, I figured, what harm would it do if we snuggled close and the guy took his photos? I'd never have to do this again. But they wanted more than two bodies facing each other. They intended it to appear as though we were having sex. We were already entangled when the model pushed my clothing out of the way and put his hands . . . in private places. The jock strap came off before I even knew what was happening. And then he poised atop me, as though he was about to . . . you know. He almost did, too. He was that close." She pinched her thumb and index finger together.

Tally's mouth hung open. "Couldn't you knee him where it hurt? You didn't agree to pose for *those* kinds of shots."

"The photographer insisted that I had. We did more," she admitted, her face flaming. "I was so embarrassed, I wanted to die. I kept telling myself this disgrace was my punishment for killing Tammy. In my unworthiness, I deserved no better."

"Oh, Marla."

Unwanted tears sprang into her eyes. Her feelings were so vivid, as though her shameful indiscretion had happened just yesterday. "I was at the bottom, Tally. My life had turned upside down. I felt I couldn't sink any lower."

Neither one spoke for a while until the waitress came to inquire if everything was all right. Hastily shoveling a forkful of food in her mouth, Marla avoided looking at her friend. She was too choked-up to speak, the morsel of eggplant sliding down her throat like a lump of clay.

"You survived," Tally said at last, her wavy blond hair swinging as she sipped her Chardonnay. "Not only did you crawl out of that morass, you triumphed in your new career and have helped save countless other children from drowning by your work in the coalition. I'd say you should be proud of yourself."

Marla smiled grimly. "Thanks for the vote of confidence." Stan, meeting her during her sojourns to his law firm, had latched on to her. Offering his support, he'd gained her gratitude during a period of intense vulnerability. Not until later did she understand he was a domination freak. At first she'd believed his belittling remarks, but finally she regained enough confidence to overcome his influence. She'd fought her way out of the swirling currents of despair and would never plunge into them willingly again.

"I won't let anyone ruin the reputation I've worked so hard to build," she gritted. "Least of all will I let Bertha's murderer get away with the crime. She was my customer and my responsibility, and no one will ever say I've shirked my duty again. I didn't kill her, even though she was blackmailing me with those photographs. The only way to prove my innocence is to find the real culprit."

"Have you told Detective Vail any of this, or does he already know about your, uh, sullied past?" Tally had given in to her voracious appetite and was rapidly devouring her spaghetti. Marla marveled at how neatly she twirled the long strands into her mouth without a single dribble of sauce.

"I haven't said anything to him. I'd hoped to get hold of the pictures myself. I've got the negatives, but I can't find the original prints. Bertha had them both, and she was blackmailing me into getting free hair appointments."

"How did she get them?"

Marla wasn't quite certain herself. "Todd must have bought them and showed them to his mother. I'd wondered if she was blackmailing other former models. Todd might know."

"Todd is the courier who takes the pictures to the printer? If his mother's name is on the business post office box listing, they must have been in on the deal together."

"I need to see Todd."

"Wait a minute. Didn't you tell me Todd was upset about his mother's announcement that she was going to publish her memoirs? Do you think he killed her to stop her from exposing their dirty dealings?"

"Bless my bones, you may be right."

"You can't go to him alone, Marla. It's too dangerous."

She bit her lower lip. "I'll have to see him. Maybe he's got the prints."

"Or maybe Detective Vail does. He's bound to find

out this stuff sooner or later. You'd be smarter to admit your wrongdoings first.''

"No, I can't. He might book me for murder."

"Well, I think you're making a big mistake." Putting her fork down, Tally gave a bright smile. "Dessert? Let's splurge."

Marla had several calls waiting on her answering machine at home. A couple were from clients who needed appointments over the weekend. One was from Dalton Vail, which she ignored. He wanted her to call him back, but she'd rather avoid conversation with him at present. Wendy's urgent message concerned her. Since it wasn't late, Marla returned the call. She'd already let Spooks out and changed into slacks. Lounging in her office chair, she dialed Wendy's number.

"Marla!" Wendy said in a breathless tone. "I'm so glad you called. I need to see you as soon as possible."

"Why? What's happened?"

"It's something I need to talk about, but I can't leave the house tonight. Zack is out of town, and I told him I'd be home in case he called."

"You can't tell me on the phone?" Marla's body sagged. After the emotional events of the day, she was exhausted. Going out again would require an enormous effort.

"Sorry. I don't want to say anything that might be overheard."

Was Wendy afraid her line was tapped? "I can come there," she offered halfheartedly.

"Please, would you mind? I'm going crazy sitting here by myself."

Stifling a groan, Marla heaved herself upright. "Hang on. I'll be there shortly."

An hour later, Marla flung herself onto a blue-silk-upholstered couch in Wendy's living room. Wendy didn't even bother to offer the social nicety of a cold drink. Wringing her hands as she paced the room, she plunged directly into her tale.

"I'm worried about Zack." Her eyes shot a furtive glance at Marla. "I didn't tell you before, but the night before Aunty Bertha died, Zack went out after we'd argued about her."

Marla sat up straight. "You mean he wasn't home all night with you?"

Wendy's slender shoulders slumped in defeat as she paused in front of Marla. "I wasn't going to say anything until I heard about that janitor, but now I'm concerned."

"Carlos . . . what did you hear about him?"

"He was poisoned. I listened to the news tonight. The police say there may be a link between his death and my aunt's." Her chin quivered. "I'm afraid Zack might be involved. He was worried about money, Marla. He'd made some bad investments. I know he felt frantic with a baby on the way and debts to pay. Do you . . . think he's capable of harming someone?"

"You know him better than I do. But I'm surprised. Zack implied you didn't know how bad things were. When I visited his office, he said he was expecting a financial windfall. It would allow him to dig himself out of his pit."

"What windfall? Surely you don't think he meant Aunty Bertha's inheritance? Oh dear, he knew the terms of her will. And I have no idea where he went that night, but it could have been your salon."

"You didn't share this with Detective Vail, did you?"

A look of misery crossed Wendy's face. "No, and I suppose that means he can accuse me of being an accomplice."

"You never confronted Zack about this?"

"I was afraid of what he'd say. Now he's not here, so I can't ask him."

Marla drummed her fingers on the plush sofa arm. "You said he went away on business?" For some reason, that bothered her. Where would he go, and who'd paid for the trip?

Wendy nodded, resuming her pacing. "He seemed excited. I-I hope he'll be back by Sunday as promised. It's a quick trip, but he said it was important. I think he was meeting someone else in Franklin."

"Where?"

"North Carolina. I wasn't even aware he had clients there."

Ken had gone away this weekend, Marla remembered, biting her lip thoughtfully. Do you suppose—nah, too coincidental.

Loud barking sounded from the back of the house. "Your dogs want in," she observed.

"What should I do, Marla?"

Sighing, Marla rose. Rolling her stiff shoulders, she yearned for a hot shower and a few hours of oblivion with a good mystery. Although didn't she have enough to solve on her own right now? Maybe she'd read the latest trade magazine instead.

"I don't know what to say," she replied, facing Wendy. The girl looked forlorn, but Marla couldn't think of any more comforting words. Zack's actions were puzzling but that didn't mean he was a murderer. "Wait and talk to

Zack when he comes home. And call me . . . I'd like to know your results if you're willing to share them."

"Of course. You've been a big help just by listening. And if you learn anything new, will you call me?"

"Sure," she lied, thinking of the mound of data accumulating in her brain. *Trouble is, I can't tie it all together.*

Wendy showed her to the door, and she drove home pondering their conversation: Zack and Ken, both out of town for the weekend. Zack left the house the night before Bertha's demise. *Doesn't prove anything,* she concluded. Nope, too many loose ends still needed completion. A weary yawn convinced her to contemplate them on the morrow.

Saturday dawned bright and warm with the promise of rain held in cotton-fluff clouds on the horizon. Marla didn't have time to think much less ponder the mystery of Bertha's death. Darlene didn't show up for work, and Nicole called in sick. The morning flew by in a flurry of activity.

Just after Marla stuffed down a bagel and cream cheese for lunch, Lucille summoned her. "Vail's on the line. Here."

"Oh, joy." She grabbed the receiver. "Hello?"

"Ms. Shore, I'd like you to come down to the station, please. I have a few questions to ask you."

Marla cringed inwardly. His stern tone of voice lacked any hint of familiarity or warmth. "What's up? We're really busy today. Maybe I can meet you later."

"*Now,* Marla. Shall I send a car for you?"

Compressing her lips, she glanced at Lucille, who was trying her best to pretend disinterest. "That won't be necessary. I'm on my way." Carefully replacing the receiver, she hung up. "Shit. What does he want?" She hoped he hadn't found the pictures. But why else would he need her at headquarters?

"What's going on?" Lucille queried, a bland look on her powdered face.

"Who knows? He wants to ask me more questions."

"Why? Were you snooping again?"

Gathering her purse, she shot Lucille a resentful glance. "Maybe, maybe not. What's it to you?"

"Someone's got to see to your welfare."

"Yeah, well, I can look after myself. Did you ever get hold of Darlene? I can't understand why we haven't heard from her."

"She isn't answering her telephone."

"Keep trying. I don't like her leaving us in the lurch like this. You'll have to reroute my clients to Miloki and Giorgio again. Sorry, guys," she yelled on her way out the door.

Vail met her personally in the lobby at the police station and herded her into the same office as before. A sterile room apparently used for questioning suspects, it held a single desk and several chairs. Motioning for Marla to be seated, the detective lowered himself into a creaky chair behind the desk.

"So." Glaring at her, he steepled his hands.

Marla squirmed uncomfortably. "Why did you bring me here?"

"Certain new evidence has come to light. Care to explain these?" Opening a drawer, he pulled out an oversize brown envelope and tossed it across the desk surface.

Marla, fingers trembling, retrieved the envelope. She didn't want to examine the contents. A sinking feeling told her what was inside. Peeking past the open flap, she felt her face lose color. "W-Where did you get this?" She saw no point in denial. The best thing would be to come clean. Pressing her shaking knees together, she tried to compose herself.

"They were in Bertha Kravitz's safety-deposit box. You'll notice the envelope has your name on it." His icy tone matched the hard expression in his eyes.

Swallowing convulsively, Marla met his gaze. "I can explain."

"I'm listening."

At least he hadn't read her the Miranda rights. Did that mean he wasn't going to arrest her? Hoping she still had a chance to redeem herself, she repeated much the same story she'd told Tally. During the recital, she kept her head bent, voice low. It was embarrassing enough to confess her sins without seeing the disgust in his face. By the time she'd finished, she felt sick to her stomach. The gunmetal gray walls pressed upon her like a prison as she waited for his response.

"Why, Marla? Wasn't there someone else who could help you? You must have been terribly desperate to pose for *those* kinds of pictures."

She winced at the inflection in his voice. "I had no one. I couldn't tell my parents. It was something I had to do for myself. When I took the job, I—I didn't know it would involve that type of work." Her throat closed, and she coughed to keep from choking.

"Yet you cooperated with the photographer, didn't you? You did everything he wanted."

"That doesn't make me a bad person. I was a naive nineteen-year-old! It was a single episode, that's all."

"Bertha got hold of the pictures and was blackmailing you. Is that why you killed her, Marla?"

Glancing at him, Marla couldn't read anything in his impassive expression. "I did not poison Mrs. Kravitz. I've been trying to find her killer. I want to bring the bad guy to justice just as much as you do. I'm not the person you want."

"No? Then why did you ask Wendy for these pictures if not to cover your tracks?"

Oh, so he knew about their conversation. "I—I figured you would construe my motives wrongly."

"On the contrary, I understand completely. The victim must have threatened to expose you in her memoirs. You decided to stop her. You've been smeared before, and you wouldn't risk it again. The reputation you've built is too valuable to be ruined by an old lady's exposé."

Inwardly, she shrank from the pain of his accusations. His regard had meant more to her than she'd cared to admit. Losing his faith, not that she'd ever had it for a certainty, dealt her a tough blow. "I didn't even know about the memoirs until Wendy told me. If anyone, Todd was the most upset. He deals in stolen goods, or at least that's what Zack said. And I believe Todd still works as a model for the photographer. Maybe he wanted to stop his mother from exposing his dirty schemes."

"Why did you visit that print shop?"

Marla moistened her dry lips. "Wendy found a porno magazine among Bertha's things, and she chose to turn it over to me rather than you. I traced the printer's post office box to that address. The magazines are being distributed by mail. Todd acts as courier between the printer and the photographer. Whether it's a family interest or a secret subsidiary of Sunshine Publishing, I don't know. You'd have to ask Todd . . . or Roy Collins.''

A strange gleam entered his eyes. "Funny you should mention Roy's name. Seems he didn't show up for work yesterday. Left the condo in the morning, and no one's seen him since."

"So ask Darlene—" Her eyes widened, and she slapped a hand over her mouth. "Darlene never came in this morning, either. Lucille has been unable to get in touch with her."

"What have you done, Marla? Darlene was getting too nosy so you bumped her off? Roy became suspicious and you got rid of him, too?"

Her jaw dropped. "W—What are you saying? Are they . . . have you found . . ." Horrified, she let her voice trail off.

"I'm the one asking questions here." Suddenly he changed tactics. "It would be best if you told me the truth," he cajoled, giving her a smile that had all the friendliness of a neighborhood werewolf. "We could strike a deal."

"Are you arresting me?"

His eyes never leaving her face, he shifted his wide shoulders. "Not yet," he said with obvious reluctance.

"Good, then I'm leaving. You can contact my attorney." Rising, she clutched her handbag. "If something happened to Darlene, you're wasting time with me. The real murderer might harm someone else. Or maybe Darlene and Roy are the guilty parties, and they've taken off. Have you considered that angle?" Anger seethed behind her next words. "I've made a few mistakes, but I'm not a killer. I'd think a man with your experience

could discern that I'm being truthful. You've disappointed me, *Dalton.*"

Sticking her nose in the air, Marla swung the door
open.

"I'll be watching you," he called.

Marla wheeled around to face him. He stood by his
desk, eyes glittering darkly.

Her defiant gaze met his. "You do that, and in the
meantime, maybe I can find the real criminal."

19

Her blood boiling, Marla marched out of the police station and headed for her car. Once inside, she turned on the air-conditioning and sat for a few moments to collect her cool. Damned cop. Who the hell did he think he was to accuse her? Didn't he recognize that she wasn't the only one with a motive?

Gripping the steering wheel, she tore from the parking lot to head back to work. No, wait a minute. Speaking of motives, she remembered their interview with the *santero* in the Everglades. *Señor* Manuel had spoken of Carlos and the light-haired woman, quoting Carlos as saying she'd looked good for her age. She'd confided to Carlos: *"I'm doing it for him."*

Partners in crime? Stan's stern image floated into her mind. She could be way out of line thinking he and Carolyn Sutton were involved. *Even if they didn't conspire together for Bertha's murder, then certainly they sabotaged my lease. No way Carolyn could afford those steep payments on her own*, she thought. Guilty, either way. Detouring east,

Marla decided Saturday afternoon would be the perfect time to pay a visit to Carolyn's salon. She needed to discern the truth for herself.

Fifteen minutes later, Marla approached the Hair 'N Care salon on foot. The shop used to have a different name, she recalled with a snide curl of her lip. Carolyn's new title was an attempt to copy the success of Marla's Cut 'N Dye.

Where once the area had thrived as a busy city center, westward expansion had pushed it into a decline. *Progress marched on, and in its wake came decay,* Marla thought. Her cynical eye caught the evidence of deterioration in peeling paint and broken pavement. *How Carolyn would love to move into my domain.*

A smug smile on her mouth, she pushed open the door and stepped inside the shop. A couple of customers glanced up, the only occupants besides the staff, most of whom appeared idle. One stylist Marla recognized was treating herself to a manicure. Others stood about chatting, Carolyn among them. When she spotted Marla, the woman's gaze sharpened. She had the eyes of an owl, large and round, and the skin of a woman ten years younger than her age of forty-three. Bleached strawberry blond hair and a slim miniskirted figure added to her youthful appearance.

I should look that good in my later years, Marla observed, noting the woman's flat abdomen as she trotted over. Even Lucille kept herself in fit shape, and she was in her fifties. *I'll have to ask what she does for exercise.* Probably works out in her garden every day. Pruning bushes and yanking weeds could be vigorous work. Not that holding your arms up every day for eight hours cutting hair was any less active.

Suppressing a twinge of envy, she told herself that keeping busy with a booming clientele was just as aerobic as following a fitness regime. She wondered if Carolyn had heard how much business had prospered after Bertha's murder. If she were involved, and her purpose was to ruin Marla's reputation, she'd failed miserably. Or maybe it had been Stan's intention to force Marla out of business, so she'd be more agreeable to selling her share of their jointly owned property. Gritting her teeth, she determined to learn the truth.

"Well. I see things haven't improved much around here," she said sweetly.

Carolyn bared her teeth. "Come to get your hair done properly?" Her scornful glance raked Marla. "Looks like a complete makeover is in order."

Speak for yourself. Your salon needs a serious overhaul. "No, dear, I just came for a little chat. Got a minute?"

Glancing at her watch, Carolyn raised her pencil-thin eyebrows. "I'm between appointments, so I can spare a few minutes. Let's go in that corner." She pointed to the coloring station, where a row of seats was unoccupied. Marla tramped over and levered herself into a cushioned chair.

Crossing her legs, she addressed Carolyn. "Uh, I hear you're interested in changing locations. You wouldn't have approached my landlord with an attempt to outbid me, would you?" Cursing inwardly, she realized she should have phoned her lawyer first. Then she might have a better handle on what to say.

"What do you mean?" Carolyn shot back.

"Someone offered my landlord a better deal—a huge raise in rent plus a larger security deposit. I'm wondering if you're involved."

"Who, me? Where would I get the money?"

"You're clever enough to have devised a plan. For a while there, I'd wondered how desperate you'd become. If someone was hoping to ruin my business by killing off Bertha Kravitz, that idea backfired. We've never done better."

Carolyn's eyes narrowed. "That's wonderful, luv, but I hope you're not thinking I had anything to do with that woman's death. I wouldn't be so stupid. There's easier methods."

"Oh, really? Whose idea was it to approach my landlord with better terms—yours or Stan's?"

Carolyn smirked. "Stan came to me. Brilliant idea, wasn't it? Flush you out over finances."

Elation charged through Marla. "I knew it. You won't succeed, either one of you. I'll bet the change in terms isn't legal according to my contract. My attorney is checking into the details. If I'm right, you can tell Stan to bug off."

"Tell him yourself."

"Maybe Stan is in this deeper than you think. He could have wanted to make Bertha sick to chase clients away, without being aware the poisons were fatal. The cops are close to catching the killer. If you know something you're not telling them, you'd be considered an accessory."

Chuckling, Carolyn regarded her with amusement. "Your desperation shows, darling. Maybe *you* did it to drum up business. After all, you're already responsible for letting a small child die. What's another victim to you?"

Resisting the urge to smash her rival's face, Marla jumped up. "If I find you've been collaborating with Stan about my lease, I'm going to sue you both. Since your cash flow is already hurting, I wouldn't risk losing more if I were you."

Carolyn rose, an ugly look on her face. "Don't threaten me, Marla."

"Why, what else can you do to me that you haven't already tried?" *Wrong question, stupid.* "Never mind answering. I've already learned what I needed to know," she chortled.

Carolyn stood frozen, watching her with a malevolent expression. Hastening away, Marla didn't look back even once.

Reaching the pavement outside, she drew in a deep breath, as though to cleanse her lungs of stale air. Well. So Stan had conspired with Carolyn regarding her lease. At least that matter was clarified.

First on her agenda upon returning to work was phoning her lawyer. "Ah, Marla. I'd just instructed my secretary to put you on my list for today," he announced jovially. "You were right. Your landlord is overstepping the terms of the lease. I've got a call in to his attorney, and we'll iron things out."

"You mean we can get him for breach of contract if he cancels me out?"

"Yes, ma'am. According to what you both signed, he can't raise you more than ten percent a year. And that extra security assessment is way over the limit. I don't think we'll have any problems getting you renewed as long as you agree to a slight rise in rent."

"Thank you! I've no problem with that." She hung up, triumphant. Screw Stan and his nasty ploy. He'd underestimated her again, the dolt.

Lucille followed her into the storeroom where she'd

made her call. "What did Detective Vail want?" the receptionist demanded after Marla replaced the receiver.

Marla turned to her. "Oh, he thinks I killed Bertha,"
she replied wearily. "I warned him he's chasing down
the wrong alley, but he didn't listen. I'm going to have
to take care of this problem myself."

Crossing her arms, Lucille scowled. "Meaning?"

"Roy and Darlene might be involved. Have you gotten
in touch with Darlene yet?"

"Nope."

"I hope nothing's happened to her."

A puzzled frown crossed Lucille's face. "Why would
you think that? And how do you feel they're involved?
You're not thinking they killed Bertha, are you?"

Marla shrugged. "I don't know . . . something Vail said
or didn't say bothers me. I need to talk to Roy."

"I called his office. He's not in. I thought he might
be able to help me locate Darlene."

What if Roy had done something to Darlene? Marla
thought with a frisson of alarm. If they'd plotted together
and she became a threat, he could have decided to get
rid of her just the same as Bertha. But where would he
go if he wanted to hole up for a while?

"Who's my next scheduled appointment?" she asked,
changing the subject. Walking into the salon, she heard
Lucille's footsteps trailing her.

"You've got two more cuts to do," Lucille answered,
rattling off the client's names. "Miloki was going to do
them for you."

"I can take over. Is she finished for the day?"

"I think so."

The phone rang. "It's for you," Lucille said, handing
over the receiver.

"Yes?" she answered.

"Todd Kravitz here. I need to see you. How about coming over to my place after work?" His words slurred, as though he'd been drinking.

Her heart thudded in her chest. "Why? What's happened?"

"I can't tell you on the phone."

Marla glanced at Lucille, who had a look of avid interest on her face. "Uh, I can meet you, but I'd rather go to the same place as before. Shall we say the same time, too?"

"Oh. Okay. See ya later, babe."

She hung up, dreading the prospect of spending time in his despicable company. Maybe he'd be able to tell her if Roy knew about the porno magazines. That would make their talk worthwhile.

Feeling her margin of time was narrowing, she headed for the Strip after dark with a sense of urgency dogging her heels. Todd was waiting for her in the nightclub at a corner table.

Marla slid into the opposite seat, wrinkling her nose at the mingled smells of cigarette smoke and liquor. From the empty beer bottles on the table, she surmised he was on his third drink. His aim was suffering, she noticed with a wry smile, surveying a couple of stains on his rumpled shirt.

"What did you tell the cops about me?" he demanded without preamble. His bleary eyes regarded her angrily.

No wonder she'd been blind to his identity. His disheveled appearance had aged him considerably and filled out his fine-boned features past the point of recognition.

"I spoke to the photographer, Todd," she said, ignoring his question. "At first, I didn't realize you were the man who . . . I'd worked with in the past. But you recognized me at your mother's funeral, didn't you?''

"Huh." Stroking his stubbled chin, he regarded her warily.

"Why didn't you remind me who you were then . . . or later, when we met here?"

"You would have remembered me if you'd come back to my place, babe. I would have made sure of that."

To emphasize his point, he sidled closer. His hand disappeared under the table to stroke her thigh in a decidedly northern direction. With a shudder, she brushed him off. "Fat chance."

Not to be dissuaded, Todd grinned. "You need to loosen up. You'd enjoy yourself, babe."

"Forget it. What were you asking about the cops?"

Giving a furtive glance around the room, he dug a few bills from his wallet and tossed them on the table. "Let's take a hike. You never know who's listening in here."

Yeah, right. Are you just trying to get me alone, pal? Marla wasn't thrilled to follow him outside, but she complied nonetheless. Maybe he'd be more communicative in the wide-open space. The evening air was warm and humid, tinged with a salty sea breeze and the hint of an approaching storm. Lightning flashed in the distance, the squall being too far away for thunder to reach her ears. They walked along the beachside path, dodging other passersby.

Todd plowed stiff fingers through his stringy hair. His blond roots were no longer visible. He must have had it colored since she'd seen him last.

"Why do you do it, Todd?" she asked curiously.

His resentful glare raised her hackles. "It's a means of making a living. Just how much do you know, anyway?"

She detected a hint of menace in his tone but forged on. "I meant your hair. Why dye it black instead of a lighter color? That's the way I would go to cover the gray."

He gave a mirthless chuckle. "You've got it wrong; I'm not so vain. I don't want certain parties to recognize me."

Halting, she stared at him. "What?"

"You didn't mark me right away. That's why I go for the hair job. Wouldn't want all the gals siccing their husbands on me, ya know? At least I wasn't doing you, babe. That was my mother's pleasure."

"Dear Lord. You mean you're blackmailing other former models like me?" She'd suspected as much, but from Bertha's viewpoint. Now that she thought about it, Todd was the more logical choice. He'd been the model, after all. And he was the link between the photographer and printer.

Resuming their pace, she tried to clarify the jumbled thoughts in her mind. "Your mother said she got my photos when she went to the photographer for boudoir pictures. Yet, the photographer said she'd never been there. You're the one who bought the photos. So how did she end up with them?"

He bared his teeth in a wolfish grin. "I brought home a batch of photos, and my mother saw them. She'd always scorned my means of making money, but this time she realized the opportunities for herself. She took the ones of you to get some personal services for free. I began ripping off other models like you who'd retired. With her publishing background, my mother thought up the idea of starting a subsidiary venture using current pictures. The magazine was mostly her ball game. I just acted as intermediary."

"Was Roy Collins in on it?"

"Nope. Ma and I made all the money, minus the cuts for the other guys involved, of course. You know Vail came to my house with a search warrant?"

Her brows raised in surprise. "He didn't say anything to me. What was he looking for?"

"You tell me." He turned to face her, gripping her shoulders. Suddenly Marla realized they'd reached an empty stretch of territory. Cars crawled past on Route A1A, but there weren't any walkers up that far. Smart girl, she'd let herself get into a compromising situation. A few steps away, the sandy beach met the water. Would anyone notice if Todd became violent?

"Detective Vail brought me in for questioning," she said, a defiant gleam in her eyes. "He'd found the original prints of our photos. He wondered if Bertha was blackmailing me because then I'd have a motive to want her out of the way."

"Did you kill her?" His grip tightened.

Shaking him off, Marla snorted. "I was going to ask you the same thing. Bertha intended to publish her memoirs. Weren't you afraid she'd expose your blackmailing scheme? Not to mention those stolen goods you fence."

"How'd you find out about that?" he growled. "Vail discovered my stash."

"Someone else told me," she said, thinking of Zack. "So how come he didn't arrest you?"

"I didn't kill my mother." His eyes glittered in the reflection from the streetlights. "Someone else got to her first, or I might have done it. Vail wasn't after me. He wanted information. But he's busted my job, babe. Like he confiscated all of my stuff and told me he'd be watching me. I'm finished, and I have you to thank for it.''

He edged closer, his gaze glinting with malice. She could smell his beer-laden breath and see the pulse throbbing at his throat. Fear rushed her like a tidal wave. "You don't want to hurt me, Todd," she said, keeping her voice even.

"No, I want to have you, babe." He grasped her arms, jerking her against his body. "I've remembered how you felt beside me, your skin soft and supple. The way you squirmed in my arms for the camera, I knew you wanted me. Well, you can have me now." His mouth descended, his kiss erasing her protest.

Marla struggled in his grip but he held fast, his strength laced with liquor and fueled by lust. Refusing to be subjugated to his will, she stomped on his instep. At his howl of pain, she broke free.

"Give it up, Todd. I don't want you now . . . or ever. If you don't leave me alone, I'll be the one who blows the whistle on you next."

Taking a chance, she turned her back on him and strode away. Her heart raced and her blood beat a staccato rhythm in her neck. As she quickened her pace, her footfalls sounded like a tap dance on the pavement. She dared not look back, or he might take it as a signal to pursue her. What a slimeball. To think he believed she lusted after him! A quiver of revulsion shook her spine as she hurried toward a more populated area.

Back home, it took a steaming hot shower and twenty minutes of scrubbing to erase the feel of his touch from her skin. Scooping Spooks into her arms after dressing in her nightshirt, she stroked his soft creamy hair. He gave a low growl, lifting his long throat so she could pet its sensitive underside. The repetitive motions, along with his warmth snuggled close to her body, brought her comfort.

That night brought her troubled dreams, however. Bertha's face floated in the water of a shampoo sink, her eyes mildly accusing. Dark fluid dribbled from a corner of her mouth. Her strands of thinning hair twisted like tentacles, gyrating about her head as though alive.

Suddenly, Marla was in her viewpoint, seeing with her eyes. She caught sight of naked bodies writhing on the salon floor, a man and a woman entwined in each other's embrace. The woman glanced up, and she had Marla's features. The man's countenance wasn't clear, but he had dark hair . . . peppered with gray. Naturally colored, not dyed.

Jerking awake, Marla sat up in bed. Her sheets were strewn at her feet, and sunlight streamed past the borders of her drapes. She'd slept well past nine, she noticed, glancing at the battery-run clock. Early for a Sunday but she wasn't surprised. Too much on her mind to sleep peacefully.

As she performed her morning routine, she reflected upon yesterday's talk with Todd. She'd been too weary last night to think about it, but now she believed his assertion that he didn't murder his mother. Guilty of other crimes, he wasn't a killer. So who did that leave? Mentally, she scrolled down the list of suspects during her walk with Spooks.

Stan and Carolyn were out as potential teammates. They might have conspired to destroy her lease, but Carolyn claimed she had nothing to do with Bertha's death. She could be lying, but Marla didn't think so. The woman's attitude was too smug over that one nasty tactic.

Darlene and Roy? They were a distinct possibility. She'd call Darlene's number today to see if the girl was in. A visit to Roy's place might be in order, too. She could always consult the gatehouse guard as to when he'd seen Roy last. So far, this investigation seemed to be leading in circles. She hoped Vail was having better results, unless he focused too much of his attention on her.

Scanning the street, she became alert to a black sedan cruising along as though the driver were a stranger to the neighborhood. Oh, shoot. Was Vail having her tailed?

Crossing the road and stepping past a swale of newly mowed grass, she headed home. Spooks cavorted after a squirrel, necessitating a firm yank on his leash. The scent of freshly turned earth rose in her nostrils. Warmed by the sun, her skin bore a light sheen of sweat when she pushed open her front door. Just after she'd unhooked the poodle's leash, the phone rang.

Tally's excited voice squealed in response to her greeting. "I just got a call from Ken in North Carolina. You'll never guess what he's been up to these past few weeks, Marla! Oh, I'm so ashamed of myself."

"Calm down. Explain slowly, please." Jamming the receiver to her ear, Marla poured herself a glass of orange juice.

"Apparently he'd made a bad investment through an old friend from business school—guess who? Zack Greenfield. To recoup their money, they invested in a risky mining operation which just struck it rich in Franklin. Gemstones, Marla. It's near that Mason's Mine where a three-hundred-twelve-pound ruby was found by Tiffany's. That stone is in the Smithsonian, or so Ken said. His group found a sixty-six-hundred-carat sapphire, uncut weight. I'm just stunned. And to think I believed he was fooling around with another woman."

"I knew he wouldn't be unfaithful, Tally." Well. Now she knew what Ken and Zack had been conspiring over. Was this the income Zack had expected? She'd bet her bonnet on it if she had one. So where did that leave her investigation?

"What about the surprise you were planning?" she asked her friend. "Remember, your plan to confront him over his avoidance behavior?"

Tally laughed. "He didn't want me to find out he was such an idiot! I'm going to take him on anyway. We've both been too wrapped up in work and other activities. It's time we were alone together to air things out. My plan is to kidnap him for some preplanned vacation fun on a cruise."

"Sounds great! I'm so happy everything is turning out all right." *For Tally, that is. Not for me.*

"Oh, there's one more thing I forgot to mention. Remember those tiny sapphire earrings he gave me for my birthday last September? They were the wrong kind— screw-backs instead of pierced—and I'd meant to have them reset? Well, he said not to bother. He's got replacements, and they're much more impressive."

"That's swell, Tally." Marla heard her own voice as though from a distance. A suppressed memory had risen to the surface of her consciousness and was clanging in her mind like an alarm. An earring . . . why was that so important?

Forcing a farewell to her lips, Marla hung up. One more step in the process of elimination was required. Placing a quick call to Wendy, she asked, "Has Zack contacted you or returned from his weekend trip? Did you have a chance to talk to him about where he went the night before your aunt died?''

"Oh, Marla." Wendy's voice shook with emotion. "The most fabulous thing has happened! Zack's big windfall turned out to be a gem mine in North Carolina. And yes, I asked him where he went that night. He said he'd just been steamed and had gone for a drive. I believe him, Marla. I shouldn't have doubted him.''

Marla wished her good luck and replaced the receiver. Conviction shook her with the solidity of rock. She knew. *She knew!* Denial slammed into her mind, but she forced it back. No, she'd kept this from herself for too long. Now it was time to face her demons.

Betrayal came in one color. One color only. *Reddish gold.*

Trembling, she punched in the number for Detective Vail's beeper. When five minutes passed and he didn't return the call, she dialed his answering machine at home to leave a message. Her heart pounding against her ribs, she grabbed her purse and dashed out of the town house.

Time was of the essence. If she was right, Bertha was destined to have company in her grave.

20

Marla approached the sprawling house as though this were the first time she'd seen it. Truthfully, her visits had been limited to the occasional holiday party. Sometimes she invited the staff over to her place, but other times they rotated. It was important for morale to celebrate seasonal rituals together, and Marla was usually the first one to plan a party. She wanted her staff to feel part of a team in order to work amicably with each other. All the more reason why she felt so bad about coming here today. Betrayal didn't sit well in her book. She preferred to take people at face value. *So much for my instincts,* she thought unhappily. In this case, she'd been wrong. Dead wrong.

Pausing on the front walkway, she surveyed the grounds. Situated in an older section east of Federal Highway, the Mediterranean-style house was surrounded by lush tropical greenery on an acre of land. Brilliant pink bougainvillea mingled with scarlet hibiscus blossoms. Oleanders clustered among black-olive trees and philodendrons. A generous herb garden off to the side rested beside a Key lime tree. Ground cover appeared well mulched and weed-free. Overall, the yard gave an impression of being cared for and tended by a person highly versed in gardening skills. Someone who might have firsthand knowledge of edible as well as poisonous plants.

Marla stepped forward and pressed the doorbell with a stiff finger. She was taking a dangerous risk in coming alone, but it wasn't her way to lay blame without confirming the facts in person. Besides, she'd left a message for Detective Vail telling him to meet her here. If she were right, he'd serve as backup providing he got the voice mail in time.

A small part of her still refused to admit she'd been bamboozled. Possibly, she'd just jumped to erroneous conclusions. That was easier to believe than the alternative: a trusted colleague had tried to harm her.

Dismay filled her gut when Lucille answered the summons. Opening the door, the older woman showed little surprise at Marla's visit. Dressed as though she were expecting guests, she'd swept her reddish gold hair into a knot atop her head. Her attire consisted of a tailored pair of black slacks, a loose overblouse decorated with silver studs, and heeled sandals. Perfume drifted on the air. With a sharp gaze, Marla noticed the tinge of rouge on Lucille's cheeks. She wore no earrings. Her lobes were smooth, absent of any pierced holes.

"Come in, Marla. I was wondering when you'd show up."

Marla strode inside, smoothing down her khaki shorts. Sneakers kept her tread silent on the ceramic-tile flooring. "Were you expecting me?" she asked, swinging around to face Lucille. It wouldn't be wise to turn her back on her employee.

Lucille gave her an oblique glance. "I thought you'd have this figured out a long time ago. You weren't so smart, were you?" Smirking, she gestured to the living room. "Take a seat. I'll get you a drink. Then we can talk."

Marla glanced around uneasily while Lucille left the room. Her house was laid out with the bedrooms on one side and the kitchen and family room on the other. If she remembered correctly, the place had three bedrooms. Lucille had renovated the master bathroom so that the marble tub overlooked a pleasant tableau outside with a rock waterfall and large glossy ferns.

"Here, honey, it's my herbal iced tea I've been wanting you to try," Lucille said, returning with two tall, frosted glasses. Marla's gaze flickered to the yellow-plastic gloves on her hands. "Land's sake, I ran out of clean glassware, so I just washed these."

She handed a glass to Marla and set her own on a cocktail table before returning to the kitchen to remove her gloves. Marla gripped the glass, moisture droplets clinging to its exterior. Cautiously, she sniffed the amber liquid. It lacked any particular fragrance. No bitter almond essence, anyway.

"Go on, taste it," Lucille urged. She smiled encouragingly, but it was more like a crocodile grin. As though to prove her concoction was harmless, she took a sip from her own glass.

That proves nothing, Marla thought, guarding her expression. She claimed an armchair, placing her drink on a side table. Waving a hand, she indicated the glass. "This wouldn't be sun-brewed tea, would it?" she inquired. "Because someone else you knew drank some homemade tea once and died from poisoning."

The liquids in their glasses looked alike, but Lucille could have poured something different into hers. Narrowing her eyes, she watched Lucille's reaction to her remark. Her plan was to provoke Lucille, to trigger an emotional hot spot so she'd talk. Getting a rise out of her might be the best way.

Lucille frowned, creases appearing on her brow. Even with a light application of makeup, her skin appeared leathery and dry from too much sunshine. "Harvey was stupid. He didn't realize oleander leaves were poisonous."

"If your old boyfriend was into natural foods like you are, you'd think he'd have known stuff like that."

Lucille shrugged. "I couldn't help it if he was careless."

"You must have been heartbroken at his death."

An odd light flared behind Lucille's eyes and then was gone, replaced by a cold, fixed expression. "On the contrary, he got what he'd deserved."

"But I had the impression from Darlene that you two were very close."

Lucille snorted. "Darlene doesn't know her asshole from a snake hole. Now there's a soul who won't be bothering us anymore."

Marla sucked in a breath. "What does that mean?"

Lucille's lip curled in a secretive smile. "You'll see. As for Harvey, we were inseparable until Roy tipped me off. The bastard never did appreciate me. He used me, you know."

"Oh? How so?"

"Let me go back to the beginning so you'll understand. It's important to me, honey, so bear with me. I'd worked for Sunshine Publishing Company for fifteen years." Lucille's pale blue eyes grew nostalgic. "I began there when I was thirty-three. Harvey Moore and I were an item then, so at first Roy didn't attract my attention except in a respectful way. I admired his energy and business savvy, but our relationship was purely professional.

"He was forty-one, six years younger than Bertha. Not being married, he confided his problems to me. We'd go out to lunch, and he'd talk, and I understood what he didn't put into words. The man really wanted to be with me, but I was too focused on Harvey then to return his regard."

"So what happened?"

"Roy shattered my world. At first, I didn't believe him when he said Harvey was seeing someone else. I'd given Harvey so much of my life." Her gaze hardened. "I meant nothing to him. He threw away my devotion to go after a floozy with more money and a younger body. Well, he wasn't going to toss me aside like a heap of trash. If he didn't stick with me, he wouldn't have anyone."

She grinned wickedly. "The dolt didn't know I switched his mixture. Oleander is highly poisonous. It didn't take long for him to croak after drinking the sun-brewed tea steeped from the leaves. I figured Roy would comfort me in my grief, but Bertha's husband had just died, so he turned to her. Again my loyalty wasn't appreciated. But I knew why he was cozying up to Bertha. He wanted to distract her so she wouldn't notice he was siphoning company funds into his private accounts."

Damnation, Marla thought, *I should have brought a tape recorder.* Lucille was confessing everything. Didn't she realize Marla would tell the police? She'd only hoped to get a clue that the woman was truly guilty. A chill of fear clawed up her spine. Maybe Lucille didn't expect her to leave. Oh, God.

Her gaze inadvertently swept to the tall iced glass, droplets still visible on the outside. She rubbed her fingers where they'd contacted the moisture. An oily residue remained, irritating her skin. She flexed her fingers but the prickly feeling wouldn't go away.

"Bertha refused to believe me when I told her about Roy," Lucille went on. "She fired me for accusing her lover, and warned me against any further action."

"You could have exposed Roy to the authorities. Why didn't you do that?" Marla asked, curious.

"Huh. Bertha was a smart cookie. She'd been recording the phone calls I made from my office. In my last message to Harvey, I'd threatened him. Foolishly, I'd scribbled down a list of poisonous plants I could use against him. She found it in my trash can. If I didn't keep silent, she proposed to turn the tape and handwritten paper over to the cops. So I shut my mouth and left Sunshine Publishing. She told Roy what she suspected I'd done to Harvey, and I hated her for that because it turned him away from me. But as long as she held those items in her possession, I couldn't do anything."

Marla glanced at her palm. The prickling sensation had been replaced by a burning soreness where she'd touched the glass, and she noticed with alarm that her flesh was beginning to redden. Idly, she rubbed at the spots with her other hand. She didn't need this distraction now.

"In the last few months, Bertha realized she was losing Roy's attention," Lucille continued in a chatty tone. "Bertha wanted to know if I were seeing him because I'd kept in touch. I denied it was me who'd alienated his

affection, but I knew Roy still wasn't happy. He was searching for love without realizing that it was right on his
doorstep. Bertha decided to publish her memoirs as a
means of revenge. Her notes would credit her with the
company's success and cast aspersions on Roy's acquaintances, including me."

Lucille's eyes lifted to meet Marla's rapt gaze. Marla
couldn't have pulled herself away for anything. "Go on,"
she urged, wishing her hand would stop hurting. Damned
peculiar how the irritation wouldn't ease off.

Lucille tapped her foot in a rhythm on the tile. "Bertha
warned me away from Roy. She was going to hurt him.
I couldn't let her publish her memoirs. She'd have
exposed him, and then any chance for our getting
together would be smashed. I knew Roy really wanted
me. He'd just gotten confused, but I'd set him straight.
First I had to deal with Bertha, though."

A proud grin lit her face. "It was so easy to add poison
to her powdered creamer jar. I knew Bertha was coming
in for an early appointment that morning and that you'd
be alone with her."

"What about Carlos and leaving the back door unlocked?"

"A red herring so the cops would think an outsider
did it. If not, you were the perfect fall guy."

"Why did you kill Carlos—so he wouldn't reveal who'd
paid him?" At Lucille's nod of affirmation, Marla queried: "How did you do it, Lucille?"

"He had a sweet tooth, so I gave him a home-baked
cake. The poison was slow-acting. I knew it would take a
few days."

"And when you found out Roy was shacked up with
Darlene?"

Lucille's face darkened. "Roy shouldn't have done that. *I* would have satisfied his needs. I understand him better than anyone. But he couldn't see that because Darlene blinded him. The tramp just wanted his money. So I got rid of her."

Marla choked. "W-What? You killed Darlene?"

Lucille's eyes glinted. "Roy wouldn't admit his passion for me. I had to make him acknowledge that we were meant for each other. Bringing him here was the only solution. He's finally confessed his need for me, but his philandering eye keeps separating us. It's like a sickness inside him, but at last, I've found a way to keep us together."

Marla lost her train of thought. She clutched her right hand, wide-eyed when she noticed blisters forming. *This reaction isn't normal,* she realized. Panic seized her, and she leapt to her feet. "What have you done to me?" she cried. Water. She needed to rinse her hand off with water!

Dashing to the side of the house where the bedrooms were located, she fled to the master suite.

"Oh, my God." She skidded to a halt inside the bedroom. Roy Collins lay on the bed, eyes closed. Was he dead? No, she could see his chest move. Forcing herself to go on, she rushed into the bathroom and twisted on the faucet. Cold water splashed on her hand but the residue wouldn't clear. As she let the water flow, her eyes caught on a ceramic dish decorated with hand-painted angels. A single earring lay inside. A pearl-and-marcasite earring with a screw-back setting.

Hastily patting her hand dry with a towel, she hurried back into the bedroom. There was nothing she could do for Roy without knowing what was wrong. Frantically, she scanned for a telephone, but none was visible. Lucille had made certain no one would be able to call for help.

"You went to Bertha's house," she accused Lucille when the receptionist appeared in the doorframe.

"That's right. I wanted to find that tape she'd recorded. It wasn't there."

Marla didn't like the menacing light in Lucille's eyes. She edged to the side of the room, relieved when Lucille stepped forward. "What did you do to Roy?" she asked, maneuvering toward the doorway.

"He drank some of my herbal tea. I'll drink my share soon enough. And now I'm afraid you'll have to join us, honey."

"Wh-what?"

Lucille wormed closer. "You've really been most annoying. I couldn't let you dig too closely into the past, could I? Warnings didn't stop you, and you didn't take the bait with those marzipans I sent you. Too bad. I really did like you. Now, come on back into the living room and have some tea."

Marla complied, thinking she'd make it to the front door, but Lucille blocked her exit.

"Get out of my way, Lucille. I don't want any of your tea."

"Oh, but you don't understand." She pointed at Marla's right hand which dangled by her side. "You've already absorbed poison through your skin. Those droplets on the glass—they weren't water. Ever hear of sarin? It's a lethal nerve poison related to insecticides. You should be feeling ill by now."

Horrified, Marla stared at her hand as nausea rose in her throat. The blisters were puffy and red, spreading rapidly. And now her left hand began to tingle. *Lord save me, some of that stuff must have gotten on my other hand, too.*

"Listen, I have an antidote."

Her heart thumped wildly. "Where is it?"

Lucille cackled. "It's in the tea. You have to drink the whole glassful."

Marla eyed the beverage suspiciously. "I don't think so. Move aside, Lucille. I need to go now."

"Roy and I will be together soon." Lucille reached for her own glass and rattled the liquid. "I've got a stronger dose here than what I gave him. We should join each other at about the same time." She tilted the glass to her lips.

"No!" Heedless of her own safety, Marla charged forward to stop her. Duty compelled her to prevent another fatality. But she was too late. Lucille thrust her away and gulped down the liquid. "Now it's your turn to die, honey, unless you take the antidote."

Pain lanced through Marla's hands. Blisters crackled on her reddened flesh. She wondered if Lucille were telling the truth. Did she have a means to save herself or was it another trick?

"Drink," Lucille ordered, reaching for Marla's glass.

"No." Marla turned toward the door. *I've got to get help.* But with the speed of a cougar, Lucille jumped in front of her. A cold, calculating look on her face, she grasped Marla's shoulders and twisted her around.

"Let me go!" Marla yelled.

Lucille grabbed her hair. Yanking a clump so hard it brought tears to Marla's eyes, Lucille hauled her into the living room. She lifted Marla's glass, bringing it close to her mouth. The rim hovered into view.

Clamping her lips shut, Marla fought against her. She

knocked Lucille away with a thrust of her hip. Pain tore at her scalp as the piece of hair ripped off.

A determined glow lit Lucille's crazed eyes. With a snarl of rage, the agile woman lunged at her, thrusting a fist into her stomach. Gasping with pain and surprise, Marla clutched her midsection. Her jaw dropped as she struggled to suck a breath of air into her uncooperative lungs. Lucille pounced forward, pushing on her forehead and forcing Marla's neck to arch backward. Liquid trickled into her opened mouth. Sputtering, Marla coughed and choked. She spit as Lucille tried to pour more of the cold brew down her throat.

"Bitch!" Lucille shrieked. "Drink it and die."

Marla summoned her strength. She pushed at Lucille, pain shooting up her arms from her afflicted hands. Years of work had honed her muscles, and she used them. Lucille stumbled back, saving the glass from breaking by plopping it onto the cocktail table. Growling, she charged again, head lowered. Marla lashed out but missed decking Lucille, who twisted aside in time. Dimly, Marla became aware of a repetitive knocking sound.

"Marla, are you in there?" shouted Detective Vail's voice.

Sirens blared in the distance, but Marla barely perceived them over the noise of her labored breathing. Before she could cry for help, Lucille swung a fist at her face. Dodging the blow, Marla grappled with her assailant. Both of them tumbled to the floor, sending a side table crashing over. A crystal vase shattered. Marla screamed, shielding her face. Fragments pelted the backs of her hands.

As she crouched, a heavy weight slammed into her. Lucille pounced on her back, shrieking like a wild animal.

Strong fingers encircled Marla's neck. Scooting backward, she rammed Lucille against the armchair she'd sat on earlier. The woman's grip loosened, giving Marla a moment to grab a weapon. She scrambled for her purse, which she had left on the floor. But she wasn't the only one looking for a tool. Lucille faced her, drool sliding from her mouth, a pointed shard of crystal gleaming in her hand. Ignoring the shooting pains in her arms, Marla whipped out the container of finishing spray from her purse and aimed it directly at Lucille's face.

Screaming, Lucille recoiled instantly. Marla used the distraction to grab an onyx paperweight from the cocktail table. Wincing, she cracked it against Lucille's temple. The older woman crumpled without a word.

"Wait, I'm coming," she yelled to Vail. Her body shook violently, but she forced herself to her feet. Tottering to the door, she let him in, falling into his arms as a wave of dizziness overwhelmed her.

"What happened? Are you all right?"

"My hands," she whispered.

Glancing down, he muttered an oath. "What did she do to you?"

"Tricked me into touching sarin, a nerve poison. It feels oily then hurts and turns into blisters. She said I'm going to die. An antidote . . . it's in the glass of iced tea. But I didn't believe her. She wanted me to drink it." Marla babbled on, aware that her mind was becoming increasingly numb. She didn't feel well, not at all. But she still had things to tell him.

"Lucille . . . she killed Bertha and Carlos."

"I know. You shouldn't have come here alone."

Her tongue thickened. She had to force the words

from her dry lips. "Poisoned Roy. Took some herself. Darlene . . ."

Her eyes drifted closed, and the searing pain in her hands receded. Awareness centered on Vail's closeness and his tender words of concern. Her body became weightless as he lifted her to his chest. He shouted orders to his fellow officers, who'd rushed inside the house after him, then he addressed her.

"I'm taking you to a hospital. Don't try to talk."

She felt herself being placed upon the seat cushion of his car and then being strapped in. It felt so good to let him take charge. Entrusting herself to his care, she allowed oblivion to sweep her into its comforting depths.

Epilogue

Marla had just finished dressing prior to being discharged from the hospital when a knock sounded at her closed door. Glancing at her mother, who hovered nearby with an anxious expression, she called: "Come in."

Dalton Vail marched through the door holding a wrapped bouquet of freshly cut red roses. "I wasn't sure if you were being released today," he said, his smoky eyes trailing over her silk blouse and slacks. Anita had to help her with the buttons. Marla could wiggle her fingers, but movement was limited by the bandages restricting her hands.

"Are those for me?" A smile came easily to her pale face. Once the shock of recent events had worn off, she'd rallied with her usual energy. Besides, being soft didn't get the job done. It was time to put the past behind her and move on to bigger and better opportunities. Her smile broadened.

Anita glanced at the two of them and hastily stepped

forward. "I'll go find something to put these in," she interrupted, snatching the flowers from Vail's hand and scurrying out of the room.

"So how's the patient?"

"Better, thanks." Marla's pulse rate quickened as she perused her visitor. His hair was neatly combed off his forehead, parted at the side. With his conservative shirt and tie, he appeared ready for a day's work. His penetrating gaze and the tight lines around his chiseled mouth revealed his concern. Although his jaw was freshly shaven, the sharp angles and deepened shadows under his eyes told her he hadn't slept well since yesterday, when he'd brought her to the emergency room.

"How's the hands?"

Marla grimaced. "They don't hurt anymore now, but as you see, I can't do a whole lot until they heal."

"At least that stuff wasn't sarin. You'd be dead if it were a true nerve toxin. Croton oil is relatively harmless unless ingested."

"The doctor said it will take up to three weeks for the blisters to heal."

His eyes glowed warmly. "The time will pass quickly. Consider it a good thing you didn't drink that iced tea. As you suspected, it wasn't any antidote. The solution contained monkshood. You wouldn't have lasted out the day."

She was almost afraid to ask. "What about Lucille?"

He shook his head. "Her dose was more concentrated than the amount she gave Roy. She must have been planning to join him quickly when his time came. He's in intensive care, but it looks as though he'll make it. Darlene wasn't so lucky. We found an area of freshly turned earth in Lucille's backyard."

"Dear Lord." Marla's eyes filled with moisture. Maybe Darlene had deceived her, but the girl didn't deserve this fate. *Hey, Marla, don't fall apart now. Crying doesn't solve anything.*

Vail gestured to her bandages. "So what will you do since you're, uh, incapacitated? Take a vacation?"

Marla laughed, and her urge to dissolve into tears subsided. "We're two people short in the salon. I can't afford to take time off. Nicole and the others will handle my customers until I can work again. In the meantime, I'll take over Lucille's job." Determination emboldened her tone. "I can answer the phone and peck at the computer keys. Plus, I've got to set up interviews for new employees. And there's always paperwork to file. I'm sure there will be enough to do. If not, my cousin Cynthia has conned me into being on the planning board for Ocean Guard's big winter fund-raiser."

"The beach conservation group?"

"That's right. I said I'd donate free hair appointments for raffles and help plan events for the black-tie gala at Cynthia's estate."

"Sounds like a big job." Clucking his tongue, Vail regarded her with admiration. "You're one amazing lady, you know that?"

Her expression sobering, Marla disagreed. "I wasn't smart enough to figure out Lucille was the killer."

"You're too trusting, that's your problem. You didn't want to concede that a member of your staff might be responsible. I have to admit, I'd found evidence on both of you. Lucille's tape and her handwritten poison list were in Bertha Kravitz's safety-deposit box. So were your compromising photographs. I wasn't sure which one of you did it since you both had motive and opportunity."

Remorse colored his voice, and he glanced away. Realizing what he must be feeling, Marla forgave him his lack of faith. He wouldn't be a good detective if he didn't consider all the angles.

"Well, I believe in the people I hire," she said. "I guess I failed to get beyond that sense of loyalty to suspect Lucille. From my past experiences, I prefer to believe that basic goodness resides within everyone."

"Maybe it does, but that attitude can get you killed."

They regarded each other in silence. Marla thought about their different worldviews, hers involving trust and his being suspicious of everyone. Maybe she was being naive, but she'd rather see things through rose-tinted glasses than view everyone as a potential criminal. How could he raise a daughter with an outlook so grim?

Gazing deeply into his eyes, she read a hint of vulnerability that touched her heart. It must be difficult for him to be a single parent. As a stylist, she was used to listening to people's problems. It gave her joy when she made customers feel better, not only by helping them look good but also by offering compassion. What could she give to this man to help him?

It crossed her mind that he might be seriously interested in her. The notion both pleased and frightened her. Since Stan, she'd avoided intimacy with other men. Her self-reliance had been too hard to come by to lose it in another relationship. Her other prospects were not serious considerations. Arnie was sweet, but he had too many kids. Ralph and she were more than friends, but she didn't envision their relationship going further. Lance was cute but devoted to his computer. *Dalton isn't even Jewish, not that it matters. Bless my bones, I'd just be agreeing to get to know him better.* Maybe it was time to plunge into the currents of change and see where they carried her.

Shoving his hands in his pockets, Vail cleared his throat. "I was wondering if you'd like to go out to dinner tonight since you can't cook until your hands recover."

A silly grin split her face. "Sure, that sounds great. I'm ready to have some fun, aren't you?"

Author's Note

This story was inspired by my visit to a hair salon to get a perm. While waiting for the twenty-minute timer to go off, I peered around at all the ladies flipping through magazines and thought, "What we need is a gripping novel to read while we're killing time." Killing was the key word, and soon my imagination soared into a romp wherein Marla Shore was created and her client got permed—to death. Hence *Permed to Death* was born. If you enjoyed this story, please look for the next two books in the series, *Hair Raiser* and *Murder by Manicure*.

Please write to me at: PO Box 17756, Plantation, FL 33318, and enclose a #10 SASE for a personal reply. Or contact me via E-mail: ncane@worldnet.att.net.

BOOK YOUR PLACE ON OUR WEBSITE AND MAKE THE READING CONNECTION!

We've created a customized website just for our very special readers, where you can get the inside scoop on everything that's going on with Zebra, Pinnacle and Kensington books.

When you come online, you'll have the exciting opportunity to:

- View covers of upcoming books
- Read sample chapters
- Learn about our future publishing schedule (listed by publication month *and author*)
- Find out when your favorite authors will be visiting a city near you
- Search for and order backlist books from our online catalog
- Check out author bios and background information
- Send e-mail to your favorite authors
- Meet the Kensington staff online
- Join us in weekly chats with authors, readers and other guests
- Get writing guidelines
- AND MUCH MORE!

Visit our website at
http://www.kensingtonbooks.com